AMONG THE SURVIVORS

A NOVEL

ANN Z. LEVENTHAL

She Writes Press, a BookSparks imprint
A Division of SparkPointStudio, LLC.

Published 2017

Printed in the United States of America

Print ISBN: 978-1-63152-236-9
E-ISBN: 978-1-63152-237-6
Library of Congress Control Number: 2017939145

For information, address:
She Writes Press
1563 Solano Ave #546
Berkeley, CA 94707

Cover design © Julie Metz, Ltd./metzdesign.com
Interior design and typeset Katherine Lloyd/theDESKonline.com

She Writes Press is a division of SparkPoint Studio, LLC.

AMONG THE
SURVIVORS

In memory of Dan'l Bracey (born 1951, died 1995)

and

in honor of Hizzonnah Jon O. Newman,
aka the husband of dreams

CHAPTER 1

Since Karla Most has been working as a maid for over five years now, she is not bowled over when she opens the back door of her new client's Manhattan apartment. All her clients live big. And in her off-duty life, she herself is no peon. Thanks to her superrich grandparents, who give her a monthly allowance and used their pull to get her registered at NYU, when she is not working, she audits courses: Art History, Language of Film, Introductory Spanish. In fact, Karla's family thinks attending classes is all she does.

They'd be ripshit if they found out she was moonlighting as a housecleaner. But being a maid reflects Karla's sense of herself as someone who needs to do penance. Even if she cannot name her crime, she has no doubt about the source of her guilt: she let her mother down. And cleaning, scrubbing, vacuuming to suck up her clients' schmutz gives her a reason to exist. Other people count on her.

Besides, Karla enjoys having a secret life; she rebels against meeting anyone's expectations. Not that she exactly *decided* to become a maid. She fell into it at age sixteen, just after her mother died. Back then, not knowing her father's parents were even alive, Karla believed that, as a person with no birth certificate, no Social Security number, no proof at all of her existence, she had no other choice. And later, when she found her grandparents and could have

1

become a full-time student, she didn't see why she should. Karla likes her life as it is. She likes starring as Cinderella in a fairy tale of her own creation.

So, today, as she checks out her new Park Avenue client's enormous kitchen, instead of asking herself, *What am I doing here?* she thinks, *Who needs a kitchen this humongous?* Everyone she knows eats out or orders in. Karla's favorite client uses her oven to store her jewelry. So kitchens, untouched, are usually the cleanest rooms. But this new guy is clearly different. Karla wrinkles her nose, disgusted by the stench of cigarettes and fish. *Well,* she supposes, *that's why he hired me.*

Groaning, Karla pulls off the seal coat her grandparents gave her this past January for her twenty-first birthday and drapes it over a chair. Her grandmother thinks that giving her things is important, but Adele's best gifts are her stories about the father who died before Karla was born.

"Every woman Michael ever met adored him," Adele likes to say of her only child, a light going on in her normally mournful face. "I could never account for it. Because, you know, he was a little pudgy, more of a Martin Milner than an Errol Flynn, if you know what I mean . . ."

Though she has no idea who either Martin Milner or Errol Flynn is, Karla nods because she does catch her grandmother's drift.

"Michael was never drop dead gorgeous. But oh, how all the gals loved him!" By this time, Adele is beaming.

So natural magnetism is in Karla's DNA. And whenever she leaves one of her sessions with her grandmother, she feels assured, attractive, joyful. No need whatever to be like her mother; Karla can be her dad's kid.

But she accepted the coat only once her grandparents agreed to her terms: any clothes they buy her *have* to be black.

Right from the beginning, her mother insisted on dressing her in black, even going so far as to dye her diapers. So always Karla has been "the girl in black," and at this point it is easiest just to stay that way. Only she hates it when people ask her why she never wears anything else. It always sounds as if they are accusing her of something, but of what? Is wearing black such a crime? As a child, Karla may have yearned to try every color in the rainbow, but now, in 1979, five years after her mother's death, she wishes people would just stop bugging her about it.

Focusing on the job before her, she recalls that yesterday, her boss said Karla was to scour and mop the kitchen and bathrooms, vacuum, dust, spray and wipe mirrors, polish wood surfaces, make up the bed, and empty wastebaskets. However, she was not to touch any of the artwork. "Is that clear?" demanded Louise, who runs her housekeeping agency with absolute authority.

Karla could never pull off such self-assurance, but she identifies with Louise's wariness. She, too, distrusts, and, recognizing their bond, Karla wishes she and Louise had more than a working relationship. But over the years Louise has made it obvious that there will be no meetings for coffee or glasses of wine, no weekend brunches or dinners, in fact nothing at all, their meetings strictly business. "Is that clear?"

As usual, Louise glared at Karla before handing over the key to this new client's apartment. And Karla played her part, faking submission although, having been raised by a control-freak mother, she harbors in herself a pilot light of defiance that can flare up at any time. "I've got it, I've got it," she reassured Louise, who, paying her cash off the books, deserved at least the pretense of obedience.

Louise said the new client was a guy named Saxton Perry. The minute Karla heard the name, she knew the type: a WASP. And, looking around his kitchen, she figures he probably wouldn't live in a palazzo like this one by himself. He'd have a significant other, probably not a guy, the room insufficiently tarted up; Saxton Perry's woman would wear Armani. Her blond mane artfully gilded and perpetually sleek, this svelte Nordic goddess would of course constantly look impeccable. Karla knows her type, too.

Imagining her, Karla is conscious of her own bushy red hair, her slapdash inadequacy. But at least she is genuine; this guy's babe is probably superficial and snobby. And, with a trophy like that on his arm and his aristocratic bearing, he would advertise his connection both to the Founding Fathers and to some club that wouldn't take Jews as members.

Karla knows all about that sort of thing because, though Mutti may have neglected arithmetic, in addition to teaching Karla about art, music, and literature, she passed on to her daughter a keen appreciation for social gradations. Not that Mutti was in awe of anyone. She might well have deemed the owner of this apartment "worthless," which, in her German accent she pronounced "vertless," so that for years Karla said it that way, too, because in Mutti's world there were two kinds of people: vertless and valuable.

It was as important to know which was which as it was to be one of the valuables who were not necessarily rich, though, Mutti often pointed out, money never hurts. It just shouldn't be too new, too obvious, or take the place of important intangibles like good taste, intelligence, or kindness. Being a nice person beat out being a wealthy one. Mutti liked to quote the Bible, saying it was easier for a camel to go through the eye of a needle than for a rich man to enter the kingdom of God. But whether this new client turns out to be vertless or valuable, right now Karla transfers her own indignation into energy. By God, she will clean him out!

She opens a closet as big as a maid's room and, instead of a bed and a sink, sees the Rolls-Royce of vacuums, along with every other high-end cleaning product in the world. She emerges with a cartful of supplies and quickly locates the source of the fish stink: a garbage pail loaded with cigarette butts and unwashed cans containing scabs of dried cat food.

As she dumps the cans into a trash bag, Karla remembers how her richy-rich, anorexic grandmother cuts paper napkins in half, saying, "Waste not, want not," and, either because she grew up in Nazi Germany or because, having lied to get into the United States, she feared she would be found out and deported, her paranoid mother believed the police were constantly watching them. In any case, Karla suspects this Perry is just one more weirdo, like the misers she reads about in the tabloids who subsist on cat food, because any actual cat around here, as far as Karla can detect, is invisible. Unless it is hiding from her, in which case it will probably turn up when it is good and ready.

Meanwhile, addressing the immediate problem (odor up the giggy), Karla sprinkles baking soda into the garbage pail before she relines it with a fresh bag, then gives it a quick sniff. Acceptable, so no point in scrubbing the pail, for it is one thing to clean and quite another to be like Mutti's cousin Viv and make a fetish out of cleaning. Besides, getting away with a cut corner or two is half the fun of everything Karla does.

Opening the fridge, she decides that no matter how gigantic his pad is, this client cannot, after all, have a live-in other, because only a loner could subsist on four Heinekens, one dried-up lemon, a jar of Dijon mustard, a bottle of ketchup, and a couple of raw eggs. Famished, Karla furiously wipes the empty shelves, bangs the fridge door, jangles the beers. Scared, she pauses. And hears nothing smash, so that's okay.

But what about this great art she's been warned not to touch? She drags the vacuum and the cart through a swinging door into the dining room, where a hidden sound system startles her with jazz, some invisible pianist stroking her spirit along with his piano keys. Is she supposed to be drinking in the music this way? Is Karla allowed to have a good time on the job?

She shivers and looks around. Is anyone other than the phantom cat watching her? Or is that sense of constantly being under scrutiny a holdover from those years of living with her mother?

Nobody's spying on you, kiddo, Karla reminds herself for the zillionth time. *You're on your own, so just figure out what's the deal here.*

A magnificent still life she recognizes as seventeenth-century Flemish from her History of Art course hangs over a fireplace. Deliberately casual fruits and nuts cascade into the body of a pheasant, an image that screams of abundance; no one who lived in any house where this painting hung on a wall would ever have gone hungry. The fireplace beneath it holds a charred log and ashes.

Since Louise has frequently warned her to be ultracareful with paintings, sculptures, and ornaments, Karla assumed today's client's art would be the usual crap. But it is possible that in this apartment, everything from the working fireplace she cleans out to the genre painting above it could be the real deal.

Mutti would have loved this place. She might even have loved Karla, despite all her deficiencies, for worming her way in here. And this thought gladdens Karla. In any case, what an opportunity! Karla abandons the fireplace to examine huge bronze double doors of the type she has seen only in art books or cathedrals. But instead of featuring saints and angels, these colossal doors portray bas-relief sailboats on curling waves, and in one panel, a kind of mini–capitol building with a smooth golden dome. And she cannot help chortling at this jokey version of the entrance to St. Patrick's.

Then Karla grasps a handle, pulls the weight slowly toward her, freezes. What if the door is one of the art objects she was not supposed to touch? But how else is she supposed to get into the living room? Still worried—*what if there are security cameras in this place?*—she pushes the vacuum and cleaning cart ahead and returns the massive doors to their exact original position. Then she gets down to work.

But as she moves through, at least one picture per room wows her. What kind of person owns paintings like these? An American Göring? Mutti told about how he looted all the Jewish collections. Who else besides someone like that would have a Rauschenberg and a Balthus in his living room, two Dürer etchings in his den, a secret cache of excellent art collected with no discernible rationale? Even if the guy stole the stuff, based on the fact that she loves every single piece in here (with the exception of the Balthus), Karla might have to revise her original take on this Saxton Perry. Whatever else he may be, he is not your average WASP.

Has everybody else heard of him and his seemingly random collection of unbelievably fabulous works? Is Karla the only person in the world who, until today, had no idea he, Saxton Perry, or it, his trove, even existed?

In particular, the painting in the master bedroom stops her cold. Framed on the wall above the bed's headboard, a peachy-gold woman sits, one naked thigh over the other, displaying a luscious haunch. With a bare arm, she clasps a white cloth, her arm crossing her chest but leaving her tawny nipple exposed. Her head tipped to one side, she has wavy black hair, long Asian eyes, a mysterious smile, her whole pose as sinuous as an S.

Of course Karla recognizes the artist. "Modigliani always painted sad because he was Jewish and knew grief firsthand," her mother used to say, as if she knew from being Jewish herself. What bullshit! Still, in all fairness, Mutti did teach Karla to recognize a Modigliani. And this sure as hell is one right here in the room with her. Who would believe it? And what would Mutti say about it if she were here now? For a minute, Karla almost misses her.

She would certainly like to tell her mother how wrong she was, because the woman in this portrait does not look sorrowful. Ripe, and therefore pluckable, is more like it. Also contagious, as Karla's own body actually absorbs the glow from that painting so that even when she turns away, she senses its warmth on the back of her head.

And when she faces the light pouring from it, reflecting the woman's open willingness, Karla remembers how, that time in the van with Vince, when she was sixteen, she, too, felt luminous.

Their encounter occurred when she was working her first job, cleaning a toy store. She hadn't been employed there long when the boss's son, Vince, showed up and invited her to take a drive with him after work. He would, he said, take her to Brooklyn Heights to "watch the submarine races." Having no idea what that meant, Karla sat without moving, once Vince parked his truck, as he leaned over and touched her mouth with his. Without thinking, she opened her lips and Vince slipped his tongue into her mouth. Even though at first his tongue flicked only a bit, when he slid it in and out, it began to go much deeper and her tongue responded, wanting to taste more. How she wanted that melting-all-over feeling to go on and on!

And go on it did. Karla still relives, from time to time, the way Vince's tongue sent thrill after thrill through her. Had her body started emitting light, she would not have been surprised. So she gets why the woman in the painting looks luminous.

That night with Vince, Karla closed her eyes and was surrounded by the sounds of their breathing, hers matching his. And when, a little dizzy, she opened her eyes just to get her bearings, she saw that the windows had steamed over, creating a cozy cocoon within the car. Aroused by the painting, she half expects the windows in this room to be clouded, too. But, though they are clear, Park Avenue is wide; no one without binoculars can see in, and if they care enough to spy . . .

No one that night could see when Vince reached inside her coat and pushed her leotard down over her shoulder. When he breathed on her naked breast and licked it, Karla felt as if she would pass out with joy. Then he raised his head and asked, "You on the pill?"

"No," Karla admitted, feeling stupid.

"You got a diaphragm?"

She let out her breath. "It's not like I can exactly leave it at home. That's how I breathe," she said. Remembering this idiotic remark even now, she blushes, just as she did in the van.

"Come on, Karla. Cut the horseshit and just tell me. Do I need to wear a rubber?"

"Why would you?" she asked.

"I'm not exactly ready at this point to have a kid," Vince said, reaching deep into a pocket and shifting around whatever was going on down there.

"I'm pretty sure babies don't happen every time." Entirely self-taught, Karla, alas, skipped reading the birth control part in *The Joy of Sex*.

How how how could I have been such an idiot? She is to this very day still asking herself.

"Hey, it only takes once. I mean, what've you used in the past?"

"Nothing."

"And you never got pregnant?"

"I never went out with a guy," Big Mouth admitted.

"Oh, shit," Vince swore and moved away from her. "Jeez, I had no idea you were a virgin."

"What difference does that make?" Staring at the windshield, where steam drops were sliding down wobbly tracks, Karla was mortified to feel tears running down her cheeks. She rooted around in her pocket and naturally came up with yet another embarrassment: an ancient Kleenex clump she shoved at her nostrils, confirming her status, then and now, as a classic jerk. Not like Modigliani's woman. Anyone can see *she* is no virgin and has no regrets.

"Popping a girl's cherry, it's, like, a lot of responsibility." Vince had by then turned on the engine, which blew a gust of cold air in Karla's face. "I mean, all your life you'll remember your first time."

"So?" She was never going to forget this disaster, either. Had he ever thought of that? Did Vince even remember Karla now?

"So I wasn't thinking in terms of a commitment," he explained then. "I thought you realized that. I mean, I've got, like, years ahead of me before I start settling down."

"I never said you should," she pointed out.

He turned on the windshield wipers, and they drove back to Manhattan in silence.

When they arrived at her loft on Canal Street, the car windows were perfectly clear—as was Vince. "You ought to talk to my mother," he advised, as he pulled up to the curb to let her out. "She'll tell you why you don't want to just throw it away."

"I've kind of had it with mothers." Karla slammed his door behind her.

Having been "homeschooled," an ordinary-sounding word that barely touched on that sicko childhood with her paranoid mother, she still has no idea how other girls grew up or what they might have experienced. At NYU, Karla is clueless about how to act around people her age. What on earth can she say to any of them? She stares at the painting, as if it will tell her.

Who are those girls, anyway? Karla studies them, wanting to know. One time after class, hovering on the fringe of a group in Washington Square Park, she saw them passing around a joint. "Want a hit?" someone asked.

"Sure." Faking expertise, Karla nervously put the slimy thing between her lips, took a quick breath, shoved the joint at the next person, choked back a cough, and, unable to imagine why anyone would let herself go like that in public, observed the other girls' goofy grins, unhinged movements, rollicking gestures.

As for the guys, Karla could not just walk up to one of them and say, "Please fuck me," though more than once she has imagined doing just that. Especially since her best and only friend, Ron'l, took her to a sex shop. If only Ron'l were straight.

Since that night with Vince, no one has even kissed Karla, let alone propositioned her. At the time, she saw Vince as her first chance to experiment. Now, four years later, she is terrified that he may have been the one and only chance she will ever have.

How could she have been so stupid as to tell him she was a virgin? Now she could die without ever having slept with a guy. Looking at the woman in the portrait, she comes close to crying. Because in the middle of the so-called sexual revolution, bombarded by articles about sex, advice about sex, sexy ads, sexy movies, sexy music, Karla is somehow missing out on sex.

The boys she sees in her classes or just hanging around act as if she is off-limits. And when one dweeby guy actually did zoom up to her, his pushiness was a total turn-off, so, instead of encouraging him, she mumbled an excuse and fled. A woman with Modigliani know-how would have encouraged his attention, even welcomed it.

Karla is probably the city's only twenty-one-year-old virgin who has no clue, despite the beds she has changed and the rubbers (used and unused) she has encountered in her years of apartment cleaning, about what sleeping with a guy feels like or how to go about finding out. She has no idea how to bridge the gap between the studs in the books she devours, and the creeps crowding the edge of her life. Gazing at the nude in this astonishing apartment, Karla just hopes that someday she will have it in herself not just to look like that woman, but to *be* like her.

That morning, not so many hours earlier, the Modigliani's owner was sitting in his office at Redstone Capital when his secretary announced that his ex-wife was on the line. "What's up?" Sax barked into the phone, instantly on guard. Pam's calls were always bad news.

"The building superintendent went into Fleur's apartment last night and found her unconscious!" Pam blurted out. "She's at St. Luke's. I'm here with her."

Sickened, Sax immediately understood. Although their daughter had had years of psychotherapy, she kept shifting from one antidepressant to another and trying new combinations. Nevertheless, Sax had been telling himself that lately at least Fleur's illness wasn't getting any worse (no news was good news, right?). And while she still had neither a loving partner nor any kind of job, she seemed to be managing her daily existence well enough—that is, she was more or less "functioning." So, up until that moment earlier today, his daughter's sadness was just another ache Sax routinely set aside while he went about the business of living his life. "Did she overdose?" he forced himself to ask.

"Yes," Pam confirmed. "She mixed valium with vodka to do the job right. Oh, Christ, Sax!" Pam couldn't hold back a sharp sob, which moved him. For once, she was allowing herself to show emotion.

"Will she be all right?" Sax became aware he was grasping the arms of his office chair as if it were a raft keeping him afloat. His daughter nearly ended her life, and his along with it. If she died like that, he could not just go on. Grasping at a chair wasn't going to change that, but he couldn't bring himself to release his grip. "Is she conscious?"

"Not yet," Pam said, her voice lifeless. "They haven't let me see her; they just say she's in serious but stable condition. So, even though nothing terminal is imminent, I thought you should know."

"Yes, of course I should," Sax replied fervently, which was his version of screaming, *Why the hell didn't you call me immediately? Were you waiting until it was too late?* Pam could be such a bitch, but she must have been floored. She would have needed time to pull herself together. At least she finally did call him—Sax had to give her that much—so he dragged out his gentle voice to ask, "Any idea what shape she'll be in if she recovers?"

"No, not really." Pam's voice broke.

"Hey, it'll be all right," he reassured her, though things with Fleur were never all right. "I'm on my way."

When he arrived at the hospital information desk, a girl about Fleur's age jotted down her room number for him; apparently, his daughter had been transferred out of intensive care—a good sign, Sax reassured himself. As she told him to take the elevator just past the gift shop to the fourth floor and turn right, the information volunteer—if only his daughter could be someone like that!—acted as if his visit were ordinary and not momentous.

Another good sign, Sax thought, as he stepped first into the elevator and then out into a miasma of rubbing alcohol, floor polish, and whatever that food was in the stacked trays sitting on a hall rack. Breakfast? Lunch? A few feet down the hall, he found himself outside his daughter's room. Trying not to expect the worst, he put on his game face before he opened the door and stepped inside.

Sax was immediately struck by how, looking more like her aging mother than like herself, the normally posture-perfect Pam was sagging in a chair beside the bed, where Fleur (presumably) lay under a sheet. A plastic mask hid the patient's mouth and nose, her eyes were closed, tubes sprouted from her body, a shower cap covered her head. It could be anyone in there. This could all have been a huge mistake.

Please let it not be Fleur, Sax prayed to a God in whom he had not since childhood believed, as he moved around the bed toward his ex-wife. "How is she?" he found himself whispering.

Shakily, Pam rose, her face dead white, save for the pale gray hammocks below her eyes. Touching his ex-wife's body for the first time in the fifteen years since their acrimonious divorce, Sax clasped and unclasped her padded shoulder.

To his surprise, Pam reached up and pressed her hand over his. "The doctors say she'll probably be okay." She sighed. "Now, she needs lots of rest."

Embarrassed by his impulsive gesture, Sax retrieved his hand. "Do you know what made her do it?" Not that it made any difference—what was done was done—but Sax just had to find out why. Assuming Fleur survived, he had to know what he could do to prevent a recurrence—if that was possible.

"She left a note," Pam murmured, as their daughter, silent and unmoving, lay still.

"What did it say?" Sax steeled himself. Fleur probably blamed him. And why shouldn't she? If he had not impregnated Pam, they would never have married. And had their daughter not just tried to kill herself, he would not be here chatting with the person who'd cuckolded him with his own brother. What a twist!

No matter how they felt about each other, Pam and he both loved their only child. Yet Fleur did this unspeakable thing not just to him, but also to her mother. For no reason at all that either of them could fathom, she did this to herself, when either of them would have given all of their own happiness to her if they could; how could Fleur not understand that?

"She apologized for putting us through this but said that turning thirty next week would be too much to bear. She asked you to take care of Sidney. Would you believe that her damn cat was all she worried about?"

Sax had recently cat sat so that Fleur and her boyfriend, Ned, could be free to work out their latest problems. Why could she not see that the problem *was* Ned—Ned and his lovers, both male and female; Ned and money; Ned and coke; Ned and you-name-it. As long as Fleur stayed with Ned, she was going to be miserable.

Sax told her that repeatedly. When that had no effect, he reluctantly tried more than once to rescue Ned and was unsuccessful. Still Fleur could not acknowledge the reality of her situation. So Sax finally tuned out his daughter's soap opera, promising himself that if Fleur was ever planning to do anything desperate, he would notice the signs in time to stop her. Benign neglect was the ticket, he thought, and had allowed himself to set the problem aside—until this morning.

"How'd the building super know something was wrong?" he asked Pam. How could he himself not have known?

"Fleur called Ned before she passed out," Pam sighed.

Of course, Sax thought. *Any normal person would have called 911, but it's been years since anyone called Fleur "normal." And at least Ned called the super—I have to give the little shit that much credit.*

"And now we just wait?" Sax asked, envying those who still believed prayer could do the trick.

"I guess. I just feel so helpless," Pam groaned.

"Me, too." He slumped into a chair next to hers and marveled that, in all their years, first together and then apart, he had never felt so close to this woman. "Did they say how long it would be before she wakes up?"

"It could be any time," Pam said. "Her vital signs have all stabilized."

So, thankful, he sat with her in silence, trying to empty his mind of everything but the quiet hiss and tick of medical equipment until finally, after what felt like days rather than less than an hour, Fleur's eyelids fluttered open.

Pam noticed first and eagerly reached out for her daughter's hand. "Hi, honey," she said softly. "Your dad and I are here."

Fleur looked blank for a moment and then focused first on her mother, then on her father. As usual, in control of his emotions, Sax squelched his explosive relief and joked, "Some people will do anything to palm off a cat."

Was Fleur trying to smile? Yes, yes, her mouth was twitching, and Sax, who'd shed his religious upbringing years ago, offered up a prayer of thanks to "whoever's up there." At least his daughter could still respond to humor. So her mind was probably intact and she wasn't going to die—at least, not this time.

When she again fell asleep, more than half-dead himself, he waited another hour before he left to pick up the cat. Then Sax managed to hail a cab, which, in his depleted state, felt like a major achievement. He paid the driver, brought the cat up in the elevator, and finally made it into the apartment, where he wanted only to collapse. But first things first.

He arrives in his kitchen with his daughter's cat in a pillowcase and instantly notices that the place smells of lemons and bleach, an aroma he associates with his mother. Sax shudders. If his mother were still alive, she would kill him for what almost happened to Fleur, her only and fully beloved grandchild. But then he remembers: the agency was sending in a maid today. And, judging from the fur coat hanging over the chair, she must still be here.

Great, he thinks. *Somebody else I have to talk to.* Surely he has done enough talking today.

Sax tips Sidney out of his pillowcase onto the floor. The cat momentarily freezes, then, realizing he is at last free, scampers around the kitchen.

Dragging himself to the counter, Sax remembers he has forgotten to pick up cat food. The nearest thing to it in the cabinet is anchovies. So Sax rummages through a drawer, finds the can-opening key, peels back the lid, and sets the can on the floor. Sidney hops down from the counter and laps up the fishy oil, his tongue clicking.

Sax consults the clock. Rather than being four in the morning, as his exhaustion suggests, it is four in the afternoon, which means that soon the maid should be finished. Sax has not had anything to eat all day. Once she is gone, he will make himself something, whether or not he is actually hungry. As he hopes to make Fleur understand, life must go on, no matter what. You owe that much to the people who love you.

Meanwhile, drained of feeling, energy, understanding, Sax takes a beer from the fridge, tosses the cap onto the counter, and wonders, as he heads for his bedroom, *What the hell kind of cleaning woman owns a fur coat?*

CHAPTER 2

Were the bottle in his hand a camera, Sax would snap a picture of the maid in his bedroom. Her hair Celtic red, she is standing before his Modigliani, a worshiper gazing at it as if it were a crucifix, this girl—or, as Fleur would remind him, "woman"—dressed like a dancer, clearly a believer in art.

Out of respect, Sax waits a moment before breaking the spell. "Hello," he finally says.

Yelping, she spins around to face him.

Though there is nothing wrong with her features—in fact, she has arresting, pale silver eyes—self-consciousness causes her beauty to morph, so the poor thing instantly becomes just that: a poor thing. "Sorry to startle you," Sax says. Today he regrets everything he has ever done, this just the latest of his colossal missteps.

"That's okay." Only she wishes she had not kicked off her shoes and been caught barefoot. "It's my fault. Your art's very distracting." And Karla has no idea how he got in here without her hearing him, no idea what she is supposed to say to a gaunt guy who looks not like Robert Redford but like Abraham Lincoln. Not exactly the preppy type she was picturing. How is she supposed to speak to someone with that kind of innate dignity? She falls back on telling it like it is. "That Modigliani . . ." She points. "It's a killer." She shakes her head in awe.

"So I've always thought," Sax replies. And now, so soon after he assumed he would never smile again, he finds himself smiling.

Having managed to think of one thing apparently okay to say, Karla gratefully reverts to her housecleaner role. "I'll work an extra half hour to make up the time." She snatches up an ashtray, dumps the cigarette butts into her garbage bag, and pulls back the covers to smooth his bed's bottom sheet, all the while wondering, *Why is he still staring at me? Was I supposed to act as if the walls in here were blank? And anyway, who is this guy?*

He could be a supersmooth burglar, surprised to find her in here. If so, she has to hand it to him—he sure doesn't look flustered. It is Karla who is unsettled. She's always uncomfortable if she's working somewhere when its owner is around, and if this guy is an intruder, it's even worse. She'll have do something, alert someone, or, at the very least, keep an eye on him to see what he's up to. She cannot believe any normal collector would allow cigarette smoke in the same room as his Modigliani. "I took a little time with the Dürers, Balthus, and Rauschenberg," she assures whoever he is, deciding, for the time being, just to play along as if he is her employer.

"That's okay." Sax is impressed with Miss Fur Coat's ability to identify his artists. "And don't worry about the bed. I'll be getting into it soon."

She checks her watch. Four o'clock, and already he's talking about bed? She blushes. Does he realize that even though he's pretty old and kind of mournful, he's also sort of studly in a sinewy way? Does he sense that looking at him is giving her the same rush the painted nude did? *I mean, wouldn't it be funny if just when I was ready to give up my search, this brilliant burglar or megabucks art collector turned out to be my Big Opportunity?*

"I know it's early," he's saying, "but it's been a difficult day." Just standing here is taking willpower.

"I'll finish up fast," she promises, noticing that maybe how he looks is not so much mournful as exhausted. "And you can lie down." Blushing again, she reminds herself her shoes still are over by the desk. "Excuse me." She scoots around him.

"Go right ahead," says Sax, wondering how old she is. Certainly younger than his daughter, obviously not underprivileged, probably a dancer or actress earning her living between auditions.

"I'll just get everything out of your way." After cramming her feet into her shoes, she quickly tosses stuff into the cart for this man swilling beer out of a bottle. She cannot picture her grandfather, the one really rich guy she knows, drinking out of anything but a proper glass. But this one seems to have his own set of rules, and, of course, Karla likes that.

Sax considers. Since she seems to be eyeing his beer hungrily — the poor thing probably can't afford much on what she makes — he lifts the bottle toward her. "Want one?" Not a question he would normally ask a housecleaner, but this housecleaner, he could argue, is clearly not your run-of-the-mill.

"Let me just finish here." Grateful for the excuse to look away from him, Karla unplugs the vac and wonders what to say next. *He could be dangerous*, the ghost of Mutti warns. But Karla would have sensed by now if he were. She would not be hoping he is as attracted to her as she is to him. "I'm almost done."

"It's fine as is." Up close, Sax notices, she smells not just of bleach and lemon oil, but also of lily of the valley, another fragrance he has always associated with his mother. "If you don't have to be somewhere else right away, why don't you stick around awhile?" he asks, astonished to hear himself add, "I could really use the company." For some reason, rather than being intrusive, this girl/woman is actually making him feel human again.

"No problem. I've got nowhere else I have to be after this," Karla replies, vacuum hose in one hand, cart rim in the other. Whoever he is—and she decides that since those cigarette butts were in the bedroom before he was and he is acting as if he owns the place, he must in fact be the real Saxton Perry—it is possible she can help him. One evening at her grandparents', when her grandfather Ben came home after a bad day at his office, he said Karla's being there cheered him up. Now, this melancholy man seems to have sensed that she is good at cheering people up.

"My daughter . . . ," he begins, then pauses to clear the sorrow from his throat, "tried to kill herself last night."

"Wow!" Feeling as if she has just landed in the deep end, Karla holds her breath. What will she say if his daughter turns out to be dead? "Is she going to be okay?" she finally makes herself ask.

"Yeah. At least, we think so." Sax nods, not mentioning that for years, Fleur has been anything but okay.

"Well, that's good." Again breathing normally, Karla looks around for further conversational inspiration. "Is that her?" She points to a silver-framed photo of a slim girl on horseback who reminds her of a similarly framed picture of the chubby father she's never known, on a hairy pony at his sixth birthday party. This kid has the same easy assumption of entitlement as he did, only she looks classy, not comical.

"Yes, that's Fleur when she was a child." Sax blinks back sudden tears. At that time, either his daughter was happy or he just believed she was happy.

"How old is she now?"

He finds the question surprisingly painful. "With luck, she'll be thirty next week."

"Do you know why she tried it?" A few minutes ago, Karla wanted to be if not the naked woman over the bed, then the girl in the photo in her leather boots and velvet hat, but that girl apparently doesn't realize how lucky she is. Karla would give anything to have this cool guy as her father.

"She probably wanted to get back at her boyfriend." Though he knows this is crazy, Sax feels like shaking Fleur for what she did to herself, to her mother, and, not least of all, to him. "She was probably furious at me, too," he confesses. "She couldn't help knowing how disappointed I was in the choices she was making."

"I don't know," Karla replies. As furious as Mutti made her when she was alive, and as angry as Karla still is about how she was brought up, she has never seriously considered suicide. Her death would bother too many people, and her life is simply too interesting. Unless she goes on living it, how will she know what comes next? "There has to be a lot more to it than that."

"I suppose so." Sax sighs, drops his cigarette into his empty bottle, hears the hiss. No point in torturing himself over Fleur now. Tomorrow will be another day. "Anyway, how about that beer?" Wearily, he heads back down the hall.

Karla glances around the room before following him. With no idea what exactly she is supposed to do at this point, she clutches the vacuum hose and cleaning cart, drags both behind her, and, though she now doubts that this chance meeting is going to get her where she wants to go, hopes she is nevertheless doing whatever it is this man expects of her.

In the kitchen, the fishy smell has recurred as a sleek, gray cat noses a can around the floor. "I was wondering where she was," Karla says.

As she puts away the vac and cleaning supplies, she is also wondering if she should not do a little more to get rid of the stink while asking herself where Mr. Perry stashes his daughter's mother. In addition to the evidence of the foodless fridge, in the bedroom Karla noticed no women's clothes, no makeup, nothing that would suggest a female lives in this apartment. But then, this place is full of surprises.

"He—the cat, Sidney Vicious—came in with me." Sax is impressed. This girl doesn't miss a thing. "So, tell me." He uncaps a couple of beers and hands her one. "What's your name?"

"Karla. Karla Most."

"And I'm Sax. Sax Perry."

"Pleased to meet you, Mr. Perry."

"Sax."

"Okay. Sax." Karla cannot get over him. Far from being the snob she imagined, this guy obviously considers her his equal, which, in her heart of hearts, Karla knows she is. But she also knows most people wouldn't see it that way. And they could be right, for the cosmically rich owner of a phenomenal art collection is apparently comfortable in his kitchen, while the woman he hired to clean is not. Until now, the only grown man Karla has ever had much to do with is her grandfather, and it is not as if she really knows how to act around him, either.

She's always embarrassed by Ben's gratitude for what she does for Adele. He says that if Karla hadn't come into their lives, her grandmother would probably have starved herself to death by now. But Karla hangs out with her grandmother because she enjoys listening to her, so why should she get credit for that? "Whatever you say," she tells Saxton Perry, repeating, "Whatever you say." She can only play this situation by ear.

"How about some egg drop soup?" Sax takes out a Campbell's can.

"That's chicken noodle, I believe," Karla points out, because she might as well fake being relaxed, enjoy herself, try to go with the flow.

"But not for long." He dumps the can into a pot, adds water, sets the pot on the stove. "I assume you'll join me?"

"Sure." Still famished, Karla envies the cat her anchovies.

"Once the soup's good and hot, you just crack in eggs and stir," Sax explains, demonstrating with a whisk.

"I never realized egg drop soup was really egg drop soup." Laughing, she also never realized a big shot could, or would, be such good company. She never realized she could hold up her end of a conversation with such a person this skillfully. "That's great to know." Relaxing for real, she amazes herself by feeling at home.

This man's macho, beery cigarette smell is oddly ordinary, like one of the bars in the neighborhood where she grew up. "Just stick with me, kid." He serves them both, treating her like an old customer as they slouch at the table, slurping. "As my mother used to say, 'I hear you're having soup today.'" Sax used to hate when she said that, but now he chuckles as if it was amusing.

"My mother always said, 'Don't be sloppisch,' instead of 'slobbish,'" says Karla, delighted. Mutti's Germanisms, or being labeled a slob, never before seemed funny, but, thanks to Mutti, Karla has coaxed a laugh out of this sad man.

One time, her grandmother said that when Michael was only nine or ten years old, her friend Marilyn came to visit and Michael opened the door, looked her up and down, and fervently said, "Oh, Mrs. Epstein, you look *good*." Marilyn swore she would never forget that. "None of them ever forgot Michael," Adele said, sighing.

Listening to her, Karla felt like one of those thin, hard sponges that, touched by water, instantly fluffs up and softens. Now, she finds herself expanding like that again. Like her father, she apparently knows how to charm a member of the opposite sex. A miracle!

"How old are you?" Sax is asking.

"Twenty-one."

"When I was your age, Fleur was a year old."

"Fleur?"

"My daughter."

"What happened to her mother?" Karla hopes he isn't noticing how intently she is waiting for his answer.

"We're divorced."

Great! she exults, maintaining the most neutral of expressions. And if his semi-smile is any indication, there is more good news: his divorce doesn't seem to have shattered him.

"She left me for my half brother," Sax adds, waiting for her reaction. When there is no giggle, gasp, or evidence of pity, he continues. "The breakup was terribly hard on Fleur."

"My father died before I was born." Ignoring the juiciness behind the breakup of this guy's marriage, Karla does some quick arithmetic. Sax was twenty when his daughter was born, and in the bedroom he said Fleur was about to be thirty, so that puts him at around fifty. Not all that old, Karla decides, though his eyes do remind her of Grandpa Ben's—sort of doleful, which is only natural after what his daughter did. But even if he is obviously dejected, she is anything but turned off by him.

"Just leave everything—I'll take care of it," Sax says, as she rises to clear the dishes. Karla can't imagine her grandfather doing that. She would be astonished to see him drinking soup with his housekeeper/cook.

"That must have been hard, never knowing your dad," Sax is saying. "Tell me how you managed." He is the one getting up, filling the kettle, putting it on the stove. "Instant coffee okay with you?"

"Sure." It's better than okay. It's all she ever makes at home; plus, somehow, unlike her other employers, this one is treating her as if she is a guest who also just happens to be a maid. He recognizes that isn't all she does.

"Are you an actress or a dancer?" he asks.

"Neither." But he can tell she has a life apart from her job. "What made you think I was?" Loving the idea of being onstage, she feels like preening.

"The way you're dressed." Except, that is, for the coat. That could, Sax supposes, have come from one of those consignment shops Pam used to like. "Are you cleaning to pay back college loans?" He offers her a cigarette.

She shakes her head. "No. No college loans."

"You in grad school? What's your field?" He lights up.

Karla laughs. "I wish I had one. Actually, I just audit courses."

"But you've obviously studied art."

"It's a long story." Other people have asked Karla about herself, but her grandparents just want to know how much progress she has made toward becoming some nice Jewish boy's wife. Her mom's cousin Viv says never mind marriage—when is she going to have kids? And, beholden to her grandfather, the college administrators just want to know when Karla will start taking courses for credit. But this man seems to want to know who she really is.

"I'm ready to hear it all," he says, and though when he arrived he looked to her and felt to him half dead, now he feels (and looks) eager to hear a story that isn't his own.

So Karla tells him. Only rather than beginning, as she generally does, with Viv's word-for-word account of her birth, for some reason she starts from her earliest memories. "My mother taught me how to read," she begins. "She named me Karla after Karl Marx and used the Communist Manifesto for my ABCs. I mean, I guess that's really wacko, but I didn't think so at the time." She waits to see how this plutocrat will react to this.

He stuns her by saying, "No child thinks their parents are nuts. That comes later." Around the time, Sax thinks, when the parent comes to the same conclusion about the child.

"Yeah, but at some point I figured out that even though Mutti kept expecting the Gestapo to break down the door, nobody was really coming to get us. She claimed that in Germany, they killed everybody in her family. Now, I'm pretty sure that was not true. But anyway, they were dead."

"Yes, well, losing relatives, especially if they were close, would be enough to distort one's view of life." Neither Sax nor his daughter has that excuse. "It's a horror for anyone to undergo."

"I guess that's right." Staring, Karla is fascinated to see the tip of his tongue darting in and out between his lips. At one point, Sax picks a bit of tobacco off it, rolling it between his third finger and his thumb, the gesture surprisingly personal, almost as if they are sharing something intimate.

"How old was your mother when she came here?" he asks.

"Fourteen." Since he already knows about her life as a maid, she has no need to keep anything secret from him. Karla is finally free to be Karla, whoever that is. Maybe this is her chance to find out. Hanging around Sax feels like a definite potential as she pets the cat curved in her lap, absorbing the animal's heat between her thighs while basking in the marvelous warmth of this strange man's attention.

"My God, your mother was so young to travel on her own. How did she do it?" he asks.

"She claimed they spared her because she was a good worker." Unable to imagine her mother as anyone but a grown woman, Karla has never wondered how she actually carried off her emigration. But Sax Perry is making her see everything differently. "Mutti made sure I knew how to cook and clean. Told me being a good worker would keep me from being killed." Karla knows how weird that must sound. "Actually, though, she just wanted to make sure I could take care of her." She trained Karla right from the beginning to be the mother.

"Did she teach you about art?"

"Sort of," says Karla, shrugging this off. "At least she dragged me through a lot of museums."

"Judging from how much you know about my collection, you're a fantastic autodidact." And he marvels that, with no father and a cuckoo mother, having obviously been through tough times, this kid still seems genuinely sunny. Contrast that with his daughter, coddled in the lap of luxury . . . "Clearly, you read and study. Why not take on a more challenging job?" he wonders aloud.

"Such as?" Fascinated by this new label, autodidact—and making a mental note to look up the word—Karla dares him to think of something else she can do. "When I was born, my mother never even filled out a birth certificate, so, officially, for a long time I didn't exist.

"And promise not to tell anybody?" She knows she shouldn't blab, but how can she help herself when this man is sitting there, caring about her? She confesses, "The agency pays me in cash because when I started there I had no Social Security number." No need to mention that she enjoys being off the record, or that the grandfather who arranged for her to get her birth certificate and Social Security number doesn't know about her job. It is not as if she can explain her reluctance to change from how she was when she lived with Mutti, or how she kept on being the same after Mutti died. Karla just knows that keeping some things the way they've always been makes her feel safer.

"Do you make enough to live on?" asks Sax, while stifling a sudden impulse to set up a trust fund for this girl he met only an hour ago. But he is mesmerized, watching that hand stroking the cat and picturing it stroking him. (Just as his widowed father lusted for the governess he'd hired to take care of Oliver—that servant later became Sax's mother.) Now Sax finally understands how his remote father must have been feeling at that critical point in his life. How grateful he must have been to the woman who helped him raise his first son and then gave him another!

"I don't have to make enough to live on. You see, I have this grandfather, Ben Zimmerman." She pauses for his reaction.

"Oh, yes. Even I, who know next to nothing about fashion, have heard of Ben Zimmerman."

"Pretty much everybody has," says Karla. Then, moving on to Adele and her anorexia and her orchids, and keen to keep impressing this guy who actually seems to get her, she uncovers storytelling skills she never knew she possessed, describing her first visit to her grandfather's estate.

"So, if they're willing to support you, why do you work at all?" Her shining moonstone eyes have, for some time now, kept Sax from thinking of Fleur.

She shrugs. "I have to do something." And Karla is not about to admit, especially to herself, that she is happiest in places where no one can see her—except for right now, when she is ecstatic to at last be seen. "My grandparents and Viv think I'm going full-time to NYU. I haven't told you about Viv."

"I think we'd better save that for next time." Hit again by his own exhaustion, Sax staggers to his feet, at the same time telling himself, *Who knows? There might actually be a next time.* He's not usually home when the cleaning help is working, but now he just might have to arrange to be here once or twice.

"Of course." Stopped in the middle of her narrative, Karla jumps up, horrified. She was boring him, going on and on about herself, and after what he's just been through. What are her problems compared with that? She does not want to just leave him, though, and end this encounter; in fact, she will do anything to extend it. The image of the nude in his bedroom flashes in her mind, and she asks, "Would it be okay if I took one more quick look at your Modigliani?"

"I was about to suggest something along the same lines." Sax smiles, looking into her intriguing, pale eyes before he leads her out of the kitchen.

Once again enfolded in laid-back jazz, they move down the hall.

"Do you keep your stereo on all the time?" she asks, smothering a wild hope as she follows him as far as and then into his bedroom.

She has at last stumbled on the man she has been looking for, some-one she finds extremely attractive and amazingly likable, and who seems to like her as much as she likes him. Although Karla has not moved quickly down the hall, her heart is galloping.

"The tape player shuts off automatically at midnight and goes on again at seven in the morning. But I can turn it off if you want." He reminds himself that, no matter what Fleur might think, twenty-one is no longer a child. And this girl has been living on her own for some time.

"No, I like this music." And, oh, God, she likes this man.

"I think appreciation of Oscar Peterson is only one of the things we have in common." If he is to get through this night without falling apart, Sax badly needs to be with someone, anyone, and this attractive young woman is so much more than just anyone. "I sense a special bond between us." He hopes she did not observe his wince because, even though it was true, the line sounded corny—maybe because he is feeling rather like Humbert Humbert, the child seducer. But surely Sax cannot be blamed for wanting a little human contact—not after what Fleur has just done to him.

"I have to admit, I do love your paintings." In fact, whatever does or does not happen between them, Karla wishes she could simply stay here with the art and him and the music. But if she had not suggested a final visit to the Modigliani, she would already be on her way home. Temporarily reprieved, she faces the sexy nude and, again absorbing its heat, thinks that after she has been visiting like this with Sax, taking the service elevator is going to feel strange.

"I could see that," he agrees, joining her to stare at his Modigliani.

"Most especially this one." She cannot wait to tell Viv and her grandmother all about the painting and its owner, and how marvel-ous they both are, so Karla will have to think up a reason to have been in this apartment. Maybe pretend she knows Sax's daughter, Fleur, from NYU?

"Would you consider spending the night here?" he blurts out. *So much for a suave seduction*, he berates himself.

"How do you mean that?" Her body already on fire, Karla knows exactly how he means it. Her big chance is finally here. She steps away to look at him. Is having sex with this man who is, for God's sake, her boss, a good idea? But what if nobody else ever asks her? It's not as if Karla isn't attracted to Sax—quite the contrary, in fact. It's not as if at this point she really gives a shit whether or not it's a good idea. "You'll have to explain."

"I guess you'd have to say I mean it lasciviously." Sitting down on the bed's edge, he kicks off his shoes and looks up at her. "Interested?" he asks.

Oh, God, is she! But will she know what to do? Or, worse, will he know that she doesn't? "Yes, I'd like that." Kicking off her own shoes as if she has done this thousands of times, she fakes casualness. She fakes calm. She suppresses her excitement.

"Great." Relieved at how well this is going—he will not be stuck all night with his own morbid recriminations after all—Sax unbuckles his belt, slides off his trousers, and drapes them over a chair.

Karla unbuttons her skirt, slips it off, and tosses it more or less in the same direction.

He unbuttons and removes his shirt.

She unpeels and removes her leotard.

He pushes off his underpants and socks.

She wriggles out of her tights and stares, unable to understand why no one has ever told her how funny an erection looks. Maybe his is different. His body is all bone and muscle, his skin a glowing white, his hair ebony black. Is this wiry guy with a knockwurst waving up out of his crotch unique?

Never mind whether this is a smart move. Sax counts on good old animal lust to wash away his fears of not meeting this strange young woman's expectations—if she has any.

Laughing, Karla slides with him under the bedcovers, and then everything happens faster than thinking. They move together, skin against skin, and never has she felt anything so thrilling. His penis, hard and unyielding, is coated in something soft as an earlobe or a rose petal. Their tongues touch, stop touching, touch again, wet becoming wetter, moistening the dryness until nothing is dry, and then he pushes into her.

And he is surrounded by her, his every idea, emotion, sensation absorbed in her.

"Oh," she cries out, because for a second, it hurt.

"Oops." Coming far more quickly than he'd like, he goes limp. "Sorry," he moans.

"That's okay." She likes him lying on her. She likes the stickiness, and his penis still in her, only now it is soft. Clasping her arms around this man's ropy back, she enjoys the feel of him resting on top of her, enjoys her sense of accomplishment. For Karla can finally check losing her virginity off her to-do list and move on to what happens next.

CHAPTER 3

S he wakes up blank. Where is she? Ah, yes. Others act according to plan, but Karla acts on impulse, as if going to bed with Saxton Perry was not so much a decision as an inevitability. "You two are *beshayrt*, destined," as Viv, if she were in the know, would say. But this morning, having achieved one long-term goal, Karla must take stock. Where besides Saxton Perry's bed is she? She came here as a maid; she'll leave here as a what? And when will she go?

The rest of the bed is tousled but empty. So where is the man who is now her boss and lover? The sound of a running shower tells her. Whenever he returns to the bedroom, will it be easier or harder than it was before they slept together to talk to him? This is a new game with new rules. Since Karla is lying here naked in his bed, pretending nothing happened would be difficult, if not impossible. She considers leaping up to get into her clothes so Sax will find her dressed.

Checking Mutti's Timex, which, incongruously, is still strapped around her wrist, Karla sees it is only a quarter past five, too early for the music to go back on but some ten hours after they fell asleep together. Amazing. She stretches, then collapses. Might as well go with the flow. Especially since it's the crack of dawn. No one is expecting Karla to be anyplace today except Ron'l, who has his own key and can let himself into the loft. She might as well lie here, taking in the sheets' silky feel and her new, funky smell.

As cars swoosh down Park Avenue and trains rumble underneath, Karla feels as if she is catching a performance of a play in which she just happens to be acting. What do people do after they make love? *The Joy of Sex* didn't say anything about that part. In movies, the camera just cuts to elsewhere. She has never seen a heroine washing, dressing, going about the business of her life after sex. All Karla knows is that she has spent the night with a man she hardly knows and that he seems immensely likable.

In reality, though the naked part of sex was megadelicious, the actual intercourse was an anticlimax, and, lying here, thinking about climaxes and anticlimaxes, Karla chuckles. She is finally in the know. What was once vague is now specific. Overnight, her *schmunda* (Viv's word for a vagina) went from being a "down there" (Mutti's expression) to having its own identity. Karla presides over a secret entrance to a cavern as welcoming to visitors as her stomach is to food.

Having often seen interlocked hearts chalked on sidewalks—"Tom loves Tina," "Kim loves Scott"—she feels like drawing one of her own to say, "Schmunda sort of loves schlong." But who knew the experience would be funny? Remembering Sax's pecker sticking out of him like a fishing pole makes her giggle.

At this point, she has no idea whether she will ever again see that rod. She and Sax could now be an item, or last night could have been a once-in-a-lifetime experience. There is the faint possibility that Karla might already be pregnant. She recalls what Vince said about avoiding pregnancy that night, years ago, when he asked if she had a diaphragm. But evidently either Sax assumed Karla was on the pill or he didn't care. He squirted his seed into her, and the book said not to believe the myth—you *can* get pregnant the first time.

Not that Karla ever believed she couldn't. In fact, after Ron'l explained sex to her, she figured that was how she herself must have been conceived, because she was surprised Mutti had had sex even that once. Impossible to imagine her ever having sex again, with Karla's father or anyone else.

How different she is from Mutti, who gave birth in the loft with only Viv and a government how-to manual in attendance! Not that Karla expects to become a mother right away, but having babies is something that, like cleaning, she can see herself doing. And if she did give birth, someone like Saxton Perry would be sure she had a doctor and nurses, in a hospital. Unless they decided she should have their baby right here, with a midwife. And why not? Karla loves this room.

She twists around for a look at her sexy guardian angel and, feeling blissfully safe, returns to her musings. Of course she knows this is all fantasy, but what harm is there in that? Pretending is fun, and wherever and whenever Karla has a kid, made-up or actual, the main thing is that it will have a live, on-site father. Boy or girl, the child will wear white diapers and clothes of every color. Karla will never dress it in black.

Snuggling into her silky-sheet make-believes, she pictures what being "with child"—an expression she has always adored—would be like. She doesn't know anyone, other than maybe her grand-mother, who could tell her how it actually feels to be pregnant, but if Karla ever does have a baby, Viv and her grandparents will be on cloud nine, while Mutti will roll over in her grave—a two-for-one.

Ben will, of course, want to design her maternity clothes, but he might not do it if she insists on black. And Karla would finally give in. Because she knows her grandparents are probably right: it is time for her to get past her mental block about wearing colors. Miracu-lously, the prospect now excites, rather than daunts, her.

She can hardly believe that in less than twenty-four hours, so much about her is new and better, and all because of Sax. How can she express her gratitude to him? The answer to that question is clear. Her first assignment is to make him realize his daughter's suicide attempt was not caused by anything he did or did not do. Karla is actually good at getting people to feel better. Look at her grandmother—until Karla advised Adele to "think of food as medicine you have to take three times a day," the old woman hardly ate. Now, they sometimes reminisce about that advice as they split a hot pastrami on rye.

Adele's turnaround is Karla's greatest victory to date, while Mutti, whose death she did not prevent, is her greatest defeat. Still, Karla knows more now than she did back then, and she wonders if, after fixing up Sax, she should look for a job in a hospital or a rehab center or a school for at-risk kids. In any case, today she will quit housecleaning, which, it turns out, has served a hidden purpose. Through this job, Karla met her first lover; after it, she can begin a new life. Realizing this, she hugs herself in delight.

Imagining pregnancy is so enjoyable that Karla decides if it is a boy, she will call him Michael, after her father. If it is a girl, Karla has always liked the name Lydia. Now, when she says it in her head—*Lydia Most, Lydia Perry* (she will figure out that part later)— it sounds perfect. If, of course, Sax is still in the picture, and if he agrees, he will probably have his own naming preferences.

This gives Karla pause. His daughter is called Fleur. How la-di-da is that? What if he wants a Phoebe or a Gwendolyn? After five years on her own, having successfully fought off Viv and her grandparents, Karla is not eager to give in to anyone else's preferences, especially not when it comes to having a Phoebe.

But the thought of spending every night in this lovely bed and waking up every morning underneath that gorgeous nude, well, what could possibly top that? And who knows? If they stay together, Sax just might let Karla do whatever she wants—not such a far-fetched notion. Certainly, up to this point, as a boss he has been the exact opposite of bossy.

Meanwhile, in the next room, the showering Sax is asking himself, *What the hell was I thinking? A twenty-one-year-old girl? Jesus!* Glancing down, he notices blood streaks on his thigh. Great! As if sleeping with the maid were not bad enough, she has her period. So now his sheets will be a mess and he can't even ask her to change them. Can he?

Wearily, Sax stands there. Yesterday's tension left his arms, ass, and legs feeling beaten up, bruised. His head throbs, but after only two beers he can't be hungover, so this must be his punishment for, first, not having kept Fleur from trying to kill herself and, second, for having invited this initially intriguing girl into his bed. Sure, it was easier to think about her than to worry about his daughter, but Fleur should have been all that was in Sax's mind.

Who said living in the moment is a good idea? Last night, he ignored the obvious consequences of getting involved with his maid. Now, having further complicated a lousy situation, Sax will have to deal with one-of-a-kind Karla, as well as with the aftermath of Fleur's suicide attempt. Without the first clue about how to go about addressing either problem, he stays in the shower.

An abundance of hot water running over him usually dissipates the worst day-after recriminations, but today the flow merely slides over Sax, leaving intact the heavy load on his spirit. Nevertheless, he makes no move to finish up so he can reckon with the maid who—at least last night—seemed so much more than just a maid.

But this is today. There is cat food to be bought. And Sax has to get to the hospital. The doctors will probably want to check Fleur into a psychiatric facility. Will she go willingly? If not, what a mess *that* is going to be!

And, as if that were not enough, at some point Sax will have to check in at his office, where things will either be in chaos or running so smoothly that he and everyone will wonder why he ever needs to be there. If he tells his secretary or his partners what happened, he will have to face questions he is no way ready to answer. So he remains in the shower, smearing soap over himself.

Ordinarily, Sax enjoys the sensation of his hand slipping over and around his body. Now he simply soaps, rinses, reluctantly twists the taps, wearily steps out.

As far as the girl in his bed is concerned . . . Sax wipes the cloud off the mirror and wonders who that baggy-eyed old guy peering back at him is. Whoever that person may be, he will have to be straight with the girl. He must explain that he was strung out, not himself, and that it will never happen again.

Sax must not, under any circumstances, mention money. Thank God he always pays the agency, not the help. He supposes that to avoid any future awkwardness, he should call and tell them to replace this one. But that might get her in trouble, which is the last thing he wants to do. Better just to make sure he is never in the apartment on her cleaning days.

He draws his razor along his jaw; then, remembering how as a little kid Fleur loved to watch him shave, he stifles a sob, chastises himself for being maudlin, finishes shaving, dries his face, wraps a towel around his waist, and walks into the bedroom, half hoping to find that the girl has already taken off.

No such luck. There she is, lying in the center of his bed, the covers pulled up under her arms, her sweet-potato hair fanned over her pillow, a seductive smile on her lips. For an admiring instant, he wonders whether sleeping with her was such a mistake after all, but the moment of self-forgiveness quickly passes. No matter how gorgeously tempting she is, twenty-one is still too young for any fifty-year-old particularly this one, on the day his daughter tried to kill herself. At this very minute, Sax should be calling the hospital to check on Fleur's condition.

Turning away from the bed, aware of Karla watching, he drops his towel and hastily pulls on clean undershorts. By the time he turns back to her, he is buttoning on a beautifully laundered, starch-free white shirt as if it were armor. "I gather you've got the curse," he announces, and thinks, *Damn it, that is not how I intended to approach her.*

"What curse?" Karla has been enjoying each detail of his reverse striptease, but now, accused by him, she stiffens.

"Your period. You know . . . I mean, that's what my daughter calls it. The curse."

"My friend Ron'l calls it my monthlies, but I'm not due for two weeks." So why does Sax think she has her period, and why isn't he meeting her eyes?

"I guess you're early, then." He ducks into the closet for a suit and—more important—a fresh subject.

She looks under the covers to see what he's talking about and realizes the sheet is bloodstained. "Oh, shit. But listen, I don't think that's from my period." She pokes her head out again, only to find him still looking anywhere but at her. What happened to yesterday's approval? Was messing up his sheet such a big deal? Is that all she did wrong?

"Never mind. It is what it is." He has his trousers on now, his fly zipped. "The main thing is that last night I was completely strung out and not myself," he says matter-of-factly. Sax does not want her thinking this is her fault.

"I guess I was kind of weirded out, too." Chilled by his coolness, rather than by the room's, Karla thrusts her arms under the covers and wriggles down so only her head sticks out. "You know, it was my first time making love," she confesses, hoping he will therefore be willing to forgive her for any mistakes.

"Really?" Sax recoils. Does she expect him to believe she was a virgin? He emits something between a snort and a chortle.

"Really." Karla does not see what is funny about what she said. She just knows Mr. Mood Swing is starting to piss her off. "You know, after last night it just could be, maybe, that I'm going to have your baby." Let him snicker about that.

"Really," Sax all but drawls, wondering if she actually thinks he is stupid enough to believe that a) he deflowered her and b) he knocked her up. This girl, who just a few minutes ago he found irresistible, either is a full-blown nutcase or takes him for an idiot. And if the latter is true, maybe she is right, as only an idiot would have fallen for her scam. "So, what makes you think you might be pregnant?"

"I believe it can happen the first time." Hoping for some sympathy, she flashes him a nervous smile.

Her bared teeth, Sax thinks, give her a feral, cunning look. "Just take it from me," he says, leaning toward the girl as if he were a lion tamer with a chair. "You are not pregnant." No twenty-one-year-old runs around having sex with strangers without using some form of birth control; she could not have known he had a vasectomy, so this has to be some sort of racket. Unless this girl is indeed insane.

"How do you know I'm not?" Suppressing unwelcome tears, she glowers at him defiantly.

Aha, so that's it. Taking full advantage of his vulnerability, Little Miss Innocent is now ready to close in for the kill. Sax was conned, punished not only for his other sins but also for his damn gullibility. This whole thing was a setup. Of course she was the one who suggested they go back into the bedroom for a last look at his nude—right from the get-go, she was scheming. "Assuming you are pregnant"—for once glad he has it in him, Sax now exudes maximum WASP frostiness—"I will have no difficulty proving that I am not your child's father." Given all he now has on his plate, she can take her attempted blackmail and stuff it where the sun don't shine.

"You'd have to be its father." Infuriated as much by the man's tone as by his words, she sits straight up while covering her breasts with the sheet and glares. What gives him the right to speak to her like this? "Like I said, I've never made love before. Or had sex," she adds, because it is now apparent that, at least on his side, love had nothing to do with what they did together last night.

"You cannot actually expect me to believe that," Sax replies, his voice still icy. Now he gets it—when she isn't cleaning, she is probably a call girl, the price naturally higher for a "virgin." And to think, last night he actually considered setting up some kind of endowment for her. How dumb was that?

"Believe whatever you want." Tempted to duck under the covers until this is over, she holds her position. The fact that all of it is her fault does not mean she has to cave. After what happened with Vince, Karla should have known better than to confess her virginal status. Now, another guy is freaking out because it was her first time. She should have let him believe she was experienced. She'll just have to show him right now.

"Don't worry," she says. Even if she does turn out to be pregnant, no way is she giving birth in a loft all by herself—that much is certain. She will stop on the way home at the drugstore and pick up a test kit, then know for sure. And whatever it says, she will somehow manage to deal with it. She might even be glad about it; left to her own devices, Karla is good at dealing with things. "I'll handle whatever happens next."

"You can't be serious." But one look at her determined expression shows him she is serious indeed. *Okay*, Sax thinks. *There are two possibilities: either this girl is an extortionist or she's being honest.* He shakes his head, confused. "Last night was your first time ever?" He peers at her, hoping to detect from some change in her expression that she has been lying to him.

"Yes," Karla admits, bowing her head, blushing before forcing herself to look him in the eye again. How incredulous Sax looks! This is even worse than it was with Vince.

The blush convinces Sax. Either the girl is the best actress since

Sarah Bernhardt or she is telling the truth, and he has the feeling she isn't a great actress. *Damn!* Shaken, he blurts out, "Oh, God, I'm so sorry." He clasps his forehead. "But at least I can reassure you on one issue. If what you say is true, and I'm sure it is"—there was the damn bloody evidence—"you're not pregnant."

"How do you know?" And how many versions of this man are there? First accuser, then apologist—how is Karla supposed to respond to the shifts?

"I had a vasectomy," he informs her.

"What's that?" she asks curiously.

Oh, Jesus, he thinks, *she is a true naïf*—someone he clearly has to educate. "My tubes were surgically cut so sperm couldn't get through them. Hence, I can't make anyone pregnant ever again." And, having spelled that out, Sax turns away, flings open his closet door, and busies himself picking out a necktie.

Whoever the maid in his bed may be, he has Fleur to deal with. He cannot spend more time on anything else. It is pointless to call the hospital; they never tell you anything on the phone. He will just go straight over there. But first, whether she is a schemer or a virgin, he simply has to get this Karla out of here. So, opting for the out-of-season madras tie his daughter once gave him for his birthday, and hoping Fleur will be in good enough shape to see that he has it on, he emerges from the closet and announces, "I have to get some cat food. That should take me no more than fifteen minutes, after which I'll come back for you and drop you off on my way to the hospital."

He raises his chin and tightens his tie while giving her a *this is it, kid* look. Sax is going to concentrate now on his daughter. "I assume you'll be ready to go when I get back." Not looking at the girl again, he leaves.

So that's how it is. My life-altering experience was his one-night stand. I should have seen that coming. The jerk is dumping me, Karla thinks. *Well, fuck that!* Still, for a moment, wondering if she misread him this morning or last night, she stays in bed for a bit longer, in case. But he doesn't do another about-face; he just abandons her. Seething, she hurls back the comforter, springs up, skips the tights, jams herself into her leotard, throws on her skirt.

Grateful for this chance to work off her negative energy, she yanks off the quilt, strips his bed, jabs the stained sheets into his bathroom hamper, and heads for the linen closet. After making up his bed, she takes a last look at the Modigliani. "You're the one I'm going to miss," she tells the nude. Then, without so much as combing her hair, Karla marches to the kitchen, grabs her coat, pockets her tights, walks out the back door, and rings for the elevator.

Last night, she thought taking the service elevator would feel funny. This morning, it feels like this is where she belongs, and that makes her want to cry.

On his return to the apartment, having failed to come up with a plan B for getting rid of Karla, Sax is relieved to find her gone. Yet, as he feeds the cat, he cannot help being disappointed in himself. He cannot help feeling sorry for the girl he just kicked out.

She is probably as nice as she seemed at first. And even if she isn't, she deserved better treatment than she received at his hands. At the very least, Sax owes her an apology for his performance last night (what a miserable sexual initiation!). He owes her another apology for his behavior this morning.

He should never have rushed her out that way. It was unkind. He looks around, on the off chance that she left a note, but of course she didn't. In fact, it is almost as if the girl was never here, and surely it is better that way. Fleur is all Sax should be thinking about right now.

Still, he wishes he'd told Karla how sorry he was for what happened last night. He wishes he'd dropped her off at her home so he would at least know where she lives. Once this horror with Fleur is resolved, who knows? Maybe they could see each other again. Sax has never before met anyone quite like Karla.

∾

Still determined after this disaster to quit her job, Karla emerges from a seemingly endless twenty-minute subway ride and drags herself back home to Canal Street. Wanting only to crash, she opens her loft door and finds Ron'l sitting in front of Mutti's sewing machine, sporting the kind of dashiki and Afro wig that have been out of fashion for at least ten years. It is almost 1980, for God's sake!

Totally unaware of how ridiculous he looks, Ron'l says, "Ben say he look at my leisure-wear line soon as I get it ready."

That first time Karla took Ron'l to meet her grandparents, Adele pulled her aside after dinner to ask, "Does your friend talk like that because of his brain damage?"

Shocked, and wanting to answer, "He talks like that because he's Ron'l," Karla just shrugged and muttered, "Dunno."

By now, when he bestows upon her his bright, welcoming grin, she knows her friend talks funny. She knows that, according to the world, Ron'l is an oddball. But at the beginning, it was different. When she first met him on the street (keeping their friendship secret from Mutti), she lied and told him she was sixteen. He was twenty-two. At thirteen, thoroughly impressed by Ron'l, Karla thought the unique outfits he wore every day were brilliant. She thought everything he said was wise. She saw nothing wrong with a twenty-two-year-old man who collected and dressed Barbies, and she thought the clothes he made for his Barbie dolls were gorgeous.

And now, no matter how weird he is, Karla still loves Ron'l. So she feels shitty because, after repeatedly assuring him that he can come here whenever he wants, she just wants him to get the hell out this minute and leave her with her rage. Yet where would she be without Ron'l?

On that fateful first visit to her grandparents, he was the one who clued her in to the facts of life. The two of them were standing on Fifth Avenue, smelling the hot pavement and auto exhaust as they clutched plastic garbage bags with their swim clothes and some of his Barbies. They were waiting for Viv and Joel to come drive them out to Forest Hills, when Ron'l said, "Look," and pointed under a bench at a squirrel that was trying to get away from another squirrel, hanging on piggyback. "They fucking!" he announced with a grin.

"What's fucking?" she asked. The squirrels were making a sweeping noise against the litter and stones between the bench and the wall.

"You know. He sticking his dick in her."

"His dick?" The bottom one, squawking, couldn't shake the top one off.

"You're sixteen and you still doesn't know about dicks?"

Karla's face got hot.

"A dick's what every guy have," Ron'l said.

"Oh, you mean a penis." Relieved, she let out her breath. "Mutti told me about them." She turned away and noticed a woman listening, smirking and nodding. Again, Karla's face heated up.

"Your mom tell you what they for?" Ron'l asked.

Ignoring the woman—why should she care what a stranger thought?—Karla shrugged.

"They for fucking."

"And what's that for?"

"Making babies."

"Isn't there any other way?" She could not believe what he was telling her.

"Not except for Baby Jesus."

"What happened to him?"

"He be God's son."

Jesus was lucky, Karla thought. *He actually knew his father.* "So what?"

"So God never fucks." Ron'l chuckled at the idea.

"And everybody else does? Everybody comes from fucking?" She was amazed to realize that Mutti must actually have let somebody do that to her. And now, after her session with Sax, she has fucked, too. Or, rather, she has been fucked.

"Yup. And they also does it for fun," Ron'l added.

"Doesn't look like fun," Karla said that afternoon. Reluctantly, she checked back on the squirrels. The front one was still squawking but stayed crouched down while the other kept shoving.

"It feel better than it look." Ron'l grinned.

"I don't know." The heat in her face flowed down between her legs. Fun? That day, when they watched the squirrels, the idea made something somersault in her. But now, it actively nauseates her. "I'm going to take a bath."

Maybe Ron'l will take the hint and go home, she hopes, as she hurls her coat onto Mutti's old chair. It is much too hot for fur, and Karla stinks from sweating inside it.

"Where you been getting dirty?" asks Ron'l, making no move to leave.

Staring at him, Karla flinches. "What do you mean?" *Oh, God, does it show?* No matter what anyone says about Ron'l, he has a way of seeing right into her.

"This be awful early for you to be out, less you be up all night."

"I wasn't up all night. I slept."

"That all you done?" Ron'l winks at her.

"How can you tell?" Glimpsing her ratty hair and bare legs in Mutti's three-way mirror, Karla assumes everyone on the subway knew, too.

"You be talking about trying it forever. Who the guy?"

"A real jerk," she mutters, and rushes off to run her bathwater.

"That's okay." Ron'l ambles after her, hanging over the bathroom partition. "Most guys be jerks," he says.

"How could I have let him?" Maybe it is good after all that Ron'l is here. Who else does Karla have to talk to?

"You been wanting to do it."

"But not with him."

"He be your first, not your last."

"You think so?"

"It feel good?"

"Some of it." Blushing, she particularly recalls Sax's penis skin.

"That's it, then."

"What?" She adjusts the water to make it hot as hellfire; that is what she needs now.

"Well that be why he ain't gonna be your last. After a while, you only remember the feel-good parts and you got to do it again."

"Look how long it took me to find even one," she exclaims, wrenching the water tap and yanking off her leotard.

"You twenty-one. It go faster now you done it once," Ron'l promises, before turning away to resume his sewing.

Oh, God! Though he is clearly trying to be encouraging, the thought of any further sex-related rejection is terrible to her. After all, Sax spurned her just like Vince did. And if no guy is going to want Karla for long, her sex life is going to be an ugly necklace, a string of one humiliation after another. How long before the next hideous bead? Right now, no matter how good some of what they did last night felt, once every five years seems to her often enough. And never again with another shithead like that Saxton Perry, Karla vows.

Sliding down into the tub, she scrubs every single place the man touched. She even twists a washrag up into her sore vagina, remembering how Sax's dick actually hurt a little. So much for feeling good—she will just concentrate on the uncomfortable part of the event.

Karla emerges from her purification ritual energized by fury. How could she have wasted her one and only hymen on a man who only pretended to like her? And, fueled by her anger at him, she vigorously dries off with a coarse towel until her skin burns. Yet, as raw as she feels, she cannot help but sense a new, even delicious beginning. For she has finally sloughed off her virginity. That much, after all, is progress.

Steeling himself to appear impassive, Sax enters his daughter's hospital room. Her body still sprouts tubes and bags, but, no longer covered by a mask, that morbidly pale face is recognizably Fleur's. So Sax feels encouraged as he asks, "Feeling any better?"

"Oh, fuck yeah," she snarls. "I'm just peachy keen."

Determined not to recoil, Sax responds, more or less in kind, "Glad to hear that."

"Like you really give a shit," Fleur says, before erupting in a spasm of weeping.

"But I do. I *do* give a shit." Sax moves to cradle her shoulder with his arm. Still sobbing, she vehemently shakes him off.

And he'd hoped Fleur would be glad to see him wearing her tie. How unrealistic was that! If anything, she is sorry to see him, period. And what, in the face of her massive grief, can he do or say? Sax just stands there, watching, until, after what feels like an eternity, her crying finally subsides. Then, reaching over, like a psychotherapist he offers her the box of tissues from the bedside table.

She snatches at them as if to claw him.

Backing off, he sinks into a bedside chair.

"Don't try to pretend you get it." She begins her next round at maximum volume as if he is down the hall and not right next to her.

"You're right," Sax softly agrees. "I don't get it."

"You never have. If you did, I wouldn't be here."

So this is his fault?

"Not one single time in my whole life did you ever try to understand me," she accuses, her voice ragged and huge.

Not one word comes to mind in Sax's defense. "But maybe it's not too late," he at last ventures.

Ignoring him, she continues her earsplitting tirade. "You were always more interested in piling up money and buying art than you were in me," she claims, her eyes flaring.

"That's not true," Sax says, even as he wonders if his daughter is right. God knows he put a lot of effort into his passion for art and his work.

"With all your connections in the art world," she is hollering, "you could easily have gotten Ned a gallery showing that would've put him on the map, but you never lifted one finger to help him, not one."

"That is not true, either." Sax restrains himself from delivering his opinion of either the so-called artist or his load of crap work, like the collage of used Kotex Ned labeled *Found Objects*.

"If you really loved me, helping Ned would have been the least you could do. But no, you just forked over checks, as if that was enough."

Silencing himself, Sax does not point out that Fleur kept cashing those very checks. He does not mention that she and her scheming boyfriend have been living off him for years.

"And did you ever once praise me for any of my accomplishments? No!" Fleur screams.

What accomplishments? A horseback-riding award when she was twelve? A high school diploma? Surely he did praise her for those. But now, trying not to absorb her words, Sax flinches as each charge pelts his soul. Though normally he would attempt to defend himself, nothing about this situation is normal.

A nurse comes in, takes Fleur's pulse, uses an ear thermometer to get her temperature, and measures her blood pressure without interrupting the barrage of bile that spews from her patient's mouth. Ignoring Sax, an aide comes in and asks if Fleur wants something to drink. Fleur shakes her head vehemently, and the aide scoots around Sax as if he is part of the chair and leaves Fleur to go right on smashing word after word at him.

Under the circumstances, what can he say? What can he do? Since Sax has heard that depression is hostility turned inward, at this point, letting her vent is probably his best move. Finally, though, he does murmur, "You do know I have always loved you, don't you?"

"You don't even know what love is!" Fleur shrieks, not missing a beat in the harangue, which is still going full blast when an unlikely savior, Sax's ex-wife, finally shows up.

Only then, like a whipped dog, can Sax slink away and flee to his office.

Once there, he licks his wounds, makes a couple of calls, and reassures four clients that, yes, their money is in good hands. The firm has excellent backup people, which is all to the good, since Sax is hardly in a condition to focus on the stock market.

Fleur's situation and her accusations throb in him like a rotten tooth, and when he switches his thoughts over to his supposedly palliative interlude with Karla, his pain is even greater. Yet he cannot get the girl out of his mind. It isn't so much the sex, which, in retrospect, was on his part embarrassing and regrettable. In fact, it was worse than regrettable. For her first time, there he was, unable to sustain an erection. Damn! Here is another young woman he cannot satisfy. If only he could forget about the whole incident. If only he could forget his whole life.

But, for some reason, he cannot erase the image of Karla standing transfixed in front of his Modigliani. Then he thinks about their talk in the kitchen as she shared fascinating things, like how she'd been dressed in black from the day she was born. And that she was an orphan, living on her own. How, after that, could he have doubted her authenticity?

She was a servant, just like his mother, the governess. But most of her life, this poor girl didn't even possess written proof of her existence. No one could make that up.

What a life she has had, and still so young! How rotten Karla must be feeling now! Didn't Fleur's near tragedy teach Sax anything? He owes this pathetic creature, abandoned by both her parents, some reassurance. He did not shun Karla because of anything she did or did not do. Facing the truth, he admits to himself that this morning he just got cold feet.

Impulsively, he reaches for the phone, calls the agency, and asks for the girl's number.

"I'm sorry, Mr. Perry. We do not give out that information."

"Then please ask Ms. Most to call me." Knowing she will not call, Sax leaves his numbers anyway. Then he buzzes his secretary. "Please bring me the Manhattan phone book, Sheila."

How many Mosts can there be? A lot more than he thought, but there is no Karla. However, there is an L. Most on Canal Street, and that is where she said she was born.

He rings the number, and someone answers. "Hello," he says cautiously. "Is this Karla? Karla Most?" Who may well not want to talk to him.

"Yes?"

"This is Sax Perry." Until he heard her voice, he didn't realize how much he needed to find her. At least he now has a chance to make things right.

"Oh." She sounds as closed off from him as Fleur does.

"I just called to apologize," he begins. If he can figure out how to get through to this girl, maybe, just maybe, he can eventually reach his daughter.

"What for?" At least she isn't hanging up.

"Well, I guess for running out on you like that," he admits, each word fraught with guilt.

"I was the one who left," she points out, her voice sullen.

"That's true." He has no right to be irritated when she puts him in his place, but, damn it, she is tough.

"So you have nothing to apologize for." Icicles drip from her every word. And she is apparently ready to end this conversation.

What next, then? Sax cannot bring himself to give up just yet. "You know, I really enjoyed talking with you last night," he says, trying truthful flattery.

"Okay." No hint of a thaw.

"Would you consider having dinner with me again tonight?" This isn't at all what he planned to say. "In a restaurant?" On neutral turf.

"I don't think that's a good idea." Karla makes sure her voice says that as far as she is concerned, he can take his Jekyll-and-Hyde routine and stuff it.

"In all fairness," Sax says, surprising himself, "I think I deserve a chance to explain in person what happened."

"I don't see why." Karla isn't giving him an inch.

"Well, you strike me as the kind of person who'd appreciate a second chance if you messed up, someone who would offer the same to others."

"You don't have any idea what I'm like." But she is beginning again to want to show him. And the guy is right; she *is* someone who likes to help people.

"But I'd like to find out." Sax does not have to fake his most persuasive voice; he really does want to know what makes her tick.

"Just dinner, then," she concedes. After all, the man is a fellow human being, not a monster. And she loves it when her grandparents take her out to one of their swanky restaurants. And Sax did enable her to accomplish a long-term goal. So she argues herself into agreeing to meet him. "Dinner." Already Karla is kicking herself. "Nothing else."

"Sounds great," Sax says.

"Where and what time?" she asks. It has to be someplace she can walk out of if he flips on her again. And even if she stays for the whole meal, she plans to make it clear to him that this will be the very last time they will ever meet. Of that she is positive.

"Quo Vadis on Sixty-Third Street, just off Madison Avenue, at seven thirty. See you then." Sax hangs up before she can change her mind.

CHAPTER 4

As the time for the dinner draws near, Karla is furious at herself. She should never have agreed to meet him. She tries calling Sax to get out of it but gets no answer, so she decides to go up to the restaurant to explain that she cannot stay to eat.

She makes a point of fixing herself up, even if she is not going to be there long enough for what she looks like to matter. Knowing she looks good gives her confidence, at least until seven minutes to eight, when she rushes into Quo Vadis to be met by a wall of heat and a grinning Sax.

He is coming at her, arms outstretched. Karla's heart slaps at her. Her head empties. She can hardly breathe. She staggers, looks for something to support her—a counter or a chair—and finds nothing except his arm, which she grasps to keep from sinking.

"I was afraid you weren't coming," Sax says, as, instead of leading her back to shore, he draws her further into the heat.

"I can't stay," she gasps. But she has to grasp that log to keep from sinking; she has to keep moving with him toward a banquette, where he deposits her. "I'm not feeling well." Indeed, she feels too weak to get up and leave.

"You look fine. In fact, you look terrific."

She shrugs. What does that matter? She almost passed out. Still feeling faint, she does not need this man to tell her she looks great when she has on her very best dress, a form-fitting number designed by her grandfather, and when she took the trouble to mascara her eyelashes. Now she takes a sip of ice water, which steadies her.

"I'll tell you why I wanted to see you tonight," he is saying. "I thought I should apologize for how I acted this morning."

Damn right you should, Karla thinks, once she can again breathe normally.

"I was upset about my daughter," Sax goes on, "and I'm afraid I took out my anxiety about her on you. I'm so sorry." Clearly, he has rehearsed this speech.

Yet, caught off-guard, Karla is moved by it. So she cannot respond by telling him she is taking off. But what else has she to say? Her first impulse is to forgive him, but, no matter how contrite he is, she is not about to tell him his behavior this morning was okay. Karla is not one of those masochists who let people get away with anything as long as they say they are sorry. But it was big of Sax to admit he was out of line. So she figures she can at least lay the napkin across her lap and ask the poor guy, "How is your daughter doing?"

"According to the doctors, she has pretty much recovered physically, but her emotional recovery will take months." Sax sighs.

Out of sympathy for his situation, now resigned to getting through the meal with him, Karla looks around. The other women here are into pearls and heavy makeup. But because Karla is wearing what Ron'l calls her "basic black," she can pass as someone who also belongs in an upscale place like this. With Mutti to thank for her camouflage, Karla waves away the menu and asks Sax, "Why don't you just order for us both?" There is something to be said, after all, for floating on life's tide and seeing where it takes her.

Sax checks on whether or not she eats red meat, then chooses escargots, *entrecôte* (rare), and a Moët, to be followed by a Médoc. This man, a somewhat younger version of her grandfather, is apparently like Ben, a flaunter of that "let's spare no expense" life-style. With people like that looking after her, Karla cannot help feeling cosseted.

After he has told the waiter what to bring, Sax talks with her as openly as he did yesterday in his kitchen. Again his tongue flicks in and out of his lips. But this time, because she knows how that tongue tastes, she keeps up her guard. Yet so intent is she on watching and listening to him that everyone else in the restaurant disappears. Only his words cross the table, as if he has been waiting all his life to have this conversation.

And Karla? At first she stayed here because she felt faint. Then she stayed because she felt sorry for this man whose daughter just tried to off herself. But now she cannot imagine leaving before he finishes what he is saying.

He tells her how, when he was still married, he started collecting art by enrolling in a course called Principles, Techniques, and Issues in the Acquisition of Art. One assignment was to attend an auction at Parke-Bernet Galleries and to hand in notes. Sax thought he might find something there for the apartment he had just bought (the very apartment Karla cleaned for him). He was also starting to make real money, and he'd decided he wanted to live with genuine art, not fakes or copies.

So, one night when Pam was going to one of her committee meetings, he and Fleur attended his first art auction. "We were both fascinated when they wheeled out these things on enormous easels and the auctioneer pulled off the cloths, announcing that, at ten feet high, the portals were really too grand to be called doors. I was enthralled by them," Sax says.

"I can understand that." Enthralled herself, Karla watches that lizard tongue.

Sax's words are covering the surface of their time together with a shimmering, silken web. "I knew the doors would fit perfectly

between the living and dining rooms. And that was all I was thinking about when I asked Fleur if she liked them. I wasn't really asking
for her opinion."

"And did she like them?" Remembering her plan to cheer him
up, Karla likes the fact that he is recalling his daughter on a happy
occasion.

"Yes. We agreed they'd be great in our new place, before I
flipped up my card to indicate the minimum bid. I'll never forget—
two thousand dollars.

"'Two thousand five hundred,' said the auctioneer, nodding
toward someone in back. Of course I turned to see who it was, but
there were too many hats and hairdos and suits. And what difference
did it make? This was my first-ever art auction, and those doors had
my name on them. 'Three thousand.' I felt like shouting, but, obey-
ing the rules, I just flipped my paddle."

"The way you're telling it, I feel like I can see it." Karla loves
being present in his past.

"'Four thousand!' came from behind us, and I asked Fleur,
'What do you think?' She said, 'They're kind of like the ones in the
Morgan Library.'

"'Your mother will love them,' I told her." Sax's quick laugh
sounds more like throat clearing than mirth.

"And were you right?" Karla asks, to distract him from his pain.
"Did she love them?" And did he love Pam? Does he still?

"You bet! So, feeling for the first time in my life like a mogul,
I turned up my card and I just kept turning it up. Seven thousand,
nine thousand, eleven thousand—the hell with it, I decided. Those
doors were not just an investment. I simply had to have them. I
knew ten thousand was, at most, what they were worth. And yet I
kept bidding to twenty-five, and finally I heard, 'Going, going'—the
auctioneer stretched it out—'gone!' He gestured at me, and he was
exactly right—I *was* gone. Was there even enough in our checking

account to cover this? I had been on the job for less than a year—would I have to write a check on the company account?

"My professor had never discussed what happened when you had to have something at any price. As I was leaving, telling Fleur to wait for me, I was trying to figure out whether my impulsiveness meant I was temperamentally unsuited to be a collector. Or was the intensity of my lust for such an object proof that I was born to collect?"

"Judging from what I've seen, you were clearly born to collect," his personal cheerleader assures him, before giving herself fully to lust. For Karla finally understands what "can't take her eyes off him" really means as her gaze melts into his lips, his tongue, his fingers, his thumb, until she manages to drag herself back to what he is saying.

"I asked a young usher, 'Do you happen to know who else was bidding?' Because by then I was wondering if even a reputable place like Parke-Bernet might plant a shill to fleece a neophyte like me. And I gave the usher my eye-to-eye, heart-to-heart, sincere-to-the-core smile."

"Are those the same smiles you've been giving me?" Karla challenges him, only half kidding.

"Probably," Sax disarms her by admitting.

"At least you're honest." Laughing, Karla has to give him that much.

"It worked on her, too. 'I think it was that woman over there.' The usher pointed to someone I thought I knew very well indeed.

"'Listen,' I told her, actually laughing as if the situation were hilarious. 'There's been a silly mistake. That's my wife.' And, seeing Pam there, I felt as if I had fallen down the rabbit hole. I mean, what the hell was she doing at an art auction, and why was she bidding against me?

"'We shouldn't have been bidding against each other,' I explained, trying to get my bearings.

"'I'm afraid that won't really make a difference,' she said.

"'It has to,' I insisted. "'She's my wife.' I signaled to Pam to meet us at the door. 'I mean, we've got to come to an understanding about this,'" I warned.

"Oh, God, I can just see it," Karla says, though what she really sees is how strong a hold his child and his ex have on him.

"'You'll have to speak to the cashier,' the usher told me," Sax continues. "At that point, I was still amused because I'd been right— Pam *was* going to love those doors. It never occurred to me to worry whether she was still loving me. I just figured I should not have to cough up two and a half times what the doors were worth because we could not see each other. The hall was designed to mislead bidders. If necessary, I was prepared to make a stink; in fact, by that time I was looking forward to taking on Parke-Bernet. 'Your people can auction off the doors again. We'll happily bid on them,' I told the girl.

"'That's right,' Pam said, as she joined us. 'I still want them.'

"'You're going to have them—that's not the point,' I told her. 'The only issue is, are we going to pay ten thousand or twenty-five thousand dollars for them? That difference is more than a year of Fleur's tuition.' By then I was feeling like my old, skinflint self. 'There's no call to be profligate,' I reminded her."

"What skinflint lives in an apartment like yours?" Karla asks.

"As my mother used to say, 'Money is meant to be wasted, not thrown away.'"

"I'll have to remember that one," Karla murmurs.

Sax is still telling his story. "'I didn't mean to go over ten,' Pam said, as we went into an office, where an imitation Englishman rose and snootily asked 'May I help you?'

"'I certainly hope so,' I managed to say, even though I was suddenly back in prep school, being called before the headmaster. 'I'm afraid my wife and I have gotten ourselves into rather a mess.' I tried throwing myself on what I knew was this fellow's nonexistent mercy.

"'Oh, yes?' He lifted one eyebrow, obviously unimpressed.

"I persisted. 'After all, I couldn't see that my wife was here, and when someone behind me bid, I kept raising, until afterward we realized we'd been competing with each other.' It never occurred to me at that point that while I hadn't been able to see Pam, she must have seen me. I just thought this sort of thing must have happened before, that they should have a system for dealing with it."

Determined not to interrupt again before he finishes, Karla sips her delicious wine.

"And then Pam took my arm. 'Could you please come out in the hall with me for a moment so we can talk?'

"Her ultrasolemn request struck me as ridiculous, but she had such a pleading look on her face, I said, 'Sure. If you'll excuse us . . .' I nodded at the Brit, who had begun to look somewhat less imposing.

"But after the door closed and we were out in the hall, I comprehended that whatever Pam had to say was going to be something I didn't want to hear. 'We just have to negotiate with the management to figure out a price for the doors,' I said, trying to deflect her and protect myself.

"'Are they to be yours or mine?' she asked.

"They'll be ours, of course—yours *and* mine," I assured her.

"'For my new apartment?' she said. 'Because I know this is the wrong time to be telling you, but I'm not moving with you. Fleur and I are moving.'

"I said, 'Of course. She's waiting for us now.'

"'We're going to live with Oliver.' Pam spelled it out for me.

"'What's my brother got to do with this?' I asked, in my last stab at denial.

"'I'm marrying Oliver as soon as our divorce is final.' Her eyes bored into mine.

"'Our divorce?' I instantly looked away. 'Jesus Christ! You're talking about my brother?' As if mesmerized, I stared at a Currier and Ives winter scene on the wall and wondered how long they'd been planning this. How could I have failed to see it coming?"

"How could you even have imagined it?" Karla asks.

"'Don't think you're getting custody of Fleur,' I said, before I went back in to pay, 'and the bloody doors are mine, too.'"

"They *are* amazing," Karla agrees, leaning away so the waiter can take away her empty snail shells.

"So, for fifteen years, I've been pretty bitter. *Pam didn't even have to change the monograms on her towels*, I thought. But now that Fleur has tried to kill herself"—Sax is shaking his head in disbelief—"Pam and I are back on the same team."

"Which has got to be weird," says Karla, reminding herself that the fact that Sax and his wife have reconnected does not mean Karla has to go back to plan A at this point and hightail it before dessert. He is still a free man.

"Not really. After all, Pam turned out to be right: she was more my brother's type."

"What type is that?" Karla asks, still wary.

"Fat-cat Republican." As if attacking, Sax stabs at his meat, slices it, and asks, "And what about you?"

"Politically, you mean?" Karla is surprised. No one has ever asked for her opinion about world affairs. "I'm a registered Independent who votes mainly for Democrats. I mean, can you believe what they're doing to Jimmy Carter because he won't give in to Iranian blackmail?"

"Do you consider yourself a liberal, then?" Sax asks.

"I guess so," says Karla, who has never really considered herself much of an anything.

"Is liberalism something that runs in your family?"

"My grandparents are like your brother: rich Republicans. But my mom's cousin Viv and her husband, they're pretty liberal." She does not mention how, the first time she met Joel, he blew her mind by calling Viv "heavenly labials in a world of gutturals." At the time, Karla thought her cousin's husband was a sicko, but then he introduced her to Wallace Stevens. Like Mutti, Sax might not get that a mere pharmacist could love poetry.

Right now, Sax is saying, "You mentioned Viv last night," because he was paying attention to Karla, remembering what she said, expecting details. "Tell me about her."

Karla pops a chunk of beef into her mouth, points at her sealed lips to underscore the fact that she is too mannerly to speak while chewing, and considers how much she wants to tell this man. After all, who is he really? The nice guy of yesterday and tonight or the turd of this morning?

Having never laid out the facts of her life to anyone, Karla wonders if she now wants to go into why Viv isn't really her cousin. Poised on a mile-high diving board, at this point, she can turn around and walk back down, or she can just dive in and hope for the best.

She sees how intently Sax is watching her, how willing he is to wait, how much she interests him. She knows by heart that "Scarlett O'Hara was not beautiful, but men seldom realized it when caught by her charms as the Tarleton twins were." Sitting here with Sax, Karla has caught him by her charms, a knack that comes and goes. In possession of that knack, she is bewitching; when it deserts her . . . Like Scarlett, she'll think about that tomorrow.

Right now, she swallows her mouthful, wipes her lips, and prepares herself to take the plunge. Because, just as surely as Sax had to have those bronze doors, Karla has to tell him everything.

CHAPTER 5

"Viv? Well, here's the thing." Karla looks around. *Oh, God, how to begin?* "I've always known her," she finally says, her eyes once again on Sax, "and at the same time, I never have."

"That's exactly how I feel about my brother." Having sopped up the garlic butter from his snails, he is sitting back and eyeing her ravenously. "Knew him all my life, without ever knowing him."

So they have that sense of alienation in common. Heartened, Karla continues, "My mother said Viv was our cousin, and I believed her."

"Why wouldn't you?"

"There are things I should have seen, but I didn't." After hearing these words come out of her mouth, Karla pauses. Has she just reminded Sax that he should have picked up signals from his daughter? "Not that I could have done much to change anything," she adds pointedly.

"No"—the word a sigh, before Sax asks, "But tell me, when you look back with twenty-twenty hindsight, what crucial signs do you think you missed?"

"Well, Mutti, my mom, was supposed to be this serious Jew," says Karla, "but we never went to a synagogue and we certainly weren't kosher. In fact, her two favorite foods were pork and shrimp."

"That sounds like just about all my Jewish friends."

"Yeah, but Mutti kept saying we were going to get rounded up and killed. I bet none of your friends said *that*." Grinning, Karla is glad to hear Sax *has* Jewish friends.

"True," he agrees. "But did Viv also believe you were in imminent danger?"

"No."

"Then how did she fit into the picture?"

"Her mother was the real Liesel Most's cousin, and when Mutti came to America, pretending to be Liesel, she stayed with Viv's family. So, having lived with Viv, Mutti called her when she was in labor. And after I was born, Viv cut the cord and stuck around."

"To help out?"

"Oh, no." Determined to make him understand, Karla shakes her head vigorously. "To fight. I grew up with the two of them screaming at each other. It was like living in a war zone."

"If they were such enemies, why did Viv keep coming back?"

The question startles Karla. Is he suggesting that she made up the fact that Mutti and Viv were enemies? Defending herself, she says, "She felt guilty because Mutti was supposed to have survived the concentration camp where her parents and her sister died, and theoretically Viv's parents could've rescued them before the war, but they didn't."

Sax nods. "So Viv thought she had to compensate."

"Until Mutti threw her out. After that, Mutti did all her yelling at me." Looking to Sax for sympathy, Karla is disappointed as he switches to his own story.

"In my house, no one fought openly," he says. "It would have been so much easier, so much truer, so much more understandable, if they had. But my father and mother sometimes went for months without speaking to each other, which kept us all in a virtual deep freeze."

Big deal. This man has no idea how easy he had it. Karla is a combat veteran. "Both Mutti and Viv kept trying to get me on their side. Viv said being in the concentration camps made Mutti crazy, while Mutti called Viv a 'know-nothing blond.'" Karla stabs a chunk of meat.

"And what did *you* think of Viv?" Sax asks.

How to answer? Karla despises herself for having absorbed her mother's contempt for the "vertless" Viv, whose mascara-empha-sized eyes and glossed lips advertise her eagerness for life. Like a puppy, Viv is fierce in her loyalty, willing always to play, adoring without complaint. So why can't Karla just love her? Why must she inwardly sneer at Viv's frivolity? "With all her bleached hair and face-paint fakery, Viv was the one honest person in my life." Saying this, a surprised Karla realizes it is true.

"My mother was a truth teller, too," Sax says, "so I can see why you would love Viv."

"She probably guessed at some point that Mutti was a phony—Mutti kept making mistakes about her family history—but it didn't matter. Viv wasn't going to let her 'cousin'"—Karla makes air quotes around the word—"down. And she didn't."

"But your mother threw her out."

"Yes." Karla cannot decide which is more delicious: the sauce she is now soaking up with bread, or the attention this man is paying to everything she tells him, his eyes never leaving her face. A little unnerved, she swallows the bread and takes a swig of wine, not that she needs it. Once she launches into the story of the day Mutti ban-ished Viv, the words bubble up. "I'll never forget. That day started out ordinary enough. 'Give me ten minutes,' Mutti said for the zil-lionth time, 'before you come home.'"

"Why? Did she bring men in for quickies?" Sax grins lasciviously.

"God, no." Though, giggling, Karla quite likes the idea. Still, she feels compelled to set the record straight. "Whenever we went anywhere, Mutti would make me stay behind until she'd made sure the 'storm troopers' hadn't shown up for us. But by then I wasn't still the scared kid who used to huddle in the subway, counting to a thousand."

"Whoa. Counting to a thousand—what was that about?"

"That was how I knew ten minutes were up, so then I could come home because she had certified it was safe." Hearing how loony this sounds, Karla checks to assess whether Sax is turned off by her weirdness and is relieved to see he seems entertained.

"Of course." He is even chuckling. "Your mother was the classic old maid, checking under the bed for a bogeyman and half hoping to find one."

"Exactly." Karla has never before felt that her early life was "ha-ha funny" and not super peculiar. "Before I went up, I had to see if the lamp was lit."

"And if it wasn't?"

"I was supposed to run to the library and use the dime Mutti sewed into my skirt band to call Viv."

"And what was Viv to do?"

"Hide me from the bad guys. Of course, by then I pretty much knew no bad guys were coming. It was just the game we played. And in my fantasies, I alternated between being the poor little match girl freezing to death on the street and believing I was such a hot shit that the day I was born I had my own star, with Viv as my wise man." Karla has never admitted this even to herself, but, turning her zany past into a comedy, marveling at how brilliant she is at this, her first effort at repartee, she decides the hot-shit part might not have been a fantasy. Right now, she is certainly a marvel. "But that afternoon in the drugstore before I went home," she reminds herself, "I stole bubble gum." Having previously confessed this to no one except Mutti, who didn't believe her, Karla looks nervously at Sax.

"One time when I was maybe eleven or twelve," he says, "I shoplifted a whole bag of marbles from Woolworth. And instead of playing with them, I threw them out as soon as I got home. I'm pretty sure every kid steals something at some point in his life."

Is it possible Karla is normal, then? Now, gloating, as if the worst day of her life was funny and not shattering, she tells about going up to the loft that afternoon and hearing Mutti scream, "Get away!" How, in a total panic, Karla ran, then looked back, expecting to see armed men dragging her mother out the street door, and was shocked when instead Viv and this uptown guy appeared.

"What's an 'uptown guy'?" Sax asks.

"You know—done up. Suit. Tie. Camel-hair coat. Noticeably holding." Surely Sax has observed the difference between his crowd and everybody else.

"I get it," he says, projecting his avidity to hear more.

"Anyway . . ." Not sure how long she can keep Sax this fascinated by what she is telling him, Karla pauses before she picks up the thread. "Funny, the details you remember. In the library, after Viv introduced Ben Zimmerman as *the* Ben Zimmerman, she draped her coat around me because I was shivering, and inside that taffeta tent I could smell her perfume, Joy."

"Scents are very evocative," Sax asserts.

"I couldn't stop crying until Ben gave me his handkerchief, scented with Acqua di Gio—you know, Armani."

"How is it you can identify perfumes?"

Does he doubt that she can? Must she justify every single thing she says? "Viv worked in Macy's cosmetics," Karla immediately points out. "She was always giving me samples, so I got to know which scent was which. But back to Ben . . . I couldn't figure out why he kept staring at me. Of course, I didn't know then he was my grandfather." And right now, in his own way, Sax is equally intent on her, which suggests that Karla may be a born Scheherazade, spinning out the tales that will save her life. "Only right then, Mutti rushed in and grabbed me," she continues. "I pleaded for someone to make her let go, but I was suddenly in a nightmare; even my voice was invisible."

"Oh, my." Sax reaches over and takes her hand.

Karla teeters on the verge of weeping, for at last someone is hearing her. But with no idea what she is supposed to do with sympathy, she reluctantly retrieves her hand and goes on, "I'll never forget Ben saying, 'I'm involved with the child no matter what,' but how? Viv had been about to tell me, when Mutti ruined everything. God, how I hated her then!"

"Do you still feel that way?" Sax asks.

"Sort of." Karla watches to see how this man who just said he loved his own mother takes that. He does not flinch. Emboldened, she explains, "Mutti accused Viv and her sugar daddy of trying to kidnap me."

"Oh, Lord," Sax crows. "I haven't heard the term 'sugar daddy' in years."

"At the time, I had no idea what it meant." Karla could not believe how great it feels to turn her personal horror stories into entertainment. "I mean, why did Viv get a sugar daddy and I never had any daddy at all? They all went on talking as if I wasn't there, until Mutti grabbed me even harder. 'Stop it!' I finally shouted. And, to my surprise, Mutti did let me go, though she kept screaming at Viv, shoving up her sleeve and smacking the numbers on her own arm as if Viv were the one who had persecuted her.

"But I wanted them to look at the nail marks, crescent moons dug into *my* arm. 'Look what she did.' I tried to show them, but I was still in the nightmare and no one was hearing me.

"'From this day on, you're dead to me, Vivian,' Mutti shrieked. 'You'll never see my Karla again.'

"I could not imagine life without Viv, but Mutti was dragging me away, any power I'd had to stop her gone, just like that." Karla snaps her fingers. "Outside, she snatched the bubble gum, which was somehow still in my hand, and yelled, 'No more of her dreck!'"

"'It wasn't Viv. I took it,' I confessed, because I had to make Mutti see that none of this was Viv's fault. 'I stole that gum.' I thought then she'd have to relent about Viv.

"But Mutti just said, 'Forget it, Karla. I know you. You're no thief.' But she didn't know me."

"Of course she didn't. My parents never knew me, and God knows I don't know Fleur. In fact, I don't think any parents know their children," says Sax, his face drooping.

How to make him refocus from his pain back to hers? "I was so pissed," Karla hisses, "I slammed my bag of nuts onto the pavement and I stomped the Planter's man to bits. To this day, I cannot eat a peanut. I mean, until six years afterward, when my mother finally died and Viv came back into my life, I basically had only Mutti for family, and what good was she?"

"There is something to be said for having no family at all, you know," he says, maddeningly minimizing her travails. "Stuck with a clan I can trace back to William the Conqueror, I've always wondered if being rootless would mean I wouldn't need to measure up to anyone."

"Believe me, growing up with no family is not good. When I thought I would never see Viv again, I was certain I was going to die." Revealing her private tragedy to this man, Karla insists that he feel sorry for her.

"You must feel marvelous now that Viv and your grandfather are back in your life," he says, still minimizing her trauma. "Yet you're still wearing black and working as a maid. How is that?"

The truth is, Karla likes working, and wearing black makes her feel safe — not that she can explain any of this. "I just really like the way I look in black." She omits mentioning that she secretly fears she is nuts, just like her mother.

"I really like the way you look in black, too." Sax lifts his glass in tribute to her, then adds, "And I can certainly see that losing your family without ever really knowing them would be disorienting, rather like discovering in your teens that you're adopted."

Since her mother was, in fact, her birth mother, though grateful for his compassion, Karla thinks it might be misplaced, for she has never identified with people who believe their parents are their parents, only to find out they are not. She sees no reason to equate herself with them now. "I mean, no wonder I'm screwed up," she murmurs with satisfaction. How can he or anyone else expect her to be anything but a kook?

"For what it's worth, to me you seem anything but screwed up," Sax insists.

"You only think that because you don't know me very well," she replies. He is hardly aware of her psychic scars.

"You sure?" Sax asks. "I, too, had no idea who people in my family actually were. They were just names, not human beings."

"But your people were rich big shots with what Viv calls 'mellowed wampum,'" Karla points out. "Old money. That's where you come from."

"What makes you so sure?"

"It's obvious," says Karla, who knows the difference between old-money classiness and new-money ritziness.

But then Sax gets to surprise her. "My mother was an Irish nanny," he says, "not an aristocrat."

That still doesn't mean they are alike. "You just said you're a direct descendant of William the Conqueror." Karla can go back only two generations. "Some of your ancestors were bluebloods, and it shows. None of mine were. Take my grandfather, for instance. Ben's always spic-and-span, he's perfect in every detail, his clothes are made to measure, his shoes are branded with Gucci horse bits, and he radiates standard luxury. Compare that with you: rumpled, individually distinctive, your clothes not particularly costly."

"So that's how I reveal my mellowed wampum?"

"Yup. Just look at your watch."

"What about it?" Sax glances down.

"It's a Timex. Ben wouldn't be caught dead without his Cartier Tank. But you can get away with a Timex in a place like this because, Irish nanny mother or not, you had childhood money, so you don't have to make a point of it. Ben had only adult money, so he needs to show off his achievement."

"And you see me as just a hereditary big shot?"

"Not just." In fact, she is mostly seeing Sax as wickedly attractive, but she isn't going to tell him that.

"How else do you see me, then?" he persists.

"Well, for once, Mutti and Viv would both would be over the moon if they knew I was in a place like this with someone like you. Mutti's communism was like her Jewishness: on again, off again. Some women change clothes according to fashion; she changed her beliefs."

"And you?" Sax is scrutinizing her. "Exactly who do you believe I am?"

Remarkably unfazed, Karla leans back. Taking her sweet time, she caresses the wine goblet as she appraises this man wearing a gray suit a shade lighter than his black hair. His red plaid vest announces that he is someone who likes to do his own thing. His domed forehead looks as if it holds tons of knowledge. Under his brow's shaggy awnings, his eyes gleam with inner brilliance. Karla cannot get over being with such a person. Everywhere on him, an overlay of light reflects a brightness she also detects in herself, before she finally discloses, "I see you as a dream. A good dream."

Karla does not tell Sax that his feel and smell were from the beginning familiar to her, that without knowing what being with him would be like, she craved this man. "A dream I've had more than once."

"I prefer that version to 'rich hot shot.'" The dream man grins as he takes out a cigarette and lights up.

"Ron'l says I've been talking about you for years," Karla says, as Sax's monogrammed gold lighter reminds her that no matter what kind of watch he is wearing, anything but poor, this man is a hell of a catch.

"And who's Ronald?"

"Not Ronald! *R-o-n*-apostrophe-*l*."

"In a conversation that's starting to feel more and more like Burns and Allen, I hesitate to ask, who, then, is Ron'l?"

"Who are Burns and Allen?"

"I guess you really are twenty-one."

"And a half."

"Let's just say they were the Rowan and Martin of their time."

"Who are Rowan and Martin?"

"You never watched *Laugh-In*?"

"We didn't have a television."

"Was your mother opposed to it?"

"She never wanted me to know about a lot of things."

"Maybe she was smart. We let Fleur watch all she wanted, and look at her!"

"Your daughter's problems can't be because she watched TV. I mean, you don't believe in the Twinkie defense, do you? The guy who claimed he murdered Harvey Milk because he was on a sugar high? Come on," Karla dares him. "Nothing's ever that easy."

"No. You're right." Sax takes a deep drag of his cigarette, then confesses, "More likely, Fleur understood how much I resented her existence, especially at first."

"Why?"

"For starters, I married Pam only because I got her pregnant."

"So?" Karla can easily top that one. "My father never married my mother. He probably never even saw her after he got her pregnant, or even knew she was. And even if I do someday have a baby, I doubt I'll ever marry anyone."

"Why is that?"

"Viv says she loves being married, but I think secretly she likes Ben better than she likes Joel." And it turns out that Karla likes gossiping about her family much better than she likes talking about herself. "Ben's with Adele, who is kind of a downer. Plus, Ron'l says married people don't have half the fun."

"And is Ron'l your boyfriend?"

"No." Karla snickers at that thought.

"Who is he, then?" As if he is looking into the sun, Sax squints.

"He's a friend who happens to be gay." And when Sax's face goes from squeezed suspicion to open relief, Karla chortles. She's not the only jealous one around here.

"I'm told every woman needs a gay friend." Sax relaxes back into her narrative.

"I couldn't have managed on my own without Ron'l," Karla confides, as the waiter arrives with dessert menus.

Sax orders crêpes suzette and coffee for them both and asks, "What was it like for you after your mother died?"

Karla, astonished, hears herself admit, "My life got easier."

And, instead of giving her the disapproval she expects, he says, "Mine, too. Once my mother wasn't around, I could stop showing up at the bank, going to benefits, living the life she wanted me to. Unlike my ex and my brother, I've always found so-called 'society' a bore."

"Mutti had nothing to do with society, but she was pretty boring, too."

"Until she died," Sax suggests.

"I guess you could say my life got more interesting afterward."

And more complicated, she thinks, like now, for instance, when she likes Saxton Perry so much even though she knows she should not trust a man who, this very morning, acted as if she were an intrusion in his life. So where does that leave her?

Standing on the sidewalk after dinner, Karla finds herself in the middle of a lusciously balmy evening, swaying as if to music. And Sax is evidently hearing that same music, for, placing each foot heel to toe, one after the other, he is walking as if the curb edge is a tightrope and he is Fred Astaire, about to expertly hail a cab. "Would you rather I take you home, or shall we go back to my place?" he asks, before opening the taxi door.

"Back to your place, please." She cannot picture the two of them sharing her single bed in Mutti's loft, and no way can Karla, at this point, just say goodbye to Sax. "If that's okay."

"It's a whole lot more than okay." Sax slides his eyes over the parts of her he has touched and the parts he has not.

And, basking in the warmth of his visual caress, Karla has a hunch that her second sexual experience is going to be a good bit better than her first.

CHAPTER 6

Being with Sax every night for the past six months has solved several issues. Now that she has checked "losing my virginity" off her list, Karla can move on to "having a relationship," which turns out to involve lots of story swapping. Thus, Sax has told her how, just months before the crash, his father fortuitously sold off stock to pay for the New York apartment and for his half sister, Gracie's, coming-out party. Sax exposed Karla to the term "Black Tuesday" and explained, "A coming-out party is when debutantes are introduced to society."

"I was introduced to society in 1958, the year I was born," Karla said. "But what happened to Gracie afterward?" Sax never talks about her.

"She died," Sax said, without emotion. "Thrown from her fiancé's Packard convertible when he skidded off the road."

"How old was she?" She must have been Oliver's full sister. Losing her like that must have been terrible for him, too.

"Twenty-two."

"What happened to the fiancé?"

"Married Gracie's best friend."

"How old were you when it happened?"

"Ten." Sax's lip trembled.

"That was how my father died, too." Clasping hands, they observed a moment of mutual silence.

But not all their tales were morbid, or moving. Using words like "schuss" and "mogul," Sax told her about ski trips to Stowe and Zermatt. Karla said Viv once took her to Radio City Music Hall to see the Rockettes. Sax confessed he'd never been. So, not long after that conversation, they went together to the show.

"What did you think?" Karla asked nervously. After all, someone as cosmopolitan as Sax might not be that impressed with a glorified chorus line.

"I don't know which was more terrific," Sax said, "the precision or the pulchritude."

Score one for Karla. And for Sax, too, their hours doing things together for the first time or hearing about what happened to them before, unified their histories and their present lives. For instance, he told her how, right before his family left Boston to move to New York, his father took Sax to Locke-Ober and ordered fried tripe with mustard sauce.

"How was it?" Karla squeezed her face in disgust.

"Surprisingly delicious," Sax said.

She said that whenever Viv took her to Chock Full o'Nuts, which Viv loved because its slogan was "food untouched by human hands," Karla ordered a cream-cheese sandwich on raisin-nut bread and ate it while she stared, fascinated, at the spangly water inside the glass-fronted dishwasher, as if she were watching television.

"Probably an improvement on most of the programs on TV," Sax said, and even if he was kidding, he made her believe her experiences were as valid as anyone else's. Plus, especially in the beginning, he acted as if he was learning as much from her as she was from him. How heady was that?

Of course, Mutti would have found Sax too patrician, too old, and too imperious, but Karla enjoys defying Mutti even posthumously.

Besides, she finds Sax ageless, hugely attractive, and masterful. That should be enough. *I mean*, she thinks, *isn't this a happily ever after?*

But what about being totally out of control? Whether or not they are making love, Karla loves sharing a bed with Sax. She cannot help herself. She has relinquished her autonomy. Sax can make her do whatever he wants. She hates him for that; she loves him for that. His very presence in her life confuses her. The fact that he is a powerful magnet, pulling her toward him, makes her want to dig in her heels and resist.

There are other problems, too. On her own for six years, she is accustomed to having her own space. But in Sax's apartment, Karla is rarely by herself, and when she is, she feels she doesn't belong. If Sax is there and she wants to chat, he is often too involved in a project of his own to pay attention to her. So why is she even with the man?

She understands that only a crazy person, staying in a gorgeous palazzo like this with a marvelous guy like Sax, would think she had gotten herself into a mess. But no truly marvelous guy would choose a nut like her. So what are they doing together? Karla thinks it entirely possible that both of them are deluding themselves about how they feel. They are in this situation only because stasis is easier than flux.

Of course, they may be in this situation because she loves him and he loves her. Often, even when they are not speaking, words hover between them like music. Yet there are times when Karla needs to be alone, unwatched, unguarded, and since Ron'l hangs out every day in the loft, she cannot count on privacy even when she is back in her own place. Somewhere, somehow, in the space between Canal Street and Park Avenue, she has mislaid her ability to just be. As much as she is cradled in the lap of luxury, she is also caught in a viselike grip of doubts.

Particularly when the alarm sounds at six thirty, as it does this morning, and Sax greets Karla by snarling, "For Christ's sake, why this early?" Right away, he starts in.

"I've got to go down to the agency to pick up a new client's key," she says, and he can just go back to sleep, instead of attacking her like that.

"Why are you taking on new clients? When are you going to quit?" She hates it when he picks on her, and lately he seems to be doing that more and more often.

"I don't know," she says, because, though right after they slept together that first time she assumed she would stop cleaning, quitting now seems like his idea, not hers. "Eventually I'll stop," she promises. But right this minute, smelling of sex, she just needs a bath and breakfast. Why can't he get that? "Did you buy Cheerios?" She goes on the attack.

"Yes, but I forgot the milk."

"Shit." She won that round. "I hate working on an empty stomach."

"Then quit working." Like everyone else in her life, he is a nag. "Being a cleaning person when you don't have to makes no sense."

"I need to do some*thing*, and I have no other marketable skills," she argues, because what is she supposed to say about herself in a résumé when the very word "résumé" terrifies her?

Why doesn't Sax get that by now? At first, Karla could do no wrong, but now Sax is quick to put her down, wants her to be different. "That's nuts," he says. "You just have to figure out what you want to do."

"Yeah, right." Karla can be a salesgirl at Macy's, like Viv used to be. Or she can give up on Sax and go back to living in, let's face it, relative squalor.

As she runs a hot bath, she remembers Mutti calling all women who dolled themselves up "parasites." For ages, Karla thought her mother was saying "pair of sights," which, confusing as it was, became Karla's goal—to be half of a glamorous couple. And in a way, by being with Sax she has indeed become a parasite, in both senses of the word. So what is that old warning "be careful what you wish for"?

Karla examines the fingernails she's bitten down. She would love to expunge the memory of how, when she was thirteen and Mutti was obviously dying, rather than worrying about being abandoned to fend on her own, Karla kept shaping and polishing her nails, Glamorous Grape the last in a long line of shades.

"Like them?" Holding her hand out for Mutti's inspection, she wondered if the banished Viv also wore purple nails.

"They look like you slammed them in the door." By then, Mutti's nails, even without polish on them, were bluish.

Yet, ignoring Mutti, Karla obsessed about her own nails, and in the days that followed, she switched from Come Again Coral to Positively Pink, then from Positively Pink to Fire Engine Red, every new color a new hope.

But on that Glamorous Grape day, Mutti did not make it to the toilet. "Go." She was gripping the back of her chair, clawing off her underpants. "Get me fresh."

Wishing she could just run out the door, Karla did as her mother asked. Then she used her foot to paper-towel the pee, pinched the wet underpants in her fingertips, dropped the stinking mess into the garbage pail, snapped down the lid, and ran to the sink to scrub her hands.

What would Sax think of her if he knew about any of that? No matter how many anecdotes they exchange, how can Karla ever explain herself to him?

"What are you doing?" Ensconced again in her chair, Mutti asked back then.

"What does it look like?" To this day, her adolescent surliness pains her. This was how she comforted her dying mother. Karla has so much to atone for. Sax must never find out what a bitch she is.

"There's nussing the matter with those bloomers," Mutti insisted.

"They're disgusting." Karla dismissed her mother's comment.

"So wash them."

Karla shrugged and turned away.

At that time, she hated the revulsion she felt for her own mother. Now, looking back, Karla is enraged. What kind of mother puts her child in that position—and what kind of daughter can such a mother produce? Thank God Sax has no idea how awful she is.

Not long after Mutti died, Viv insisted on treating Karla to a manicure. Afterward, as if to disassociate herself from the memory of her behavior during her mother's dying, Karla felt as if she'd been fitted for red-capped finger puppets that flitted around without knowing what to do with themselves. She never again wore nail polish.

As far as she can tell, Sax is fine with the fact that she bites her nails and rarely wears any makeup besides lipstick. He pretty much likes the way she looks au naturel. And in all these months, despite the nagging, they haven't had a single real fight. But is there more to being with someone than sort of getting along with him? Karla slept with Sax because she needed a guy to sleep with. If, by some miracle, he really is her "it," shouldn't she know that for sure after being with him for six months?

She twists the water off, sticks a foot into the tub, yanks it out, examines the pinkness ending like a sock above her ankle, and decides she can stand it. So she steps in with both feet, telling herself, *Hot is cleansing*. She crouches in the burning water, gasps, lets go, stretches out, and warily adjusts to being purified.

"You're not Cinderella." Having joined her in the bathroom, Sax flips up the toilet seat and readies himself to pee. "No evil stepmother is forcing you to be a maid. When I was your age, I thought I was stuck with working in a bank for the rest of my life, but I wasn't. And you can figure out something more suitable to do on your own."

"Suitable?" Her privacy again violated—can't she even take a bath alone? "For what, exactly, could I be more suitable?" She dares the son of an Irish nanny to despise domestic workers.

"Whatever you want." Sax fails to grab the bait Karla offered, and why should he? Once his mother married up, she stopped working. He expects Karla to do the same. "You're intelligent, attractive, energetic, reliable. You have no idea how few people have all those attributes."

"Even in the toy store, the boss just wanted me to clean," she points out, as, fascinated, she watches Sax's pee arc move closer as he finishes, watches him shake and twitch his cock tip. Is that how they all do it, or do civilized men use toilet paper? Ron'l is the one person Karla can ask.

She met her only real friend almost nine years ago, in 1971, when she was thirteen and out doing errands for her relentlessly dying mother. To postpone the awful moment when she had to go back home to Mutti, Karla jaywalked across to the discount furniture store with the televisions in the window. She watched a contestant on *Truth or Consequences* walk through the audience with a potato balanced on her forehead. The contestant sort of looked like Viv, who had stopped calling because whenever she did, Mutti immediately hung up.

Password came on next, and Karla stayed to watch, even without sound. Wasn't Mutti the one who said fresh air was good for her? So it was almost as if her mother approved when a skinny brown guy in a red ski hat topped by a huge purple pompom joined Karla. He said nothing, but as she turned to leave, he waved goodbye.

The following day, he was there before she was. "I bet you she gonna lose." He pointed at a *Price Is Right* contestant. "Gonna guess too high."

"How can you tell?" Pretending to look at the television, Karla kept sneaking peeks at this boy. Or was he a man? Anyway, he was too old for a high school kid, with his cigar-colored profile; his zippered satin jacket, orange in the front, with bright blue sleeves; his hands humps stuffed in slit pockets.

"I just know." He turned and grinned at her, his surprisingly white teeth flashing as he spun himself around, his feet agile in black basketball sneakers. "So, what you betting?"

"I don't have anything to bet." She was not about to tell this multicolored stranger, who might even be one of the hooligans Mutti was always warning her about, that she was clutching a $10 bill in her pocket to buy lightbulbs and a chicken.

"How about information?" he suggested.

"Like what?" Other than revealing the treasure in her pocket, she had no information.

"Whoever lose . . ." Thinking, he licked his lips, his bubble-gum-pink tongue, friendly. "Got to tell their name."

"Okay, it's a bet." She decided to say she was Caroline Kennedy.

"Watch, then."

The contestant guessed low.

"You win. Now I got to tell you my name." Pulling a hand out of his jacket, he offered it to her. "It's Ron'l. Pleased to meet you."

Karla squeezed fingers that felt as roughly familiar to her as RyKrisp. "Hi, Ronald."

"Not Ronald. *R-o-n*-apostrophe-*l*," he said. "Ron'l Gamble." He giggled. "Could be because I bets so much."

"I liked Ron'l the first time I ever saw him," Karla has told Sax. "Same as the first time I ever saw you."

The next day, he was there again, so she told him her real name, Karla Most.

"Most what?" Ron'l chuckled.

She had to think about that one. "Most curious." ("Curiosity killed the cat," Mutti had often warned.)

"I bet you real young," Ron'l said.

"I am not." She already had her period. "How old are you?"

"Nineteen."

"Well, that's only a few years older than me."

"How many?"

"Three," she lied, halving the six years between them.

"You don't look that old."

"Well, I am." And for a long time, she insisted on it, though her age never mattered. Ron'l was Ron'l and Karla was Karla, and they both accepted that.

In a way, even though she didn't know about him, Mutti accepted Ron'l, too, never questioning Karla about her longish absences. So one afternoon, after *Truth or Consequences*, Karla agreed to walk her first friend ever back to his place. She followed him into Chinatown, past a window crammed with dusty dragons and fat, bare-bellied statuettes. On one of those blocks that is more like an alley than a city street, they stopped at a heavy metal door, which Ron'l unlocked. Holding the door open, he expected her to go in.

Karla wavered on the threshold. What if he turned out to be a foreign agent in disguise who had been sent to get her? Mutti always said it would happen one day. What if Mutti found out where Karla had gone? What if she didn't? If Karla disappeared, who would know where to look for her?

Karla has tried telling this story to Sax, but she has never been able to convey how scared she was that day when the door swung behind them with a thick *click*. Ron'l was taking the dark, steep stairs in front of them two at a time. Behind him, Karla groped for the railing. As she climbed, the smell of gift-shop sandalwood became the stink of old grease and poor people. "I can't stay long.

I told my mother I'd be home soon," Karla pretended, belatedly regretting her decision.

Just as she regretted her decision the night she said she would meet Sax at Quo Vadis. And look where that got her. Hard even for her to say it isn't a step up from where she was before. She is forced to give herself credit for not permitting her fears to rule her.

"We almost there." On the fourth-floor landing, Ron'l unlocked another door.

Her heart drumming, Karla looked back at the gloom. "Who else lives here?" she asked. Until that day, she had never realized anyone actually lived above the stores she passed by or went into. "Anyone?"

"Other peoples," Ron'l said. "But they ain't going to bother us none."

Behind one closed door, a little dog was yipping. *What could be more normal than that?* Karla thought. Comforted by the invisible pooch, she scooted by Ron'l into a room crowded with hundreds of Barbies.

Though Sax has now met Ron'l a few times, he has not yet been to his place, and Karla cannot imagine how, if Sax ever does go there, the great art collector will react when he sees Ron'l's collection of Barbies, their stiff arms reaching out from the shelves, a mass of yearning fairy-tale princesses dressed in tulle and fur. "Where'd you get these?" Karla asked that first day, awestruck.

"That what my social worker always asking." Ron'l latched the door behind them.

"What's a social worker?" With no one but Mutti to teach her anything all these years, Karla had so very much to learn.

"The one gets assigned to take care of different peoples. Mine sure I rip off my Barbies."

"Rip off?"

"You know. Steal them."

"Do you?" Karla wished she had the nerve to steal Barbies. She wished—oh, God, how she wished—she had a social worker! If only Karla had spoken up when, not long after Mutti banished Vivian, someone from the city's Social Services Department came to the loft to investigate a claim that a child living there was being mistreated, maybe then Karla would have had a chance. But Mutti told her to stay hidden behind the coats in the closet while she assured the investigator she had no daughter. She explained that her jealous cousin had made up that story to get back at her for stealing her boyfriend.

Afterward, how Karla wished she had stepped out of the closet that day! Then she could have ended up with a social worker. But she found out that was a possibility only after she followed Ron'l.

If she weren't willing to take risks, there would be no Ron'l in her life. There would be no Sax. She would not be here on Park Avenue, remembering. So at least she is doing something right, just as she was that day in Ron'l's room.

"I helps down at the toy store, and Mr. Cardullo give me two Barbies a week." He smiled in triumph. "That way, nothing go into my disability check, and the store get away cheap."

"Where do you get their dresses and everything? They're gorgeous."

"I makes them," Ron'l said proudly. "They my models."

Mutti said Barbie dolls were a capitalist scheme to get children to pay for "vertless," overpriced dreck. This just proved to Karla once again that Mutti had no idea what was what.

"How come you get a social worker?" Karla hoped if he told her that, she could figure out some way to qualify.

"I got brain damage to my head," Ron'l explained, "when I born."

"It doesn't show." Yet she knew right from the beginning there was something a little off about him.

"'Cause I got my hats. See?" He pulled away his red ski cap and showed her. The back of his head was flat and shiny, with odd hair-tuft islands here and there.

The day she introduced Sax to Ron'l, Karla had no idea whether Sax's urbanity stemmed from an actual absence of distaste or hid his disapproval of her for hanging out with such a person. At the time, Karla assumed it was just another manifestation of his WASPiness. Now she is not sure and not yet comfortable enough with Sax to ask him about it. Karla may never be comfortable enough with him, but she can understand, if he was turned off, why.

As Ron'l lifted a box off the floor and dumped a beret, a fez, a sailor hat, an Afro wig, a Greek fisherman hat, a hard hat, a straw hat, even a yarmulke onto a studio couch littered with bits of thread, Karla had to pretend his deformity did not repel her. If he was willing to reveal to her his secret malformation, she had no right to be disgusted by it. Instead, she concentrated on his hats. "These are great," she gushed.

"One for every occasion," he said, as if he'd memorized the phrase.

"So you're always ready," she assured him, and escaped back to his Barbie collection. "You have any boy dolls?"

"One." Ron'l grinned and slid out from the end of a row the only brown doll. "But he not Ken."

"I bet I know who he is."

"Now you be like me, betting."

"Is he Ron'l?"

"Junior," he smirked.

"I thought so."

"I see you be smart."

"Not really." But Karla was hatching a plan.

She is still hatching plans. Maybe if she brings Sax to Ron'l's place, he will understand her better. Maybe if she brings Sax there, he will think less of her. Maybe it is more prudent to keep things just as they are.

That first day with Ron'l, she tried out one of her plans. "Listen," she proposed, "would it be okay if I use your phone?" She thought she could get Viv to meet her in Ron'l's place. And even if she couldn't come there, they could at least talk without Mutti catching them.

"For a local call?" Ron'l couldn't afford long distance.

"Macy's."

"Sure." He shrugged. "Be my guest."

Karla dialed, gave the operator the extension, and waited while Ron'l watched her. When Mutti watched, Karla felt trapped, but Ron'l was gazing at her because what she did interested him; he was not trying to catch her doing something sneaky.

Sax watches her either because he loves what he sees or because he disapproves of her. Karla goes back and forth about which it is. She just knows, one way or another, people she loves have a way of disappearing from her life.

"May I please speak to Miss Margolis?" she remembers blithely asking.

"There's no one here by that name," said some woman.

"Is this the Elizabeth Arden cosmetics counter?" Karla assumed the woman was stupid.

"Yes."

"Well, then, Vivian Margolis. She's worked there for ages."

"Oh, sure, that Vivian! Yeah, she quit after she got married."

"Viv married?" That had to be wrong. If she were married, Karla would know. "What's her name now?"

"That, I couldn't tell you."

Karla carefully replaced the receiver in its cradle. Staring at a Barbie with red hair only a little brighter than her own, she felt lost.

"That color be good on her." Ron'l picked up the doll and

displayed her brown velvet pantsuit. "Be good on you, too." He looked at Karla. "How come you always in black? You loss somebody?"

"My mother," she said.

"Thought you say she be waiting on you."

"My mother makes me wear black, I mean." Because Karla used to think that, except for Viv, everyone in their family was dead. She believed the number of relatives they'd once had was the number on Mutti's arm.

"Oh." Ron'l fit the redheaded doll back into her place on his shelf. "You want me to see can I fix you something vibrant to wear when you visiting here?"

"Would you?" Through the tears that jumped into her eyes, he shimmered before her in his goofy cap. So that was the trade: Viv gone, Ron'l here. "My mother's really sick," she confessed to him.

"They gets like that sometimes," Ron'l said philosophically.

"And what should I do about it?" She already felt better thinking that Mutti's sickness might be ordinary.

"Ain't nothing you can do."

"What about your social worker? Can you ask her what to do?"

"She say long as Mommy keep drinking, I can't be with her."

And Sax's drinking? Karla's grandfather is the only other person she knows who has a drink every day, and her grandmother is always after him to quit. Maybe Karla should be telling Sax to stop. "No," she told Ron'l that day, "I meant about what I should do with my mother."

"I ain't telling my worker about you," Ron'l said.

"Why not?"

"She probably not approve of me and you."

"Why not?" Karla asked again.

"'Cause you so young." He looked away guiltily. "And all."

"But what if you tell her I need help?" Karla was too desperate to worry about what shamed him.

"You got me for that." Ron'l gave her one of his creamy smiles.

Hugging his shoulders, Karla hoped he was enough for her, though even then she knew he would not be. And now, at least for a while, she has Sax.

"But if you wants a custom dress, you need to get me the cloth," Ron'l said, as if creating clothes for her was the important issue.

"Okay," she agreed. Ever since Mutti had stopped going out, Karla cashed the checks and did the buying. She could easily skim off some fabric money.

Ron'l bounced down onto his studio couch. "Then you sit here by me and we look at some pictures." He spread a *Vogue* open on his lap. "What sort of dress you want?"

"I read that green looks good on redheads." She plopped down beside him.

"Green's kind of a redhead's cliché." Ron'l pronounced it "clitch." Behind his back, first Karla and now Sax calls it a clitch, too. "I think nothing beat chocolate brown with your color," says Ron'l, unaware that Karla sometimes makes fun of him.

"Brown's too close to black, which I have to wear because my mother was in a concentration camp," she explained.

"What that?"

"You know, in Germany."

He shrugged. "I never did no geography." He looked apologetic.

"That's okay." Fingering an electric-blue sheath on the satiny page, she felt that somehow, Ron'l understood.

In the beginning, surprised by how much they had in common, Karla thought Sax understood her, too. By now, though, she is aware of the chasm that yawns between her and Sax.

So is her grandmother right? Would she be better off with a "nice Jewish boy"? Or is Karla destined always to be separate and other with anyone and everyone?

That first day at his place, she quizzed Ron'l: "Could you make me this?" But what she meant was, could he make her into a normal person? Can anyone do that for Karla?

"For something human being–size," Ron'l explained, "I need a sewing machine."

"My mother's got one." Karla instantly regretted blurting this out. Of course, she could not let Ron'l come and use the Singer, at least not until two years later, when Mutti finally died. After that, he could come to the loft every day to sew.

When they'd been together for a month, Sax finally came downtown with Karla to see her loft. As they walked up the dark stairs, he muttered, "Leave all hope, ye who enter here," turning her horror into black humor, which was great. Only, Karla wondered, what was he hiding beneath his joke? His own horror? When she unlocked the loft door, there was Ron'l at work, and, viewing him from Sax's perspective, she could not help seeing how bizarre he looked.

There was nothing for it but to pretend he was nothing but ordinary. "Ron'l, Sax; Sax, Ron'l," she said, grateful for the conventional lines that allowed her to fake offhandedness.

"How do you do?" Sax strode over and, exactly as he would have done if he had been meeting President Nixon in the Oval Office, bowed slightly and extended his hand.

Karla felt a rush of affection mixed with envy. Ingrained in Sax was that automatic graciousness that made him treat Ron'l as if he were both special and standard. What a contrast with how Karla was brought up! Mutti thought and acted as if everyone were "vertless." Karla has had to learn manners elsewhere.

And Ron'l was one of her teachers. "I doing real good," he said, placing his hand in Sax's, "'specially now you here, 'cause maybe then Karla gets to talk about something else and not just Sax, Sax, Sax."

The ice immediately broken, they laughed together. But there was still another part of this test.

"You like him?" Karla asked in the cab on their way back uptown, not knowing what she would do if Sax said no.

"How could anyone not like Ron'l?" He smiled.

"Some people," Karla admitted, "think he's weird."

"Aren't we all?" Sax asked.

At the time, she thought that meant Sax loved her, no matter how crazy she was, but today, five months later, lying in the bathtub, watching him at the sink, Karla is not so sure. "You think I'm weird because I want to work."

"With the allowance your grandfather gives you, you don't need to clean toilets." Sax flushes, as if to say, *So that's that.*

And maybe it is. Though she should be hurrying, Karla cannot help but prolong this moment, slowly soaping an arm because she loves sharing intimate activities with this man. "That's not the point."

"Then what is?" Now Sax stands at the sink, squirting foam lather on his fingertips and smearing it on his face.

"You're not going to shower?" She loves to watch him go through the personal routines that reified his miraculous presence in her life.

"Not with you in the tub."

"Okay, I'll hurry." Which she should already have been doing. Finishing up, she feels as she often does with him when she lets her guard down: chastised.

"No need to rush. I prefer to shave before the mirror gets steamed up."

"I never thought of that." *There is so much I have never thought of, like what I really want to do with the rest of my life, exactly who I want to be, what is possible for me,* she muses, as she sits up, runs cold water, and splashes her face to close the pores. *When am I going to deal with any of the underneath stuff where my real life is happening?*

"You haven't answered my question," he insists. "What is the point of your continuing to be a maid?"

"I like getting out and having something to do." Not to mention having someplace to go where, instead of pointing out her deficiencies, people sometimes leave thank-you notes with extra cash to show how happy they are with her. "And my job isn't all that awful." Restoring order to other people's lives makes her own feel less confusing.

What I don't go for, she reflects, as she pulls up the stopper, *is the repetitiveness of the work, and the clients who accuse me of cheating them on time or who assume that when something is missing, I've taken it. And I have to agree with Sax about that one thing: the toilets are a little icky. But so what?*

"My mother trained me to clean." Karla does not mention Mutti's other plans for her, which, as far as Karla can tell, were that Karla was supposed to take care of Mutti forever. Neither of them thought about what Karla might do for herself on her own, or what else, exactly, she was equipped to become. "I suppose I could be a waitress, or a bartender." Sax could teach her everything she'd need to know about drinking, at least; his own alcohol consumption is part of what makes him a quintessential WASP.

Karla whisks away her misgivings, reminding herself that just because Sax often gets a little high after work doesn't make him a drunk. With his money, his taste, and what he sometimes sarcastically refers to as his "breeding," Sax has access to power. And, more than anything, isn't power what Mutti wanted Karla to have?

"And your father?" The bottom of it half mown, half foamed, Sax's mirror image stares into her. "Would he want you to be a maid?"

"Who knows?" And what right has Sax to suggest that her father would be disappointed in her? Not only does the man look ridiculous with that half-a-clown face, he is saying a ridiculous thing. Karla's father is dead and always has been, so why worry about what he would think of her career choices?

And yet, hauling herself up out of the tub, she slides her eyes away, as if Sax has caught her betraying her heritage. Once again, he's caught Karla, just as Mutti used to do, not measuring up.

Okay, so no Zimmerman would want his daughter to be a cleaning woman. What, then, *would* Michael hope Karla to be? A model? She knows that's what Ron'l would like. She wraps herself in a bath towel, shivers, gazes at the unshaved legs that assure her she is a natural woman, not a mere sex object, and shivers again. Not exactly model material—and probably inadequate to hold on to Sax for much longer.

Once he finishes shaving, she succeeds him at the sink and, leaning close to the mirror, squeezes a zit on her chin, relishing the pain it causes, because she deserves it. "My father never even knew I existed," she calls over to Sax's back.

"But, based on what you know of him," Sax continues, waiting for the shower to run hot, "what do you imagine he would have wanted for you?"

"He might not have cared what I did." So why should Sax? She drenches the sore spot with alcohol, wincing when it stings.

"I care."

"You're not my dad." Karla has no blood connection to Sax. He will probably like her only as long as she keeps him amused. And, complain though he might, at this point she senses that something about playing Prince Charming to his Cinderella turns Sax on—which means that once Karla stops being a maid to become a full-time consort, he might lose interest in her. And she is not about to take a chance on that. She is not about to let him forget what a sad life she's had. "When my dad died, he was only four years older than I am right now."

"There's no reason to think you are going to die young." Entering the shower, Sax curtains himself off from her.

She drifts back into the bedroom, aware that he is right. In truth, she is not looking forward to yet another day of vacuuming and scouring. She is wasting her life. Perched on the mattress edge as she pulls up her tights, she is tempted to flop back, bag the cleaning, and become what—a kept woman? That isn't exactly her life goal.

The trouble is, Karla's goals are as mixed up as she is. *All I've ever wanted was not to be like Mutti. Sure, Sax says I can get past having a crazy mother, but how does he know that?*

When Karla was little, as Mutti and Viv's war raged around her, she was caught between the two sides. Now, poised between a vast reservoir and a dam holding it back, Karla feels as if she is about to drown. Whether she wants to or not, she is sinking deeper and deeper into love. She tries constantly to stop herself, but how can she when she so enjoys being with this man—who could dump her at any time?

Even if he doesn't get rid of her, any male, particularly one from such a different culture, will always be alien to her. Karla can never feel entirely at home with Sax—except, that is, when she is telling him everything about herself and he is advising her on what to do. Then she is again with Mutti and, in a way, safe. But oh, God! Does she really want that kind of safety?

And even if she does settle for stability, can she have it with that daughter of Sax's in her life? Not long after he released Fleur from the Payne Whitney Psychiatric Clinic, Fleur's shrink advised Sax not just to tell Fleur about Karla, but to introduce them. So, three months ago, his daughter was the one who rushed into Quo Vadis by herself. She was the one who got to grab Sax's steadying arm.

"This is Karla Most." He maneuvered Fleur so she and Karla were face-to-face.

"How do you do?" Karla extended her hand.

"Fine." Fleur kept her eyes on the chilly fingers she brushed against Karla's, those fingers, like everything else about Sax's daughter, wraithlike, her face wan, her pale hair a cloud, as if her return from death were only partial. Fluttering back to her father, she clung to him like a moth.

That night, Karla trailed the two of them to the table, where Sax deposited Fleur on the banquette, then motioned for Karla to sit there, too, as if the two women side by side were the couple and he the observer.

"God, I haven't been in this place since before Granny died." Words spurted out of Fleur. "I didn't know it still existed."

"Very much so," said Sax, seating himself opposite her. "As far as I know, it's thriving."

"I see the menu hasn't changed," Fleur continued.

"Why should it?" Sax asked.

"So I suppose we're in for escargots and *entrecôte, comme d'habitude.*" Fleur accepted the cigarette Sax offered, while Karla smarted. She'd thought Sax had ordered that same meal three months before just for her. Now, come to find out, it was just what he always ate here.

"If you'd prefer, by all means, order something else." Sax held out the flame from his lighter.

His daughter cupped his hand with both of hers. "No." She then sat back, content. "I rather like the idea of returning to the days of yore." Tilting her face up, she blew smoke at the ceiling.

"How about you, Karla? What would you like to eat?" Sax asked.

"I'm fine with snails and beef." Karla just wished she were next to him, with their thighs touching. As it was, Sax felt fully separate when she turned to examine his daughter's profile and the perfect little pearl earring below her skimpy, fair hair.

During the entire meal, wearing a clingy blond cashmere sweater that made Karla feel her own jacket was baggy, Fleur never once looked at her. She never once addressed Karla. And whenever Sax spoke to Karla, Fleur simply waited, her colorlessly varnished nails rat-a-tatting against the tabletop, until their exchange was over.

Then Fleur brought the discussion back to Sidney, her cat; Ned, her ex-boyfriend; Pam, Sax's ex-wife.

At one point, Karla excused herself. When she returned from the ladies' room, Sax rose to greet her. Sliding back in across from him, Karla motioned for him to relax. Meanwhile, Fleur went on speaking only to him, saying she was looking into becoming a docent at the Metropolitan Museum. She asked what he thought of that, and whom he knew for her to contact.

"You might ask Karla. She's studying art at NYU," Sax said.

Ignoring this suggestion, Fleur replied, "I thought you'd have an in at the Met. Someone who could be useful to me."

The good news was that, sitting there that night with the two of them, Karla did not need to think of anything to say. The bad news was that neither Sax nor his daughter seemed to care whether she spoke or not.

Outside afterward, before lunging into the first cab, Fleur kissed her father's cheek and, as if Karla were something just too disgusting to look at, hastily averted her eyes as she tossed a "bye" more or less in her direction.

Sax shut the door, and the taxi took off. "Well, that wasn't too bad, was it?" he asked, turning to an astounded Karla.

"It was fine," she fudged, for if Fleur had physically attacked her, it would have been worse. As it was, Karla had been made to understand that if ever there were a conflict between her and Fleur, Sax would automatically take his daughter's side. So the sooner Karla gets herself out of this relationship, the better off she will be. But then what?

Sax is obviously right. She must not squander her life on being a maid. But what should she do? She is not going to be one of those "ladies who lunch" her grandmother hangs out with. Choosing what to wear is Adele's biggest decision of the day. There has to be something more in life than that.

Karla has no clue, so far, what that might be. Much as she is enjoying her courses, she isn't in the least tempted to marry the nice Jewish boy her grandparents will find for her, or to be the student they think she is. Ben still doesn't realize she's never officially enrolled in a degree program at NYU. One of these days, even though she dreads his disapproval and quite likes living clandestinely, she will have to tell him what she's actually been doing for the last few years. But first she has to come up with the right alternative. "Dilettante" is not going to cut it.

She stuffs her head into her sweater and pauses inside its dark, woolly warmth before reemerging into the slight chill of morning. Not that long ago, Karla often sat with Ron'l, watching television and imagining herself under a spotlight onstage, like Barbra Streisand, belting out songs. Except that not even Ron'l ever praised her singing voice.

Then, for a while, Karla liked the idea of being a famous feminist, like Gloria Steinem, until she realized she had nothing similar to offer women. No one cares if Karla agrees with them or not.

After that, she thought, since she likes to keep up with what's going on in the world, maybe she could be one of those people on television who report the news. Only she has no idea how to get into broadcasting, and the competition for those jobs has to be fierce. The most likely route for her would be to clean a TV executive's apartment and be "discovered." After all, that is how she met Sax, who is now coming out of the bathroom, a towel wrapped around his waist, another slung around his neck. Karla has only to glance at the man to know how lucky she is to be here with him. And how did she come by him? Maybe her new client on Eighty-Second Street will be her ticket to a television career.

"If you quit work and moved in here full-time, you could stop paying rent on the loft." Sax is poking his towel-wrapped finger in his ear to dry it — another of the private gestures she finds so reassuring.

If she did not belong here, he would not be letting her watch. "So, are you ready?" Asking her to make that commitment is, after all, a commitment he is making. So he is not planning to break up with her anytime soon.

This takes a moment to sink in. He wants her here full-time. The thought of being a full-time anything, giving up all her other possibilities, terrifies Karla. But she must not let Sax see that. "Is that an invitation?" she asks coquettishly, dreading and desiring his reply. For if she moves in here for real, her status as a kept woman will be official. Remembering Mutti's scorn for kept women, Karla likes the idea of being one, not just because of the money but because *I'll be kept for good*, she tells herself, *or be put out to pasture as soon as he gets tired of having me around.*

"You could say that," he agrees.

"You want me to answer right now?" She doesn't feel ready. Not yet.

"You're already here every night. What would be the difference?"

"But I don't want to give up my place." She'd have nowhere to go if she did. At least when Ron'l isn't around in the loft, she can go there and fart, pick her nose, examine her craps. Karla imagines that if Sax knew she did any of those things, he would immediately give her the ax.

"It's rent-controlled," she points out. No matter how rich he is, as a New Yorker he has to know that no one voluntarily gives up a rent-controlled apartment.

"As long as you don't sublet," says Sax, who seems to be up on the rules of everything, "you can keep paying the rent and still move up here."

"But why should I? We're doing just fine as we are." Any change could be for the worse.

"That's one way of looking at it, but I don't like not knowing when I open the door whether I'll find you here." Sax's eyes dive into hers.

"I always tell you where I'll be and when I'll be back." Karla looks away so he won't see how much she treasures the hours when he is *not* around. "But I need my independence."

"You'll still have it, even if you commit to living with me," Sax promises. "Without that assurance, I feel as if someday I'll come home and find you gone." Now he turns away, slump-shouldered and forlorn.

Clearly, she is supposed to feel sorry for him. "But that's ridiculous!" Yet, for the first time, Karla understands what Vince was talking about that night when he said he didn't want her depending on him. The thought of Sax counting on her is every bit as terrifying as the thought of her counting on him. "If I did move in here, I wouldn't always be around." But Sax would be like Mutti, always waiting for her. He would be her anchor, providing stability while dragging her down, down, down.

"But this would be your home." He goes back to dressing. "I'd like knowing that." He is buttoning his shirt, getting ready to leave her.

Because he is gone every day, if she were not working, she would have this place to herself for hours at a time. "I used to pretend I lived in the Frick," she confesses.

"I used to dream of living in a remote shack. So maybe I should chuck all this and move down to Canal Street with you."

"You don't mean that." At least, Karla hopes he doesn't. Only a crackpot would give up this apartment to live in the dungeon where she grew up. "You're not serious, are you?"

"Not really. Look, if you move in, you can figure out how to make this place cozier," Sax proposes. "That could be your new job."

"Interior decorator. Hmm." Looking around at the room—so different from the loft's rancid grit, its bland walls are the perfect background for the Modigliani—Karla suspects that, despite his protestations, Sax will not go for a serious redo. Anyway, where would she even start? The one decorator she knows is Viv's, whose apartment, with its grass-cloth walls and zebra-print sofa, looks like a Disney version of Africa. Karla would hate coming home to anywhere like that. But does she want to go on living in a virtual museum that belongs to someone else?

"Fleur's more or less on her feet," Sax is arguing. "She could handle it if our relationship became more visibly committed."

But can Karla cope with Miss Hostility, the suicidal daughter? "I'm not so sure about that," she says.

Shirt buttoned and belt buckled, Sax has now gotten to her favorite part, the necktie. Crisscross. Round and up. He tilts his head and twists his mouth as he slides the knot to his neck. Then, voilà, he approves of himself in the mirror as she approves of him in the flesh. All wrapped up, Sax is his gift to her.

And that is the problem. "God, you look great!" She can no more resist longing for him and his body than water can resist pouring through a sieve.

"You've spoiled me," he says, as they head down the hall.

"How so?" *He* is the spoiler, holding Karla in his thrall.

"I dread going back to Oscar Peterson for companionship," he admits, with a wry grin.

Oh, God, he *does* depend on her. "Got any orange juice?" Seeing to it that he keeps his fridge stocked is not her responsibility. Nothing here is her responsibility, which is part of what is so nice about it. She is living in a virtual hotel for free. But once she moves in . . .

"What does orange juice have to do with anything?"

"I can eat my cereal with it, instead of milk."

"If you want, I'll take you out for breakfast."

"No time."

"When you quit work, I'll set up an account for you."

"So I'll officially be your mistress?"

"You'll be a member of my household."

"A dependent."

"So to speak."

"What if I meet someone else?" Like a guy her age, maybe a Jewish doctor? God, how her grandmother and Viv would love that!

"Have you somebody in mind?" Sax looks stricken. "Though no longer a bachelor, my brother might be interested in cuckolding me again."

"Oh, God. I'm sorry." Karla snatches at the cereal box, pours, sloshes in the juice, and watches the Cheerios twitch. With Sax, as with Mutti, she is always saying and doing the wrong thing. Yet, resigning herself, Karla reaches across the breakfast table to stroke Sax's shoulder, playing her part in a fate determined by the gods. "I'm not looking for anyone else. Honestly."

"Well, then . . ." He gives her an endearing, almost bashful smile.

"Well, then . . ." She sighs, a deep, collapsing kind of sigh, as, withdrawing her hand, she gives in to forces beyond her control, just as she did when she was a kid. "If that's what you want, I guess I'll quit my job and move in here with you." Instead of extricating herself from this situation, she has just agreed to immerse herself more fully in it, to give up even the semblance of control. And this fills her not just with fear, but with joy.

CHAPTER 7

Eight months later, Karla is no longer a maid. Nor is she unattached, her life these days a series of "thises" and "thats." She tells anyone who asks that she is "in transition" or "finding herself" or a "perpetual student." At NYU, her only class this semester is Nineteenth-Century European Art, but, encouraged by Sax to branch out, she is also auditing Medieval Art at the Cloisters and is taking Introduction to Applied Art, or Name Your Poison, at the Learning Center.

There, every Saturday morning, the instructor, Harriette Marcus, a gray-haired woman shaped like a snowman, enthusiastically demonstrates new methods for applying color and gives her students a chance to try them out, never criticizing what they produce. Karla loves this. If only Mutti had been more like Harriette, Karla believes, she would have felt loved and would therefore have turned out much better than she did.

While finger painting, free of anyone's expectations, she experiences the delicious pleasure of muck manipulation. In the weeks after finger painting, she learns to use crayons, poster paints, pastels, acrylics, oils, watercolors, and aerosols. "It's like we're back in kindergarten," says Bessie Shelton, one of her classmates, possibly snidely.

"Yeah," Karla pretends she knows from kindergarten, when, homeschooled, she has never before squished, colored, smeared, brushed, rubbed, or sprayed on paper, wood, canvas, cement, and, most recently, cloth. Now, doing so, she is finally getting to be a kid.

Harriette says the exercises are not so much a how-to for artists as a "how to understand the opportunities and limitations" each medium offers. What Karla is realizing, though, is that work is not necessarily drudgery; indeed, it can be fun. After years of cleaning, she had forgotten that.

In the spring semester, Harriette teaches the class how to print using potatoes, sponges, stencils, wood, linoleum blocks, silk screens, collages, and cameras; she shows that every depiction requires specific skills that can be learned. Closer to Harriette's age than to Karla's, like Bessie, a widow whose bright eyes and deeply dimpled cheeks framing short, upturned lips give her a cartoon chipmunk's merry-malevolent look, most of the other students are empty-nesters who want to become artists. They are choosing their preferred forms of self-expression, studying according to a plan. Karla is studying, if that's what you call drinking in an education, according to her whims.

These days, Ron'l is her serious project—at least, ever since last month, when he showed up at Sax's place all but incoherent. After quite a lot of confusion (hers) and hysteria (his), Karla finally understood that Ron'l's landlord had sold the Chinatown building, and the new owner wanted the rental tenants out so he could convert the property into co-ops. Ron'l's social worker said he could do nothing to prevent the eviction. And, having found Ron'l a studio apartment on the Lower East Side, the social worker was making himself scarce.

But there was Ron'l, wailing about how he just could not move to the Bowery, where he did not know a single person. In a one-room apartment, he would have no space to display his Barbies. He could not walk to get to Mutti's sewing machine. It was too far. There was no subway. "What I gonna do?" he howled.

You mean, what am I *going to do?* Karla felt like yelling back. For, having never been comforted by anyone herself, she had no idea how to go about comforting him. But, excoriating herself for not doing it without thinking, she made herself reach out, put her hand on his forearm, and say, "Listen." She paused to let that command sink in.

Which it evidently did, as, miraculously, Ron'l sniffed up his tears. He calmed down. He nodded as if Karla were naturally, not self-consciously, kind.

"I'll see what I can do," she promised, meaning she would ask Sax to help. "Maybe you won't have to give up your apartment."

"Praised be the Lord." Raising his wet face to hers, Ron'l rewarded Karla with a born-again smile that left her embarrassed by how very little she deserved to be deified.

Still, desperate not to disappoint him, as soon as he left, she sat down at Sax's kitchen table to work out a plan. Clearly, if she let Ron'l move full-time into the loft, she would be breaking the terms of her lease, thus losing her rent-controlled status and probably the place altogether. So that option was out.

If she asked either Sax or Ben to buy Ron'l's apartment as a co-op, with that asset, Ron'l would no longer qualify for state aid, and Sax or Ben would be financially responsible for him. Karla couldn't expect either of them to take that on. And since all her money now came from these two men, buying the apartment for Ron'l herself would amount to the same thing. The only thing she could think to do was to appeal to Sax to come up with something.

So that evening, even before he hung up his coat, she said, "Ron'l is about to be evicted. We can't just stand by and let them do that to him."

"Not so fast." Sax made his way to the library. "Give me a minute to decompress." Not until he had a drink in hand would he listen.

"Say when." Karla dropped herself into a chair in the library and watched him clatter a few of the cubes she had put out in the ice bucket into his glass, pour his Dewar's, press a quick soda spritz, take his first sip.

After which Sax finally looked up and said, "Okay. Now."

So she told him everything Ron'l had told her. And afterward Sax said he was confident they could at least delay the eviction and maybe prevent it.

She threw her arms up in triumph, saying, "I knew you could do it," just as she had known from day one that this man was her savior.

"First thing you have to do is find out Ron'l's status," he said, then went on to explain their strategy. He said she should get Ron'l to give her any court case documents he had. With those in hand, Karla should go to his social worker and light a fire under him. Most important, she and Ron'l had to consult a lawyer. Sax said he would find her a good one.

"Do you need me to come with you?" he asked the night before the first appointment with attorney Burton Feingold.

Of course she needed him, but, not about to admit this, Karla said, "No, thanks. Not necessary." At least, she hoped to God it wouldn't be. "I'll call you at work afterward." Knowing Sax was there for her might just give her the aura of authority she would need at the meeting.

The morning of the appointment, acting as if she knows what she is doing, she meets Ron'l outside a depressing-looking building near city hall whose inside matches its exterior. The lobbies and hallways, tiled like an old bathroom, do not actually smell of urine; they just look like they do. Where did Sax find this guy? Karla expected the lawyer to have a posh office, not unlike Sax's own carpeted high-rise aerie. But here the self-service elevator up to the fourth floor trembles.

Unsurprisingly, the lawyer's "suite" is cramped; the front room barely accommodates four straight chairs, a corner table, and a steel desk, behind which sits a thin-lipped gorgon with dust-colored hair and skin. The opposite of eye candy, she nevertheless greets them with surprising friendliness and confirms that Mr. Feingold is expecting them. "Please, take a seat," she suggests. "I'll tell him you're here."

Mollified by the woman's manner, Karla sits and hopes she and Ron'l, in tuxedo trousers supported by black suspenders, a ruffled salmon-pink shirt, a bolo tie, and the genuine English derby Ben gave him, are passing muster.

When the receptionist returns, she begins speed-typing on an IBM Selectric. Karla knows about Selectrics because Sax says they revolutionized his office. So if this woman is an expert typist with first-class equipment, maybe her boss is better than his office suggests. In any case, the secretary looks up and says, "He shouldn't be too long."

Indeed, at that moment he comes out, saying, "You must be Ms. Most." The neatly bearded, forty-ish Lenin look-alike extends his hand to her, and then to Ron'l. "Hello, Mr. Gamble. I'm Burton Feingold." With seeming ease, he makes eye contact. "Come on in." He presses back against the wall to allow them to precede him into a cell decorated with diplomas and certificates.

Burton R. Feingold is a graduate of Brooklyn College and Fordham Law School and a member of the American Bar Association. *So far, so good,* Karla thinks. The guy is a New York stiff—nothing wrong with that. His office decor is even starting to grow on her—the no-nonsense approach—and she likes the idea of a Jew going to Fordham, a Catholic school.

"So, tell me, what's the problem?" A brass-tacks kind of guy, Feingold could be the experienced professional they need.

Karla has to hand it to Sax.

"They making me move," Ron'l says.

"Who exactly do you mean by 'they'?" the lawyer asks.

"The building owners," Karla chimes in.

"Why is that?"

Feeling on top of things, or at least good at playing the part of someone who knew enough to come equipped, Karla hands over the paper that says when Ron'l is supposed to show up in housing court.

"Landlord say he need my apartment," Ron'l explains.

"How long have you been living there?"

"It be eight years this June," Ron'l says.

The lawyer makes a note of this answer as if he is not noticing that his new client is in any way disabled. "And you have a lease?" he asks.

"Oh, yes." Fully prepared, Karla proudly passes over a copy thereof.

"Excellent." Feingold obviously appreciates her new competence. "Rent is paid on time to date?" He riffles through the pages she handed him.

"Uh-huh," Ron'l says, nodding vigorously.

"Do you have the rent receipts?" The lawyer looks first at Ron'l, then Karla.

"I didn't know we needed them," she says in a panic.

"My social worker have them," an unperturbed Ron'l says.

"She couldn't be here today?" the lawyer asks.

"He"—Karla puts a little stress on the word—"has a tremendous caseload." She does not say the social worker already said Ron'l could not stay where he was. "I tried every day this week to reach him, but he never returned my calls. Do we really need him?" If they do, she will figure out a way to get the creep here if she has to track him down and drag him in herself. When it comes to doggedness, Karla gives herself an A plus.

"Well, just give me a minute to take another look at what we have here." Feingold again leafs through the lease. "Seems like you're rent-controlled." He looks puzzled. "So what grounds would the owner have to evict you?"

"He say 'cause I got arrested." Ron'l matter-of-factly tosses out this bombshell.

"Arrested?" As if smacked, Karla jerks back.

Ron'l is nodding as though being arrested is an ordinary event.

"What were you arrested for?" Karla shouts, because how could he not have told her before?

"They say indecent exposure." Ron'l just keeps nodding.

"Oh my God." Her best friend is an exhibitionist. "What happened?"

"Up at Times Square, last summer in a movie, they catch me, you know, jerkin'." He finally bows his head.

"So your landlord is claiming you've committed wrongful acts," says the lawyer.

"That be it." Looking up, Ron'l again nods, his cheerfulness restored.

"Oh my God." Karla drops back into the hard, straight chair. What is there about her that turns everyone she thought she knew into a nutty stranger? Her Jewish mother was really a Nazi, her best friend a sex offender . . . What does that say about Karla herself? What shockers does Sax have up his sleeve? And why isn't he here with her when she needs him? The fact that she said he didn't have to be is no excuse. He should have insisted on coming.

"What was the disposition of your case?" the lawyer asks; then, seeing the blank look on Ron'l's face, he adds, "How did the case against you end up?"

"Guilty as charged." So why is Ron'l beaming with pride?

"And your sentence?" Feingold wants to know, but probably not as much as Karla does. She can hardly wait to go home and tell Sax about this new twist.

"Fourteen days suspended," Ron'l says, still beaming.

Either a nervous reaction, decides Karla, or else he is not just a flasher—he is bonkers.

"Any fine?" the lawyer asks.

"Fifty dollars, 'cause it be a first offense. Mr. Cardullo loan me the money."

"Mr. Cardullo?"

"My boss."

Cardullo owned the toy store where Ron'l worked in exchange for Barbie dolls. Years ago, Cardullo gave Karla her first job; his son took her on her first, disastrous date. In some ways, today feels like a continuation of that experience. "Can we do anything about this?" she asks the lawyer, blotting from her mind the image of Ron'l, pecker in hand, watching porn in a public theater. And anyway, why should the police pick on him? Isn't that what every man who frequents those places does? They probably just targeted Ron'l because he is black. The more she thinks about it, the angrier Karla gets.

"Remember," Feingold is instructing Ron'l, "the crime was not a felony. It did not occur on the building owner's premises. And as long as you stay out of further trouble, Mr. Gamble, we can certainly delay any eviction and ultimately, in all probability, defeat it."

What great news! Feingold is terrific. "Please, please," Karla begs him, "do what you can so Ron'l can stay put."

"Believe me." The lawyer's simultaneous eye-to-eye and hand-to-hand is either well practiced or honestly sincere. "I will."

After this meeting, he sends Ron'l and Karla a list of the documents they will need to bring with them to housing court:

The lease.

Rent receipts for the last twelve months.

Proof that Ron'l has satisfied the judgment against him.

Testimonials from other tenants saying he has been a good neighbor.

Statements by character witnesses.

Employment records.

Any other corroborating materials.

That evening, Sax tells Karla, "I'm really impressed not just by your efficiency but by your determination, too."

"Do I have a choice?" Karla asks.

"After you heard about the arrest, you could've dropped the whole thing and let the chips fall where they may."

"Not really." She brushes off the compliment.

"I just did what needed doing," says Karla—determination and efficiency two characteristics her mother had in spades, and who really wants to emulate *her*?

Karla spends hours accumulating the evidence. She writes a registered letter to Ron'l's social worker, enclosing a self-addressed stamped envelope for copies of the rent receipts. She leaves a daily message for him. She calls his boss. Finally, then, the receipts arrive.

Karla canvasses Ron'l's Chinatown building. Everyone likes him, but most people are too scared of the owner to sign anything. Karla persists until she finds an old Italian woman who probably didn't understand the letter telling about Ron'l, her fine neighbor. However, when she signs it, *la signora* swears to the Chinese notary that yes, she knows exactly what the letter says.

Karla next drops in on Mr. Cardullo to pick up his reference letter. While she is there, Karla asks about Vince, hoping Cardullo never knew his son dumped her when he learned she was a virgin. It seems Vince now has his own auto-repair shop in Jersey, a wife, and two sons. *Bully for him*, Karla thinks. *I've got Sax*.

While Cardullo is attesting on paper that Ron'l is a longtime, trustworthy employee, Karla speculates, *If Vince and I had slept together that night and then married, I could be a New Jersey wife and mother now. What might that have been like?* The one thing she knows about mothering is what she learned from Mutti—how *not* to do it. *Someday, though*, she thinks.

However, going back uptown with Cardullo's reference letter deliciously in hand, Karla is pleased to be living high on the hog right now. And, fortified by her successes on the Ron'l front, she decides she is at last ready to introduce Sax to Viv, Joel, and her grandparents. A mistake, as it turns out. Had she accurately anticipated how that first meeting would go, she would have waited until never to introduce them.

The debut brunch is more of a Senate confirmation hearing in Washington than a social occasion in Forest Hills. Watching as if she were a spectator and not a participant, Karla cowers as her relatives shoot question arrows into Sax.

"You were born where?" they ask, after he has already told them, "Boston," as if Boston were an outlandish place for any civilized person to come from.

"You grew up there, too?"—the clear implication being that that made his Bostonianism much worse.

"Where did you go to college?" Though they do not dare sneer at Harvard, Ben makes it obvious that he refuses to be impressed.

"What did your father do?" Adele asks.

"What is it exactly that *you* do, Sax?" Ben could not sound more suspicious.

"How did you and Karla meet?" Adele wants to know.

"I was taking an art course"—Karla jumps in before Sax can blow her cover—"and he owned one of the Modigliani paintings I was studying." Never mind that she leaves hazy exactly how they met. As she hoped, her grandparents go back to shooting questions into Sax, and, though he remains astonishingly cool throughout, Karla pictures him as one of those paintings of an arrow-pierced Saint Sebastian.

But somehow, this martyr manages to survive. And afterward, instead of swearing vengeance, Sax says he is touched by how protective of Karla her family is. He admires them for that; he even likes them. As for their opinion of him, that evening, Adele and Viv, no doubt speaking for Ben, too, phone Karla to say that Sax seems "very nice," which is, of course, the kiss of death. (Only Joel, at one point during the inquisition, muttered, "Let me not to the marriage of true minds admit impediments.")

But Sax may well have minded the ordeal more than he lets on. For now, he leaves Karla, ostensibly to go on an overnight business trip. He leaves her to go to court without him. He says he will be back tomorrow, but how can she be sure? And, just as she did right after Mutti died and abandoned her, Karla turns to Viv.

Like one of his building's residents, Karla greets Pedro, Viv's doorman, and rushes into the elevator. No need for her to be announced. At the door to 5B, she lets herself in with her own key. "Hello," she calls out.

"Hello, darling." Unmistakably delighted to be visited, Viv sweeps into the foyer and envelops Karla in a Joy-scented embrace, before she steps back and says, "Come on into the kitchen. I'll make your favorite: cheese blintzes."

"Great," Karla says.

Leading the way, her high heels tip-tapping along the floor, Viv pulls an apron from its peg and, looping and tying it on over her brass-buttoned imitation Chanel suit, goes to work. "Won't take me but a minute." She lights the fire under a frying pan and scoops in butter.

"Great," Karla repeats, figuring that she'll wait until they are at the table to tell Viv all about her marvelous victory in court that morning.

But while beating up her eggs, flour, and milk, Viv has already launched into today's topic. "You know, darling," she says, "I can see that this Sax of yours is a very nice man. Certainly presentable. Even impressive. Despite all that, Joel and I think he's just too old for you. You should find someone a little nearer your own age. Can't you see that?"

"No. I certainly can't." What Karla can see is that coming here was another of her mistakes.

"You do understand, darling"—Viv ladles glop into the pan and turns away from her stove—"I just want to see you happy." This comes with heartfelt eye contact.

"And that's what I am—*happy*," Karla emphasizes, while making sure to keep her eyes from lowering. After all, what she says is true. Only what right has Karla to be happy, especially today, when Sax has left her?

"What about the future?" Returning to her task, Viv carefully flips her pancakes, takes each one out, spoons in cheese, folds the blintzes, and lays them back in the pan to sizzle side by side. "Don't you want a husband?"

"Why should I?" And even if she did, why should Sax or any other good man want to marry someone who right this minute is doing nothing to stop people from starving, or, with two apartments to live in, to shelter the homeless, or to stop racism, sex abuse, or war? Furious at herself and at Viv, Karla grabs the offensive. "*You* seem to have had plenty of fun when you were single." Though they've never discussed Viv's time with Ben, Karla is geared up to do it at this point, when they both know what she means by "fun."

"Yes, I had fun," Viv surprises her by instantly admitting. "But having fun isn't everything."

"Why isn't it?" Karla challenges her.

"What about kids? Don't you want them?"

"I'm in no hurry."

"But you can't let it go too long."

"I'm only twenty-two."

"You still have time, but time has a way of getting away from you, darling." Viv's voice quivers. "You know, I never told you this before, but I will always regret not having had children of my own." Lifting out the blintzes, she tenderly lines them up on plates, as if the four of them were her missing infants. "By the time I married, it was just too late." Teary and sorrowful, she carries her babies to the table, sits down, peers across at Karla.

What now? Clearly meant to feel sorry for Viv, sighing, Karla can offer only, "Look, you have me." But, of course, that is nowhere near enough.

"And believe me, I do thank God for that," Viv says.

"Besides," says Karla, who at this point does not want again to bear the weighty burden of being anyone's child, "you could still adopt a kid of your own." Why has she never thought of this before? Cheered by this new, brilliant scheme, Karla loves the idea, loves chewing and swallowing Viv's creamy blintz, loves solving other people's problems, loves shifting the focus from her own.

Viv instantly dismisses Karla's recommendation. "At our age, Joel and I could never get an infant. And he won't consider an older child." She shifts her gaze to the window, her face in sunlight the pillowed interior of a jewelry box, puckered into sections. "But, listen." Turning back to Karla, who can't help being touched by how old Viv has grown, Viv says, "If you had a baby, at least we'd get to be honorary grandparents." She pours water into their waiting cups, dissolving instant Sanka clumped like dirt.

With that, she dissolves Karla's compassion, too. For what right has Viv to expect Karla to produce babies on demand? *What am I, some kind of breeder put on Earth to make other people happy?* "I forgot." She pokes at her wristwatch, tosses her napkin on the table, and jumps up. "Thanks for the deliciousness, but I've got to go for a haircut." Though her appointment is not until three thirty, she cannot wait to get out of there.

Karla does not realize she never did tell Viv about this morning in court until she has walked many blocks, expressing her determination with each stride. No matter what Viv wants, no way at this point is Karla ready to tie herself down to a kid. She isn't even sure how long she and Sax will be together. Assuming, that is, he even comes back from Cleveland.

As soon as he said he was going on an overnight business trip, Karla called Viv to say she'd like lunch, called the hairdresser for a booking, called her grandparents to ask if they could meet for dinner. Karla's idea then was that whatever happened with Ron'l, afterward she would not have to face a frozen dinner alone in front of the TV. Now, on her way to the hairdresser, she wishes she'd just gone back to Sax's place. One of her first acts after her mother died was to cut off her long braids with Mutti's pinking shears.

That day, Karla stared into the mirror at the hideous girl with the gashed hair and sobbed for her undamaged, old self in a way she never sobbed for her dead mother. But this time, again left to fend for herself, she at least had the sense to entrust the haircutting to a professional.

You've come a long way, baby, Karla tells herself after she is shorn, when, instead of sobbing, she strides over to the Seagram Building, confirming her daring new look in store window after store window. With her hair springing out like Medusa's snakes, the repeatedly reflected girl looks superchic and as lithe as the dancer Sax thought Karla was the first time he ever saw her.

This newly gorgeous étoile enters the Four Seasons and spots Ben and Adele already seated at their usual table in the far corner. Instead of being her normal agonizingly bashful self, Karla, flush with today's victories, glides past the regulars, all of them centuries older than she is. These may be the Beautiful People who run everything in this city, yet, right this minute, the girl with great hair who won her case in court can pass serenely through the Establishment's maze.

"You've had a makeover, darling." Reaching up to fluff the new 'do, Adele crows, "It's terrific. Who did it?"

"Raymond, at Raymond and Nasser."

"Where'd you find him?"

"Ron'l read an article in *Harper's Bazaar*." Karla enjoys giving him credit, for, without their ever having said so, she knows her grandparents don't approve of her friendship with him. In fact, the only person who does is Sax.

A week ago, he took Karla down to the police department, where they finally obtained a copy of Ron'l's arrest record. She'd already gotten the city court docket number and the paper attesting to the satisfaction of the judgment. She had called Feingold to make sure the copies of these records qualified as legally certified.

Between the lawyer and Sax, Karla had everything they needed in court that morning. What with her new hair, she assumes she has everything she needs this evening, too.

"Now you just have to acquire some clothes to match the great coif," Ben says, rising to greet her.

Jutting out her chest and fingering the real pearls Sax gave her, Karla slips into place across from Ben without kissing him. "You don't approve of what I'm wearing?"

"It's not a question of approving." Ben waves off that notion.

"We're just a little concerned," Adele adds, "about you and this Saxton Perry." They no doubt planned this assault.

Well, who the hell isn't concerned? Karla feels like shouting. Only Ron'l thinks Sax is perfect for her, and, let's face it, Ron'l is brain-damaged. Everyone else is telling Karla what, by now, she has discovered for herself: it isn't just the age difference; it is the culture chasm.

Sax's friends summer in the Hamptons, the Berkshires, the South of France, on the Cape and Nantucket. They all drink, sometimes even at lunch. Their wives guide museum tours and belong to the Cosmopolitan Club or the Colony Club; they sit on boards and organize benefits for nonprofits; they serve on search committees for headmasters; they talk to one another about private schools, au pairs, and SAT tutors. Dining at the Four Seasons, without any beauty makeovers or court victories, they belong.

When these women deign to talk to Karla, it is about Sax, and they make it clear that he is their only possible connection to her. "Oh, yes," one of her art teachers said, "you're with that collector. I don't suppose you could get him to come by to see my paintings? But anyway, why don't we have coffee sometime?" Clearly, many of the people Karla is meeting these days see her as their entrée to Sax; otherwise, it is unlikely that any of them would bother with her.

Of course, she realizes that anyone lucky enough to bag a prince has no business kvetching. However, kvetching is ingrained in Karla's DNA. And as far as happiness goes, not only is she not entitled to it, but if she has to pursue it, it is probably not worth the bother. Let Sax's first wife, the Yankee, go that route. Sax evidently prefers Karla, which is almost as much a mystery to her as it is to Viv and her grandparents. But Karla has a theory.

Sax often speaks to her about how he grew up as the younger son of a notorious Boston Brahmin widower who was cast out of society after he married his motherless children's Irish governess. Sax says he doesn't know which of the sins his father committed was socially more damning: marrying an Irish woman (Sax's mother) or marrying a servant.

In either case, Karla assumes that by taking up with her, a Jewish maid, Sax is replicating the past, following in his father's footsteps. But so what if that is what is going on? She applauds Sax's willingness to crash through class barriers, just as his dad did. She is okay with having been a maid, as long as—please God—Sax comes back to her.

But how is she going to explain any of that to Ben and Adele?

How can she tell them she is bowled over by how much Sax knows, by his stories about the places he's been and the experiences he's had?

Karla adores hearing about what it was like to go to Harvard and be invited to the lavish coming-out parties no one could afford after the stock-market crash. She figures that, like most people, Sax needs an audience. He needs to be needed, which is perfect, because no one needs him more than she does. But if he ever finds out how badly she needs him, Sax might be turned off. He once said he wished his secretary weren't so needy.

No. Even though she and Ron'l could never have won the housing fight without his help, Karla is never going to tell Sax how much she needed and still needs him. Tailoring herself—letting out a little here, taking in a little there—she has to make him admire her. She has to make him think she is fully independent. She has to make herself believe she could in fact be independent. And, as far as Ron'l's case goes, ultimately she was.

That very morning, while Sax was in Cleveland, Ron'l and Karla showed up at housing court. Feingold had warned Ron'l that he must wear a neat, dark shirt with dark trousers, shoes, and socks. He'd warned that once they entered the courtroom, Ron'l must also remove his hat. But in the hallway outside resolution court, again sporting his British derby, Ron'l looked like a dapper stagehand. In fact, he looked almost normal, a vision Karla would not have thought possible.

But where was the lawyer? Searching the hall for him, she noticed a little girl huddled on one of the benches next to a woman who was probably her mother. This child sat inert, any expression on her face erased. What had destroyed her soul?

For the first time, Karla felt a rush of gratitude. With her warm, stolid body and her sharp surveillance, Mutti, for all her craziness, had seen to it that no one crushed her kid's spirit. She had fueled Karla's passion to live.

Turning away from the child, Karla was relieved to see Feingold hurrying toward them. Then she had only Ron'l to worry
about. How would he feel in the courtroom when he had to take
off his hat and expose his skull, misshapen because his mother was
a drunk, or maybe because she had bad obstetrical care, or just
because Mother Nature occasionally enjoys playing one of her
vicious tricks?

Karla has never had anything like that to contend with. Maybe,
she is beginning to realize, Mutti was, despite everything, not a total
disaster. And if she had redeeming qualities, perhaps Karla inherited
some of them.

Now, at dinner, instead of having to defend her attachment to
Sax, she would prefer to talk about her morning in court, but no one
is asking about her day. She would have liked for her grandparents
to tell her what they thought of Mutti when she worked for Ben. But
then, they never really knew Mutti, just as, even now, they know
almost nothing about her daughter.

They have no idea what Karla did for Ron'l in court this morning, or what Sax does for her. Karla cannot possibly explain any of
this to Ben or Adele. "I'll just tell you this," she says: "Descartes had
it all wrong." At least the Descartes she knows about from Sax. "It's
really the *examined* life that's not worth living."

For what does it matter if she is the very definition of Mutti's
parasite or a pinball bopping from one chute to another? Let other
people worry about their couplings and careers.

Noticing that the menu in her hand is shaking, Karla lays it
down. She visualized this evening as an occasion to wear mascara,
show off the pearls, flaunt her new hair, and celebrate her triumph
over the greedy landlord. She pictured herself on this very banquette. But she forgot how stultifying places like this are. She forgot
how very far from living up to her grandparents' expectations she is.

At least, though, she can say what they expect to hear, so, as if speaking memorized lines, she asks, as she has so often heard her grandfather ask, "What's good tonight?"

"Everything," Ben replies.

Nothing new there. "Then why don't you just order for me?" At this point, Karla just wants to get this meal over with.

No such luck. The minute the waiter leaves, her grandparents start in again. "You want us to think you're happy, darling, but look at you," Adele says. "How happy can you be if you're still dressed in mourning?"

"That's not why I wear black." Karla regards the money-flaunters around them. The color that once marked her as special now causes her to blend in. And since everyone on the earth came from fucking, all of them presumably fuck, too, though it is hard to imagine any of them, in their tinted aviator glasses and Armani outfits, going at it. "I just prefer it," she says, for the zillionth time.

"And how does Sax feel about that?" Adele asks.

"Fine," Karla lies. Only a few days ago, he said yet again, "You've been adventurous in so many ways, Karla—why haven't you tried wearing colors?"

"I thought you liked me the way I am. You used to tell me you liked my nun look." She lifted her chin and squinted at him.

"I also like variety," he countered.

Does that mean he is tired of her? Why should Karla believe he is in Cleveland on business and not with a girlfriend, cheating on her?

"Plate's very hot," warns the waiter, as he sets down three overlapping slices of duck framed by a squiggle of glossy sauce.

"Thank you," says Karla, who sees too late she would have been better off wearing Sax's bathrobe in the apartment's library, sharing the night's news with Walter Cronkite and digging into Swanson's sliced white-meat turkey, mounded over mashed potatoes slathered with butterscotch-colored gravy next to shockingly green peas.

Instead, presented with a skimpy, pretentious entrée, she is forced to speak well of her possibly treacherous consort. Well, the hell with that. "What difference does it make how Sax feels anyway? I don't dress just for him."

"Good," says Ben, encouraging her spunk.

"By the way, Sax has excellent taste," Karla insists.

"His taste isn't the issue," Adele hisses.

Karla knows better than to ask what *is* the issue, but that doesn't stop her grandfather from explaining, "We had hoped you would settle on a Jewish boy," while Adele solemnly nods her agreement.

"Why? My mother may not even have been a Jew, so I may not be, either," she says, though she cannot see herself as anything else.

"Your mother raised you Jewish," her grandfather claims, his voice rising. "That counts for something."

"So perpetuating the religion is my responsibility?" Karla is outraged. Do these people expect her to personally make up for the Holocaust? Is that because of her German heritage? Was that what Mutti had in mind for her all along—Teutonic atonement?

"You can't do the whole thing," Ben admits, "but you could contribute."

"If everybody lit a single candle . . . " Adele offers.

"Sax says that candle stuff is just an excuse for the government to cut back on social programs," Karla replies. "And anyway, even if Jews do become extinct, we will have existed, like the Incas and the Aztecs. Whether I produce more Jews or I don't isn't going to change that."

"But didn't your mother try, in her own way, to keep Judaism alive?"

"That has nothing to do with me." Stuck with them, Karla wants no part of her mother's ambitions. In fact, she wants no part right now of any relative.

"Of course you'll make your own decisions," Ben says, "but I have to tell you, Karla, that even with all his wealth, your Saxton Perry strikes us as somehow insubstantial. The way he talks so much about his paintings, and not at all about his daughter—I mean, if you hadn't mentioned it, we wouldn't even know he *had* a child—he almost seems more serious about his art collection than he does about the people closest to him."

Karla sets down her glass and gives her grandfather a fierce look. The man is nuts if he thinks she is going to dump Sax just because he loves his Modigliani more than he loves her or maybe even Fleur. No way, José. Her grandparents' disapproval only binds Karla more closely to Sax. She looks around at the restaurant's display of wealth and power. These are the people she disdains, but they are also the people she wants to be.

You can't have it both ways, Sax reminds her, his voice, whether Karla likes it or not, embedded within her.

CHAPTER 8

Of course, Sax returns from that trip and from every subsequent one, too. What's more, if he is going to be away for more than a few days, he invites Karla to join him. He never leaves her for long. And when he is anywhere near her, she has only to look at him to feel a rush of love. Whether it is the dark, longish hair that frames his ear, the adorable pinkness of his earlobe, the smooth prominence of his cheekbones, or everything about Sax that stimulates this response, Karla cannot say, but always the fact that this man lets her live with him thrills her.

She figures he likes her only because she is not run of the mill. But many other originals would love being with him, so why her? Clearly, he finds her amusing. Karla sighs. For how long can she manage to entertain him? Once he sees through her charm, he'll be finished with her. The story of Scheherazade is never out of her mind.

Yet just as, charmed by his virgin wife's tales, the sultan daily spares her life, Sax allows Karla to enchant him day after day. Maybe it is a chemical interaction. In any event, as the years—ten of them—add up, their lives together follow a pattern whose repetitions imply they will go on this way forever. Nothing, as far as Karla can tell, is changing.

Without exactly deciding anything, she drifts into perpetual studies and a constant "neither here nor there." The only door that slams behind her is the one that ended her cleaning job. Karla still pays rent and retains her lease on the Canal Street loft—nothing different there.

Since she has been with Sax, no one significant in her life has died or been diagnosed with a serious disease. Sax has yet to run away with another woman. Karla regularly sees Viv, Ron'l, Ben, and Adele, all of them about the same as they have always been. Fleur has come, if not to like Karla, at least to accept her existence in Sax's life. When they meet, say, to celebrate a birthday—Fleur's or Sax's—Fleur sometimes looks directly at Karla and occasionally addresses a generic remark like "How are you?" to her. Once, she even leaned slightly forward to receive a goodbye kiss, which Karla was happy to give her.

Other than that, life with Sax maintains its pattern. Daily examining her reflection, Karla detects no obvious bulges, wrinkles, sags, or gray hairs. The magnifying mirror reveals the same moonstone eyes and prominent cheekbones, with no aging, at least none that she can see. But once in a while, she reaches an unmistakable milestone, like the time last year when she turned thirty, a true occasion for self-assessment. Of course, having achieved nothing, she flunked.

Never mind the A's she gets in every course she takes for credit. Karla is astonished when no one else is astonished by her grades. They just expect her to be good at things. She, on the other hand, knows better. Looking back, she berates herself because she squandered her youth, has no plan for her future, and, in her mind, has accomplished zero. Making any change in her life, though, seems pointless. After all, she is far from miserable.

So she continues to live with Sax. Though occasionally she plays with the idea of leaving to strike out on her own, she quickly rejects the notion.

"Have you considered the possibility of marriage?" Sax asked one morning a few years ago as they finished breakfast on the balcony of a hotel on Capri.

"Not really." As her skin sopped up sunshine, Karla gazed out toward the sea far below. Why change a status quo as marvelous as this one? "You?"

"Not really." Mimicking her response to his question, Sax chuckled. "Marriage didn't work out so well for me last time." Having once been dumped by Pam, Sax depends on Karla to stick with him. "But if it was something you wanted . . ."

"Not now." Though, truth be told, she depends on him to put up with her. At this point, she does not want a life without Sax. But marriage is another story.

In the midst of a feminist revolution, Karla is an island of uncertainty. There is, first, the issue of her identity. For years she set the question aside to concentrate on day-to-day challenges. Now, when her existence is one of almost paralyzing stability, she finds herself revisiting the issue of who she really is. However, the more she looks into it, the deeper she falls down the rabbit hole.

Other women her age are giving up their fathers' surnames, assuming their mother's maiden names or, like Karen Tigerlily, one of her classmates, making up new last names for themselves. But Karla never had her father's name, her mother's real name is oddly in question, and any alias would seem Hollywood-ish, as if Karla thought herself a starlet.

In fact, being anybody but Karla Most would feel fake. Karla Most is who she has always been, and even if she eventually does marry Sax, his name will always belong to him, not her. Karla cannot see herself, and she cannot believe anyone else would ever accept her, as a Perry, or even as a Perry-Most.

How, by any other name, would she be different? Far from being oppressed by men, for the first half of her life she was subjected to an almost complete absence of them. When a man did enter her scene—Ron'l, Ben, Joel, Sax—he enabled, rather than suppressed, her. So, much as Karla would like to blame men for making her a "nothing," she cannot. Why, then, can't she be a more significant person in her own right?

She keeps thinking it was Mutti's fault because Mutti told her over and over what she did wrong and how she failed. When Karla's contemporaries—doctors, bus drivers, lawyers, mothers, waitresses, artists, saleswomen, politicians—were building their careers, she wasn't even in school. Other women had mothers who egged them on, while her mother impressed on her that she was never any good at anything and never would be. So what could Karla ever become? She never so much as made it out of the starting gate.

Whenever she asks Sax, "Why do you love me?" she is really asking, "What makes me special?" And when he answers, "Because I just do," though she knows it exasperates him, she persists in asking again and again, "But why? Why?" Why won't he explain her to herself?

"Why do you keep asking me?" he asks. "Why can't you just accept that I do love you?"

"I just need you to tell me," she says, as if once she sees what he sees in her, she will finally know who she is.

"I never met anyone else with mother-of-pearl eyes," he once explained, which was all very well and good, but that was about what Karla *looked* like, not who she was.

"I love you because you respond passionately to art," he said another time.

"You mean I respond passionately to *you*," she joked, and pushed him away so she could take his art comment and examine it privately.

She wants to think over the implications of being this abalone-eyed art lover. What does that make her, really? There has to be something pretty good about her, since Sax still wants her around. But after a close self-assessment, the best Karla can come up with is that she does not say or do the expected, which makes her "refreshing."

She also still gets off on sex, and not just with Sax's cock in her twat—in her mouth, too. Of course, Sax loves her for that. It may even make her a rarity, because now, thinking about, say, her grandmother's mouth, so often reluctant to admit even food, and Viv's meticulously outlined, carefully glossed lips, Karla cannot imagine either of them giving anyone a blow job. But surely hers are not the only mouth, lips, and tongue that savor the feel and taste of a dick. So what else is there about her? Karla has no idea.

These days, she tries to avoid going places where she will be asked, "What do you do?" Occasionally, however, confronted with that question, she's learned to reply, with a shrug, "Not that much," or to admit, as if it is a joke, "I'm a dilettante."

"You're lucky," a woman with an advertising firm once assured her. "Most of us have to work."

Yet Karla doesn't feel lucky. She feels "vertless." And the fact that other people consider her lucky just makes her feel worse. No one understands. Some years back, Ben and Viv took her to city hall and Viv officially swore she'd witnessed Karla's birth. Now Karla has a birth certificate, a surname that may have belonged to her mother, and a Social Security number, which, theoretically, allows her to take courses for credit.

But in order to get credits toward a degree, she would need to be officially admitted to a college, and for that she would have to have a high school diploma or its equivalent. When Sax bought her a study guide for the GED, Karla took one look at the math section's foreign words and symbols and permanently shelved the book.

In any case, she has little motivation to go after a degree. The courses she sits in on are not coalescing into an obvious major. Her status as a "nothing" bothers her, at least when she thinks about it, but she has not come up with anything she wants to do that she isn't already doing. She occasionally reads want ads that suggest she might qualify as a saleslady, but the money would be the only reason to do that work, and she has no need for money. She sometimes thinks about volunteering to do something useful but balks when she remembers that she would have to commit to showing up on a certain day, at a certain time, week after week. She delights in owning her own time.

When she was a maid, she was expected to appear on appointed days at appointed hours. Now, even though the classes she attends are scheduled, she can choose to blow them off at will. No one expects Karla to do anything. And, after growing up under Mutti's perpetual vigilance ("Did you have a BM?" "Did you take your vitamins?" "Did you wash your neck?" "Why did you say hello to that woman?"), she finds this lack of supervision thrilling. At last she is free just to be.

She has her passport and can go wherever Sax wants to take her. She just needs to be available. She adores their travels, each trip better than the one before. Sax introduced her to sailing in the Caribbean and for her twenty-fourth birthday took her to Paris and the Louvre. Another time, they flew on the SST to London and went to the theater and the Courtauld Gallery. The following spring, they toured the Prado in Madrid and the Vatican in Rome. For Sax, these excursions are vacations from work. For Karla, they combine extensions of her art education with vacations from the vacation that is, in fact, her life.

"It is actually the examined life that is not worth living," she likes to remind people, expecting but not receiving points for her cleverness in misquoting Descartes. Typical, because when she is proud of an achievement, everyone else takes it for granted. But when anyone does compliment her—a teacher, for instance, praising one of her ideas—Karla feels as if she has put something over on them.

Still, there is no doubt that by auditing, she is learning. Her most recent choices are The Journey from Gentileschi to Chicago; a course in feminist art; and Film Noir: An Overview. If it weren't for school catalogs, she would not even know these subjects existed. Now Karla knows what they mean.

She takes up cooking, her latest achievement: home-baked croissants, beef Wellington, and chocolate soufflé. She starts piano lessons and aerobic dancing at the Y. Every few days, she tunes in to the soap opera As the World Turns. Karla has so many guilty pleasures. And, feeling guilty about each and every one, she manages to stave off the contentment she does not believe she deserves.

Her grandparents regularly accuse her of wasting her life. Viv still warns Karla that she is letting her biological clock run out. Meanwhile, Sax promises that soon she will stumble upon her true identity. "Look at Fleur," he advises, apparently unwilling to face the fact that his daughter and his consort, with only a ten-year age difference between them, pretty much come from different species.

Fleur had riding lessons, summers in the Hamptons, debutante parties. If any of Karla's ancestors had been lucky enough to own a horse, that animal would have pulled a cart full of goods, not ridden to hounds. Karla once got to go with Viv to Coney Island. Fleur has breeding; Karla has happenstance.

It is only natural that Sax's daughter, having left her psycho, drug–fueled past behind, has become Mrs. Endicott Chalmers the third, a Brooks Brothers, Greenwich, Connecticut, wife, and her father is so relieved by her transformation into a stable, functioning member of society that he doesn't even mind that she has become a Republican. But what has her situation to do with Karla's? All that talk about Fleur finding herself—never really lost, she was just delaying the inevitable moment when she stepped into the armor that was always right there, waiting for her.

No one ever hammered out a similar suit for Karla, unless she counts the black to which she is still limiting herself. The conformity in Fleur that pleases Sax cannot be what he expects from Karla, but if it is, does she want to be with someone who has this goal for her? Is he only a stand-in for the father she never had? If so, isn't it about time she outgrew him?

Right now, Karla cannot take time to think about moving out. She is too busy making the most of her situation, too busy doing too much, for, in addition to her other activities, she is obsessed with the "Who the hell am I?" project.

Other women her age are talking about their biological clocks, but turning thirty set off Karla's psychological alarm. If she could be that old, she could someday even be dead. So if she ever wants to know who she is, she'd better hurry up and find out. At this point, she suspects the weirdnesses in Mutti's past but does not know the details. If she is going to uncover the secret to her own identity, she will have to face exactly where she came from.

Karla begins by going back to the astounding picture she stumbled on when she was sixteen. Mutti had just died, and Karla immediately tracked down Viv, the clean freak. Right after the burial, Viv's first solid piece of advice was that even though Mutti's illness had not been contagious, Karla should go home and strip her bed and turn over her mattress.

So, that very day, Karla tilted Mutti's mattress up. And before she flipped the bulky thing, she spotted, pressed against the box spring, the old photo of her father, Michael Zimmerman, in his army uniform, which Mutti had confiscated right after Viv showed up with Ben.

Recovering this lost treasure, Karla took some minutes with it before she noticed another snapshot. Then, repelled by the image, she read on the back, in Mutti's unmistakable handwriting, "Maria Werner and Hilde Knecht, 1942," the names of the people and the year they were photographed.

It was an ordinary, old-fashioned, studio portrait—one of those pictures that look as if they have been dipped in tea. In this particular one, a somber, uniformed man with a swastika armband—his other arm missing—posed with a stubby Teutonic woman, her fair hair lifted from her temples in double pompadours. This quintessentially World War II mother and father flanked a girl, presumably their daughter, a dark-haired preteen wearing braids. She, for some reason, was glaring. How often Karla had seen that same expression on Mutti's face!

Karla took out her mother's magnifying glass from her mother's sewing table drawer and examined the *Mådchen*. Same dark hair as Mutti. Same eyes, nose, lips, chin.

During the night, Karla kept getting out of her bed to go back to the photograph. As if picking at a scab, she lifted, examined, and reexamined the Knecht family. Tempted to destroy this somehow incriminating evidence, she resisted her urge to rip it into pieces or, in poetic justice, to cut it up with Mutti's shears. She considered flushing the thing down the toilet or burning it over a gas fire like the Nazis gassed the Jews.

Near dawn, the photo fluttered, a moth in Karla's hand. She gently opened her fingers and dropped the family into Mutti's chair, where she left it until morning. Once anyone else saw that that picture, the image could never be destroyed. Karla picked it up, laid it under Mutti's sweaters in the dresser drawer, and for fifteen years did not look at it again.

Until now. Consumed by the need to know for certain who, exactly, she is, instead of just suspecting who she may be, Karla goes down to Canal Street, retrieves the photo, and takes the train up to Viv's.

Once in the door, after the usual preliminaries—kisses, declined offers of coffee, Danish, tea—Karla pulls out the photo and asks Viv point blank, "Who are these people?"

"I have no idea." Viv shudders and quickly hands it back.

"Doesn't that girl look to you like Mutti?" Holding the picture out where Viv can still see it, Karla challenges her.

"Give it back to me," Viv says, and this time she studies the photo. "Of course, I see what you mean. She does look like my cousin Liesel, but she can't be."

"Why not?"

"She is a member of a Nazi family, and it says right here on the back. She is Maria or Hilde Knecht. That's not your mother."

"Then why did she keep this picture?"

"They could've been friends."

"A Nazi soldier? And why conceal them if they were friends?"

"Who knows? Liesel was full of secrets."

"She never mentioned these Knecht people to you?"

"Never." Viv shakes her head vigorously. "Never."

"How can I find out about them?" Karla persists. She is tired of being lied to.

"If they were Jews, I'd tell you to go to YIVO."

"What's that?"

"The Institute for Jewish Research. But Nazis?" Viv scowls. "And anyway, why do you need to know?"

At the YIVO office, a buxom woman wearing dangly earrings asks, "What can I do for you?"

"I need to find out about my mother. She came out of Dachau alive," Karla can't help boasting. "Number one seven eight four three."

It turns out there was indeed a Liesel Most. She was born in 1931 in Heidelberg, Germany. Her father was Friedrich Most, her mother Greta Rosenstock Most. They lived on Hauptstrasse.

"And Liesel's sister?" Karla asks.

"No sisters. Just a brother, Stefan, born in 1929."

Mutti always claimed she had a sister. Could there be another Liesel Most? And if not, what happened to this one?

In November 1940, Liesel Most and her parents, brother, and maternal grandmother were rounded up and deported to Ravensbrück, where they all perished. Ravensbrück—not Dachau, which, according to Mutti, was her camp. And she could not have been one of the Mosts who died in Germany, because Mutti died right in front of Karla in the Canal Street loft.

But what about 17843, Mutti's tattoo?

"That number was not issued to anyone in Dachau," the YIVO woman says, without even having to look it up. "Dachau inmates had no numbers."

But with her eyes closed, Karla can see and recite the blue 17843 on her mother's arm.

"No, not from Dachau," the woman repeats.

"Where, then?"

"Might've been Birkenau. There, that number would've been possible."

"But why would she have said Dachau?" Karla asks.

"I wish I could tell you."

Maybe, Karla thinks, Mutti decided Dachau was more impressive than Birkenau. It would have been just like her to upgrade herself.

In any case, Karla did not invent her mother's tattoo. There *was* a number 17843, but apparently it belonged to a man named Gerhard Goldschmidt, born in Frankfurt in 1930, perished in Birkenau in 1943.

There could not have been two Jews with the same number. Always meticulous about record keeping, the Germans reused numbers only on people sent to camps for limited periods of what they called "reeducation" because they'd been caught criticizing their leaders. None of those inmates was a Jew.

But if they did not label Mutti with that number, who did? And what about the Nazi soldier, Werner Knecht, with his Maria and Hilde? The YIVO woman directs Karla to the German consulate. Filthy Nazis, they represent everything she hates, including and especially her mother. But she has no choice; she must deal with them.

It takes repeated visits for Karla to find out that Werner Knecht was born in Nuremberg in 1910, graduated from university, and stayed in Heidelberg, where, in 1929, he married, in a Catholic ceremony, Maria Viktoria Knaus, a local dressmaker three years his senior. Werner served in the Afrika Korps for two years. His son, Wilhelm, born in 1924, was killed on the Russian front in 1942. In 1943, a year after the picture Karla has was taken, Maria died. But her daughter, Hilde, was still registered as alive.

After the war, Werner was unemployed until 1950, when he resumed his work as a high school history teacher. He died in 1957.

And Hilde? She was born in 1930 and attended a *Gymnasium*. But there is no record of what became of her after 1944.

Having worked on this for weeks, Karla finally leaves the consulate with Hilde's last known address. At home, she compares that address to the one she still has from YIVO for Liesel Most, and she is not altogether surprised to find that the two girls lived on the same *Hauptstrasse*, Liesel in *Haus* 22A, Hilde in 22B.

So, at long last, Karla is able, based on the evidence she has, to surmise what happened. Her mother was always a stranger to her, but Mutti was no stranger to the girl whose identity she stole. Two neighboring kids, same age, in the same class, both with older brothers. They were very likely friends until one of them was made to wear a yellow star and was expelled from school.

Did Hilde and Liesel go on meeting, playing with dolls? Did Hilde share with Liesel the school lessons the Jewish girl was missing? Or did she turn her back on her friend, the new pariah?

When Liesel and her family were sent away, did Hilde know where they were taken? Did she realize what had happened to them? What was it like for her to see pictures of concentration camp liberations, like those Karla found once in that issue of *TIME* her mother immediately confiscated?

Karla's answers spawn questions that burst in her head like tough little corn kernels in a popper, snapping at her, spitting, then fizzling. Every night she tells Sax what she needs to know. Whose idea was it for Mutti to go to America after the war—hers or her father's? Was she perpetrating a scam or doing penance? Who took her to have the numbers tattooed? She was right-handed and could have stabbed them into her own arm with a needle. Or did the one-armed Kraut do it to her? Was he the man in uniform her mother feared?

"Who knows?" Sax asks.

Who indeed? But it is no wonder "Liesel" never talked about her time in Dachau. No wonder she was terrified of authorities. If anyone ever found out about her Nazi father, she would have been kicked out of America for stealing the real Liesel's reparations, Hilde Knecht would have been sent to prison. If the authorities had discovered she had given birth to a bastard (Karla!), she would probably have been deported.

Now, after years of shoving out of sight the only photo she has of Mutti—what if her Jewish grandparents saw the swastika?—Karla has set the antique image on her bureau in Sax's room and become a detective, searching obsessively for clues to her heritage.

Certain things are what Sax would call "givens": Mutti is still her mother. There is no getting around the fact that Viv saw Karla come out of Mutti's body. But that body belonged to Hilde Knecht, not Liesel Most. If Karla's mother was not Jewish, Karla is not Jewish. She and Sax are both goys. They have that in common.

She tries some of his scotch and rejects it. It tastes like medicine, without curing her sickness. Her sickness is part of her. Again and again, without intending to do so, Karla stares at the faded Germans with their swastika armbands. It is possible that these people really are her family. Yet nothing feels more alien, or even more repulsive, to her than the name Karla Knecht.

But there is the evidence. She has known for years that her mother lied about Michael Zimmerman. He did not, as Mutti always claimed, die a soldier-hero's death. According to his parents, Karla's playboy father died crashing his sports car in Long Island. And if her mother altered those facts, just about everything else she ever told Karla was probably bullshit, too, so everything Karla ever believed about herself is false. She is, in fact, no one she knows.

She is a stranger to herself, just as her mother was a stranger to her. Something made Hilde assume another girl's Jewish identity. Was she a heroine who knew what she was doing, or was she someone so delusional that she actually came to believe she *was* Liesel Most? If so, when did she make the switch? Did she mean for Karla's initials to be KK? Was the old Nazi thinking KKK? Either this Hilde/Mutti/Liesel was insane or she was a skilled con artist, or, conceivably, she was a penitent trying to atone for her country's sins.

When Karla was little, she used to pray the Vietnam War would end, as if she, with all her powers of persuasion, could get God to make this happen. Karla was the one who made everything happen, and when so much of what was happening was appalling, what did that say about her? Could that be how her mother felt, too?

Combing through German records, Karla discovers that Hilde's mother, née Maria Viktoria Knaus, had a brother, Otto Knaus, who had two daughters, Charlotte, born in 1932, and Gertrud, born in 1936. Gertrud died in 1943, but, according to the records, Charlotte is still living.

When she discovers the existence of this cousin's family, Karla is a prospector with a gold nugget. She now owns a hard lump of valuable fact, and this fact brings yet another: Charlotte, Mutti's first cousin, is a history professor who lives in Karlsruhe, Germany, married to Oskar Kessler, a judge.

"Can you believe it?" Karla asks Sax that night. "I've got a living German cousin."

"I can believe you do," he said, "but that you tracked her down, that's the miracle." He lifts his glass to her. "Congratulations."

"Listen, maybe I should've let sleeping dogs lie," Karla says, waving off the compliment. "This Charlotte could turn out to be a terrible person."

Yet Karla spends most of the following Monday writing Mutti's cousin a letter:

Dear Charlotte Kessler [what is it with these K names?],

My mother, Hilde Knecht, grew up in Heidelberg. She was the daughter of Werner Knecht and Maria Viktoria Knaus Knecht, whose brother, Otto, had a daughter, Charlotte. If you are that daughter, I think this makes us first cousins once removed. In any case, after changing her name to Liesel Most, Hilde moved to New York City, where, in 1958, I was born. My mother died in 1972.

Now I would very much like to learn about my mother's life in Germany, and about anyone there who might be related to me. My father died before I was born, and I have only recently connected with his parents. At this point, I would also like to know more about my mother's side of the family. [She does not ask what she really wants to know: Were they Jew-hating Nazis, or did they only look like they were?]

I would greatly appreciate any information you could give me on this subject.

Sincerely,
Karla Most

After reading what she wrote to Sax and gaining his approval, she takes her letter to the German consulate, where Ursula, the gap-toothed woman with an accent just like Mutti's has been helping her with the records. Ursula now agrees to translate Karla's letter into German. What's more, when Karla offers to pay her, she vehemently rejects the idea. Ursula is as eager as Karla is for her to reconnect with her German relatives. So much for filthy Nazis. Like Karla, Ursula is simply a person.

Two weeks later, Karla exchanges a box of Asbach chocolate-covered cherries for the translation and sends both versions, English and German, to Charlotte Knaus Kessler. Then she waits for a reply that may never come.

Nevertheless, while waiting, Karla lists the questions she wants answered: What were her grandparents on that side like? Why did Hilde/Liesel leave them when she was what—eleven, twelve, thirteen, fourteen? Why did she take someone else's identity? Did she need to escape from something horrible? Was she, say, sexually abused by her Nazi father? Or was she simply grabbing her chance to move up in the world?

"Why do you think she did it?" Karla asks Viv over lunch at the Whitney.

"Listen, darling, after the war, everyone wanted to come here," Viv says. "There's no mystery about that. And even though displaced Jews could get in, I don't think there was much appetite for Huns."

"But after Mutti got here, she kept being Liesel," Karla says, ignoring a shrimp salad that would normally have occupied her full attention. "She never went back to being herself."

"She was probably afraid they would deport her, and who knows what that would have been like?" Viv shakes her head, as if to dispel a nasty image.

"Aren't you pissed at her? I mean, her whole relationship with you was based on a lie. Or did you know all along she wasn't really

Liesel Most?" Scanning Viv's face, Karla looks for some sign that she, and only she, was ignorant of Mutti's true identity.

"Who else could she be?" Steady-eyed, Viv looks interested, rather than guilty or repelled.

"Hilde Knecht, the girl in the picture." Karla detects nothing furtive in Viv's reaction.

"She said she was my cousin Liesel." Viv shrugs. "And that was good enough for me."

"But I'm pretty sure she was actually that German girl. So you and I aren't really cousins." Saying this, Karla is on guard for the slightest of recoils. After all, she now has Nazi blood. "We aren't even related."

"You'll never get me to believe that, my little *schiksele*," says Viv, laughing. "Because, you know, I did once really have that cousin Liesel. And it was wonderful thinking she survived; it was marvelous helping her give birth."

"But that didn't make us cousins."

"Think of us as adopted relatives, and without your mother and her impersonation, I would never have had you." Suddenly weepy, Viv dabs at a tear while deftly preserving her mascara. "And look, who can blame anyone for trying to better herself?"

"I don't know." Isn't bettering herself exactly what Karla is doing with Sax? Like mother, like daughter? Is her life genetically determined, then? Does that mean she can stop worrying about who she should become and just let it happen?

But before she gets too cocky, she remembers that Mutti's diseased heart could also be a hand-me-down. Something killed Karla's German grandmother early. According to the records, she died at only forty-four. Reaching under the table, Karla surreptitiously takes her pulse. Yes, her heart is beating, but who knows if it is too fast, too slow, too jerky? Who knows how much longer she has to live?

CHAPTER 9

Though, like Mutti's writing on the back of the Knecht photo, Charlotte's handwriting is spiky and foreign, her English seems to be excellent.

My dear cousin Karla,

You have no idea how happy I was to receive your letter. For a long time, I searched unsuccessfully for news of your mother, my cousin Hilde. She and I were very close as children. Indeed, after her mother so tragically died, for a time, Hilde moved in and lived with us. So there is much I can tell you about her, at least from when she was a girl.

And perhaps you will be good enough to tell me about her years in America. We completely lost touch and were never able to reestablish contact. Of course, you have my utmost sympathy that you lost your mother when you were both so young. This must have been very difficult for you.

I will ask you to come visit me here in Germany, but before that happens, my husband, a judge on the German constitutional court, and I are about to leave for a conference on global justice at Yale University in New Haven, Connecticut, after which we will spend a few days in New York. Might our first meeting be possible during that time?

We will be staying in Manhattan at the Hotel Kimberly from September 7 to September 10. If no days during that period are convenient for you, perhaps we can arrange something else, either in the States or here in Germany.

She concluded with her phone number.

Sax tells Karla there is a six-hour time difference, and at noon the next day, he shows her how to make the call.

About to connect with a missing part of herself, Karla controls her excitement—how hard she has worked for this possibility!—and tries to ignore her fear. But what if she says the wrong thing to this stranger—assuming, that is, someone even answers the now inexorably ringing phone? How will Karla know, without seeing the person she is talking to, how they are reacting or how she should proceed?

Clamped by tension, Karla resists a strong urge to hang up as a woman's voice says, "Hallo?"

"Yes, hello." Karla forces herself to reply. "Is this Charlotte Knaus Kessler?"

It is. And the new cousin, whom Karla is to call Lotte, is delighted to hear from her and is so very happy they can make plans to meet soon.

After she hangs up, Karla's knees give way, as if she has in fact come unhinged. In ten days, she and Cousin Charlotte—Lotte—will face each other.

To prepare for that, Karla returns to the German consulate and looks up Oskar Kessler. Born in Frankfurt, he taught law for a while at the university in Heidelberg, then moved to Karlsruhe when he became a judge. As Lotte said on the phone, they have one son, Johann, who is twenty-four, just seven years younger than Karla.

Had Mutti stayed in Germany, there might have been a child, someone maybe like Johann, but Karla would not have existed. Mutti's life would most likely have been much like her cousin's.

They might have lived near each other and hung out together. Even though Mutti left, will they still look alike? Will they *be* alike? Whether they are or not, what will this Lotte expect of Karla? Can she be whatever that is?

They agreed to meet at the Kimberly, which, Lotte said, has a rooftop cocktail lounge where they can speak quietly. Having never previously heard of the Kimberly, Karla finds it ironic to learn of the hotel from her German relative. What other news will Charlotte bring? There may be things Karla would rather not hear, but, she reassures herself, if the meeting goes badly, she can just take off. After all, this whole thing is an experiment.

Karla simply has to keep calm. She pushes the hotel's revolving door and spots a woman who, sitting in the lobby, looks at her expectantly. "Lotte?"

"Karla?" She stands and tentatively holds out her arms, leaving Karla to decide whether to hug or to shake hands.

The choice is easy. Though Lotte does resemble Mutti, Mutti always looked closed and immersed in darkness; her cousin is open and full of light. Seeing Lotte, Karla has to smile. Seeing Mutti, she used to cringe. "Yes." How naturally they embrace!

She is not bulky and solid, like Mutti, but narrow and pliable, like Karla herself. They break apart.

"So," Karla's cousin says, standing back to assess her American relative while allowing herself to be assessed.

"So," Karla repeats, grinning at her very first for-sure blood relative (Michael, after all, despite the evidence of his red hair, was probably but not definitely her father—hence, his parents are just possibly not her grandparents).

This new cousin of hers was obviously once pretty and is still attractive. She wears her pale, chin-length hair loose around her face, her north-country skin like a plant deprived of sun. But what Karla cannot get over is her wide-set, luminous eyes. Of course Sax has frequently spoken of Karla's "abalone" eyes. But, as often as she has stared at herself in the mirror, until this moment she has not seen for herself what he was talking about. However, neither blue or gray, Lotte's eyes are mother-of-pearl.

And as if that were not a sufficient corroboration of their shared ancestry, astonishingly, Karla's cousin is wearing a black blouse with her black pantsuit, this inky propensity possibly inherited and not chosen. "Oh, God," Karla says. "I can see right away. We are related."

"Oh, yes." Lotte smiles. "You and I are family."

"Family," Karla repeats, as unshed tears and unexpressed laughter thicken a bit awkwardly the space between them.

Lotte adroitly breaches the gap by asking, "Then shall we go right up, where we can talk?" She nods toward the elevator, stepping back to let Karla go ahead, her diffidence unlike Mutti's forcefulness.

"Sure." Karla takes the lead.

On the roof, ensconced in deep armchairs, each with a glass of white wine, they continue to size each other up. Lotte has on light pink lipstick and just enough mascara to frame her pale eyes with small black Vs. She has taken the trouble to make herself attractive. Rather than frowning, as Mutti always did while searching Karla for flaws, Lotte is smiling at her, as if she expected to like what she sees and is not disappointed.

Wearing only her usual lip gloss and no mascara, Karla wishes she had done a little more to fix herself up. But because she automatically responds to her cousin's friendly receptivity, she can remind herself that clearly Lotte is going to care more about what she *is* like than about what she looks like. If only Karla knew herself well enough to tell her new cousin what she is like.

Lotte is German. Catholic. Calm. Cultured. She comes across as a normal person, not a nutcase. Karla would love to be just like her. But Karla is American. Quasi-Jewish. Mercurial. Ignorant. Still, she might share some important hidden trait with her cousin.

Lotte's past could just possibly shed light on Karla's future. "Right after Mutti died, I found this photograph." She reaches into her purse and extracts it. "That's how I learned about the existence of my mother's German family." Reluctantly, she hands over her picture.

"*Ja*. That is Uncle Werner and Aunt Maria and my cousin Hilde." Lotte's face suddenly crumples.

It never occurred to Karla that this confrontation might be as emotional for her cousin as it is for her. Now, feeling it is only right for Lotte to hold on to the photo, Karla waits until the air clears before asking, "So, what was it like for you, growing up?"

"Well, of course it was wartime." Lotte nods ruefully. "There came at night planes overhead, distant explosions, rumors about destructions. Sometimes, even in the day, strafing from the sky."

"That had to have been very scary for you." Karla has never before felt any sympathy for a World War II German. But in the middle of a war she did nothing to cause, Lotte would have been a terrified child. Karla knows how that feels.

"You would think so," Lotte says. "And, deep down, I suppose it really should have been frightening, but I was so young, it was just our family routine: some nights, into the shelter with the neighbors; daytimes, staying close to the buildings when we walked on the streets. None of us little children ever believed it was going to be one of us who was killed." And now, it seems, no past terrors bubble up to trouble the surface of her life. "But it was different for your mother."

"Why?"

"She was a *Kriegskind*—a child of war. You know this term?" Lotte takes a sharp breath, as if she were hissing. At what? Her own pain? "Hilde was four years older than I, so she knew girls and boys her age from school, and several were injured, sent away, a few even killed."

"Did you ever talk to her about that?" When Karla considers

her mother's experiences, Mutti's fears seem, after all, maybe not so insane.

"No. I was too little then," says Lotte, pronouncing the word "then" as "zen," just like Mutti used to. "I just worshipped my Hilde."

"How old was she when she came to live with you?"

"Just past thirteen."

"And how long was she there?"

"It was not quite three years—from 1943 to 1946, I think. During that period, she was my big sister."

"What was she like in those days?"

"It was almost as if she was one girl when she lived with her parents"—Lotte paused as she thought back—"and then, with us, she was entirely another person."

"You mean after she called herself Liesel Most," Karla prompts.

"Oh, no." Lotte shakes her head vehemently. "Before any of that. There was a time when Hilde was a merry girl—what we would call *eine frohliche Mädchen*—full of pranks. And, seeing her, one had to laugh. She made us all so happy." Lotte sighs.

"And so what changed her?" Karla can't imagine her grim mother either laughing or inspiring anyone else to do so. She never saw Liesel make anyone happy. On the contrary, when Karla displayed any sign of joy, Mutti would pat the air, tamping it down, and command, "Not so much exuberance," as if elation were a crime.

"First, the storm police arrived for the Most family." Lotte shudders. "They took away Hilde's best friend. We never saw her again."

"Would my mother have been there when they did that?" Karla can see Mutti watching, powerless to stop her friend from being herded like an animal out of her home. It would have been like the time when, cowering in the drugstore doorway, her heart flickering, Karla thought the SS had come for Mutti. Except, in that case, they hadn't.

"Or it could have happened when Hilde was at school," Lotte says. "Either way, she quickly knew that her one intimate friend was never coming back."

"I don't understand how, after the Nuremburg Laws, they could ever have been close." Karla still cannot think of her mother as "Hilde." She cannot visualize a "Liesel" who seems, at best, imaginary.

"Hilde's mother, my aunt Maria, often reminded us very quietly that Our Lord was also Jewish. And Hilde and Liesel, they were from birth what we call *herze fruenden* — friends of the heart. Tante Maria said no law could ever change that."

"She sounds terrific." And she was Karla's grandmother.

"Oh, yes, she was." Lotte reaches over and clasps her hand, confirming this honor that now belongs to Karla. "And then, about a year after Liesel disappeared" — Lotte takes her hand away — "Hilde's mother died."

"Was my mother with her when that happened?" Missing her cousin's reassuring touch, Karla remembers her last day with Mutti — that convulsion, the white arc of milk and the broken glass and then Mutti's return to consciousness, her cheeks wonderfully rosy. "Are you okay?" Karla asked that night, not knowing what she would do if Mutti said no.

"I'm fine. Just go. Get the broom," Mutti ordered.

But by the time Karla came back with the broom and the dustpan, the Mutti part of Mutti was gone, replaced by that dead thing in her chair.

"Although I was already nine years old," Lotte is saying, "I just cannot recall Tante Maria's actual death or know who witnessed it. I am not even sure that Uncle Werner got leave from the army to be with Hilde. If he did, he was soon away again, so that was why she came to live with us."

Karla remembers backing away from Mutti's corpse and figuring out how to call Viv, who quickly arrived to take charge. "How old was my mother then?"

"Thirteen."

Three years younger than Karla was when Mutti died. "According to Jewish law, that would make her a woman."

"She certainly aged so suddenly that she became all at once old, quiet, passive, like someone living in a world where she did not comprehend what was happening." Lotte is watching Karla as closely as Mutti used to watch her, but this time, as she is not under suspicion and is indeed not guilty, Karla has no trouble looking back. "And that was the way Hilde stayed," Lotte continues. "No more laughing, not even much talking. I would do silly things—you know, imitate circus clowns and such, trying to get her to at least chuckle—but never, not once after Tante Maria died, did I hear Hilde laugh. Before, she made us all so happy, but after . . ." Lotte sighs.

"What did her mother die of?"

"It was not sudden." Lotte looks down at the table. "She was ill for several years."

"So was my mother."

"What was the cause of your mother's death?" Lotte asks.

"Congestive heart failure." Karla got this diagnosis from Viv only years later. At the time, she simply saw that Mutti, her legs and feet so swollen, chose to spend most of her waking hours sitting in her chair—that chair still in the loft. Karla thought Mutti was just lazy. How she wishes now she had shown her mother more sympathy!

"*Ach.* For Hilde's mother, it was breast cancer." Lotte hisses these words, as if she were revealing a secret.

Which could explain how Mutti maybe reasoned in her craze of grief that by changing identities, she could protect Karla from the embarrassing disease she could never bring herself to name. For whenever Mutti knew anyone with cancer, rather than use that word, she would just shake her head, purse her lips, and say, "Not good," as if it were something cancer victims brought on themselves.

"Did you know Liesel Most, too?" Karla is still trying to absorb the fact that the person with that name was not actually her mother.

"Of course. She and Hilde were inseparable. Until . . ." Lotte trails off.

"What was she like?" Karla asks.

"Liesel was a sweet child yet a bit of a prankster, too. She and Hilde used to love to play their tricks together."

"Like what?"

"Like jumping out from behind a door and shouting, 'Boo!' to startle the poor housemaid."

"Were the two of them a lot alike then?"

"Mmm . . ." Lotte stops for a moment to think. "Your mother was more the ringleader, the instigator, and Liesel the adoring disciple. But I think they truly loved each other the same."

"So, when did my mother start impersonating her?" What Karla wants to understand is, why did she do it? Was it a scam to get Mutti to the States, or was it a manifestation of mental illness?

"I can't really tell you that. I just know that after Hilde's mother died—"

"Do you remember your aunt?"

"Oh, sure. She used to make for me doll clothes. Tante Maria was a skilled dressmaker. Before she got sick, even in hard times, she made good money."

"Like my mother." So much seemingly inherited, but no way did Karla get the sewing genes. She can barely stitch on a button.

"But I don't know. After a few months with us, Hilde became obsessed with her missing friend. Liesel was all she talked about. I think she even started to wear her clothes, though how she would have gotten them, I do not know."

"But wearing the clothes would maybe have been the beginning."

Not exactly a deliberate decision, but a gradual transformation, Mutti having possibly grown to believe that not everyone close to her was gone. "Do you know exactly when she stopped being Hilde"—and became the desperate little girl Karla is only now getting to know?

"Maybe I should have thought of this possibility, but until your letter, I did not realize she had stopped being herself."

"So you have no idea why she did it."

"I think maybe it was her way of keeping her friend alive. And if my mother understood that, the tattoo might have been okay with her, but, after years of living with this terrible sorrow and her own grief, my father and my sister by then dead, my mother felt she had no other choice. Even though we had almost nothing to eat, all of us starving, she had kept Hilde with us until my *mutti* hurried one day into the bathroom, not realizing it was occupied, and she saw Hilde shivering, naked after a cold shower, with the numbers on her arm. 'What is this craziness?' my mother screamed. I'll never forget it."

Karla can see the scene, too—the young girl, accused by the very person who was supposed to take care of her.

"My mother thought this tattoo was insane. Who knew what else Hilde might do? She was afraid for me because my little sister was already dead from measles. So, on that day, she ordered Hilde to pack up and report to the authorities, the Americans. And what Hilde did when she got to them was her business."

"And you? Did you agree with your mother's decision?" Or was Lotte as shattered as Karla was when Mutti banished Viv?

"I felt I had not done my job to keep Hilde happy. I felt that if I had, she would still be with me."

"So you thought it was your fault when your mother threw my mother out?"

"Exactly."

"Well, that's exactly how I felt when she died—that it was all my fault—so it cannot have been both of us who are responsible for what happened to her." And now Karla does laugh.

And Lotte joins her. "Today, looking at you," she says, "I see my cousin Hilde when she was young." She lifts her glass for a toast.

Clinking, Karla wonders what, other than guilt feelings and mother-of-pearl eyes, she shares with this adorable woman. What craziness did Lotte, too, experience as a child? Karla recalls the packed suitcases under the beds in the loft: one her mother's, one her own. Was Mutti always at the ready to escape from being deported or to escape from being jailed? Karla knows only that whenever her feet grew, Mutti bought an extra pair of shoes in the new size and threw out the ones in her suitcase, like someone refreshing an offering to the gods. But maybe, in the back of her mind, Mutti was leaving open the possibility of returning to Germany and rejoining her family.

"I will never forget," Lotte is saying, "a few months after the war was finally over, we were staying at our summer house in Constanz, and we had no food, only the fish we could catch in the lake." When she talks, Karla notices, Lotte lifts her upper lip, exposing her teeth, just as Mutti did. Karla needs to remember to ask Sax if she does that, too.

"And no fuel to cook it with. We had to eat everything raw. Even today, I cannot look at fish."

"Mutti said, like cattle, she ate grass." So maybe she was not a total liar after all.

"Ja. And once a farmer's son made a little fire with sticks, and he roasted on this a rat, which he gave to Hilde because he wanted her kisses. 'That rat was a better gift than gold,' she afterwards told me."

And here they are now, cousins in their armchairs, munching almonds, sipping wine. "Did he get his kisses?" Karla has never been able to picture her mother showing any sort of affection to anyone, let alone a guy. But there was that girl Lotte is bringing to life. She somehow managed.

"Oh, yes. We'd do anything for food. You cannot imagine what it was like," Lotte says. "You know, when Hilde disappeared from my life, just like Liesel disappeared from hers," Lotte says, shaking her head sadly, "for a long time, I was obsessed and I kept trying to find her. But there was no record."

However, Lotte did not go so far as to try to transform herself into her beloved cousin. Only Mutti took it that far.

"Though it should have, it never occurred to me to look under Liesel's name," Lotte confesses. "So your letter came as such a wonderful gift." She reaches over to clasp Karla's knee in a gesture that expresses both gratitude and sympathy. "But Hilde was already gone." She sits back in her seat. "So tell me, what exactly happened to her in the years when she lived here in New York?"

Then it is Karla's turn to tell about Mutti's arrival in 1955 and how somehow she found a job as a seamstress in Ben Zimmerman's design studio. There she met Ben's son, Michael. Karla tells Lotte about Viv, the cousin who turned out not to be her real cousin but who helped Mutti give birth in the loft, and about Ben and Adele Zimmerman. "But I didn't know that until after Viv brought Ben around, because she thought Mutti was ruining me by dressing me from the day I was born only in black, even my diapers."

"And here we are, still wearing black," says Lotte, chuckling. "I for travel purposes, and today, at least in Germany, among our young there is quite a fashion for this," Lotte assures her. "With the pins, too, sometimes even in the nose."

"So Mutti was just ahead of her time on my behalf," Karla jokes.

"Exactly." In the corners of her eyes, Lotte has merry crinkles.

"After she died, Viv took me to meet Ben and Adele, and up until now they've been my only family."

"How splendid that you found them!"

"Yes," says Karla even though sometimes, when Ben and Adele question her choices, for instance, she feels less lucky and more burdened by having relatives. This new German one, though, at least so far, is a treat. "Do you remember Mutti's father?" Karla still cannot bring herself to call her mother Hilde, or to refer to a German army officer as her grandfather. "Your uncle Werner?"

"Oh, sure."

"What was he like?" Karla means, *Did he molest Mutti? Is that really why she ran away?*

"As a child, I adored him. He had, how you say it, a real belly laugh. I remember him dressed as Kris Kringle. But after he lost his arm . . ."

"How did that happen?"

"He was shot, and he always said he was so lucky this happened. Most of his friends lost their lives on the Russian Front; with him, it was 'only an arm.' But after he would say this joke, though he never mentioned the son he lost, he would become very quiet, very contemplative."

"Like his daughter."

"Yes. And, like her, hard to understand. He once told my father that as soon as the National Socialists finished with the Jews, we Catholics would be next and would have to wear purple crosses. Still, after he was wounded, working in the Reichsbureau of the Criminal Police, my uncle helped round up gypsies so they could be shipped to the camps."

"Why did he do that?"

Lotte's eyes meet Karla's eyes as she says, "I have asked myself this question many times." And each now seems to detect in the other the same true bafflement. "Like so many of us, Uncle Werner did just as he was told. For that, he was convicted of a war crime and sent to prison, but his worse punishment was that by 1952, when he got out, Hilde was gone. She never contacted him. And he never forgave my mother for sending his only living child away."

"Your mother was trying to protect you," says Karla, because it seems important for Lotte to understand why any mother could have viewed poor Mutti as a possible threat. Didn't Mutti see everyone else like that?

"*Ja*, but in reality, that hurt me. My uncle stopped communicating with us. My father was already killed in Belgium. My sister was gone. Hilde had disappeared. Once my mother passed away, until I heard from you, I had no blood family. And this for me was the most terrible of punishments."

"But you have a husband, a son, a job." Might such a life be a possibility for Karla, too?

"Yes, yes." Lotte waves them off as if they do not count. "But you must meet them, and they you. This semester I am on sabbatical from teaching, so it is a perfect time for you to visit us. I will show you Heidelberg. And you will meet your cousin Johann. Here, see . . ." She takes out a photo of a blond twentysomething boy, tall and skinny and Aryan, like his mother.

But his face, especially the eyes . . . Karla studies yet another new cousin's image and wonders what it would have been like to have his mother, instead of hers. "He looks very happy," she says, handing the photo back.

"Oh, *ja*. Why not? He is living in Berlin, madly in love with a filmmaker who wants to make a documentary of our reunion, yours and mine, and to tell your mother's story." Lotte is opening possibility after possibility: Karla, starring in her own film; Karla, retracing her mother's journey; Karla, seeing out of Mutti's eyes.

At Lotte's request, using her camera, a waiter takes their picture. Lotte insists on paying the bill.

"But I haven't even told you about Sax," Karla says.

"You have not. So, who is this Sax, then?" Tilting her head, Lotte looks at her with amused attention.

"Oh, what to say? We live together. He's an art collector, a little older than I am. I think you'll like him."

"Of course he is welcome to come visit with you, too," Lotte says.

"Thank you," Karla says, even as she realizes that, at least for a while, she wants her German cousins all to herself. Though she will, of course, tell Sax everything, she thinks as she follows her cousin into the elevator, down to the fifth floor, and into the Kesslers' suite, where Lotte introduces her to Oskar.

Tall and reedy like his wife, he wears his silver hair straight back, and with his silver-framed, precisely rectangular glasses, dark suit, white shirt, and pearl-gray tie, Oskar, the judge, embodies the suavely continental.

How impressive that this man is also in Karla's family! So maybe she should bring Sax when she goes to Germany to show them off to each other.

After Karla leaves the Kesslers, having passed inspection, she cannot wait to tell Sax about Lotte's eyes and her invitation. Skipping up Lexington Avenue, Karla smiles at every passerby whose eyes touch hers, because not since she fell in love with Sax has she experienced such glorious euphoria.

CHAPTER 10

As soon as he hears about the planned trip, Sax offers to accompany Karla to Germany. She considers letting him do just that. After all, she has never traveled anywhere by herself. She has never gotten her own boarding pass, never tipped a baggage handler. Karla has always trailed Sax through security and to the right gate. Embarrassed at thirty-one to be so dependent, Karla does not so much decide as leap to seize this opportunity to have her cousins all to herself, at least for a while. This is something she must do herself.

Yet she does not speak, understand, or read German. Nor does she get German currency. Three nights before she is to leave, Sax brings home 100 deutsche marks and gives them to her, saying, "It's good to have a little local cash when you arrive."

"How much is this in real money?" she asks him.

When she is in Germany, he will not be with her to answer these questions. If she needs more money, she will have to go to a bank and make her needs understood. As a stranger to all things German, she will not know how to find anyplace. She hardly knows these newfound cousins. What if they turn out to be like Mutti? What if they are even worse? Can Karla stand two weeks with these people? She doesn't even know how to make an international phone call. What if she gets sick? Who will take care of her?

As fears bombard her, Karla knows she has only to ask Sax to join her for self-loathing to replace her fears. Mutti tailored her adult life to repel terror. Karla has sworn to herself she will not do the same—she will not be ruled by angst. If anything terrible happens as a result of her decision to go to Germany, she will deal with it, or, if the terrible event kills her, she won't have to deal with it. Time now to find out which it is to be.

Karla reminds herself that for five years after Mutti died, she lived on her own. But instead of remembering how Viv and her grandparents took over the management of her life, Karla recalls that in those days she pretty much owned all her time, each day her personal construction. However, for the last ten years, having spent almost every night and a chunk of most days with Sax, she has shaped her time around his.

Being away from him for a while is bound to give her fresh perspective, she tells herself. Outside his magnetic orbit, she might be able to decide if she wants to spend the rest of her life attached to him or to break away, even if that means hurting him.

It is possible that Viv and her grandparents are right: Karla settled too early. Not many women her age have had sex with only one person. This separation from Sax might finally give her a chance to check out someone else. Recalling *Summertime*, a movie with Katharine Hepburn and Rossano Brazzi, Karla imagines an amazing European who, throwing himself at her feet, will sweep her off them for, at the very least, a fling. If she gives in to the temptation to let Sax go with her, she could not even fantasize this whirlwind affair. As it is, the whole adventure, in prospect and in actuality, is hers to imagine.

Yet how Karla misses Sax when the travel agent books her flight to Frankfurt! Should she have chosen TWA or Lufthansa? The travel agent thought it was all about scheduling for Karla's convenience. But is the plane they settled on the one destined to crash or be hijacked? Will her luggage be lost? How is she going to buy a train ticket to Karlsruhe? How will she even find the railroad station?

Should she have gotten the tetanus shot her grandfather recommended? Does anyone these days get lockjaw? Karla thinks she is more likely to contract a new condition, "lock ears," that will preclude her understanding what people are saying to or about her. And she will not understand German street signs.

"Most Germans speak English," Sax says. "You'll do just fine," he promises.

"So you say," Karla says, because Sax never admits, either to her or, as far as she can tell, to himself, how incompetent she is. So of course he is confident that she will have no problem. "And I don't even think you'll miss me."

"I will miss you. I will, if there's time. You'll only be gone for two weeks, not forever," he points out.

Karla suspects Sax is looking forward to being by himself for a while. She wonders if he is fantasizing about his own zipless fuck.

She buys a book and cassettes and, in the weeks before she leaves, practices every day reading and speaking German, a language that, thanks to Mutti, fits into her mouth as if it has always been there.

"*Guten tag. Guten abend. Wie gehtes ihnen heute?* Is this seat taken? Are you alone here? May I buy you a glass of wine?" Evidently, if this is what Berlitz is teaching travelers to say, she is not the first person to consider the possibility of a roll in the hay in Deutschland. Not that she mentions this to Sax.

Not that she has to. "You *are* planning to come back, aren't you?" he asks a few days before she is to go.

"Of course I am," she assures him, despite knowing there is an outside chance she will not. After all, she is going to Germany partly to see if that is where she actually belongs. Having spent most of her life striving to be as unlike her mother as possible, Karla is now planning, as much as possible, to reenact her mother's life, to part the heavy curtain of lies that kept her from seeing and knowing the person who birthed and raised her. It might be that once she finally knows her mother, she will better understand herself. And that self might not belong with Sax.

Mutti was someone who would have slept with a guy to score a rat. What might tempt Karla to do the same?

Giddy with potential, in the last week before she takes off, Karla wakes up daily by 4:00 a.m. And, peppered with what-ifs and must-remembers, she lies in bed, first snuggling her naked front against Sax's naked back, then flipping over and pressing her butt against his.

"What time is it?" he groans.

"Four sixteen," Karla whispers, though she is already wide awake.

"Go back to sleep," he demands.

As if Karla can. She has to remember to buy a present for Lotte, but what? Something typically American would be good. Maybe pancake mix and maple syrup. But will that be enough? And what if it makes her suitcase too heavy to manage? And what if the syrup leaks? What could be worse than that?

She must remember to pack towelettes. Aspirin. Her German dictionary. Slipping out of bed, Karla retreats to the bathroom to compose yet another list.

Maybe Lotte would like a silk scarf. Does she, too, wear only black, or was that just her travel outfit? Karla never asked. Other than one phone call to discuss logistics, she and Lotte haven't really said much of anything to each other. What if they run out of things to talk about? What if they just stop getting along? Much as Karla loves Viv and Adele, she would hate to be stuck alone with either one of them for two weeks. Maybe she should have insisted on staying in a hotel.

Then again, nothing says Karla has to stick it out for the whole two weeks. If it isn't going well, she can always pack up and come home—if, that is, she can figure out how to change her ticket. On the other hand, nothing says she can't decide to stay longer. The uncertainties of this whole venture are a source of panic and titillation. Karla is about to be tested.

When Sax drives her to Kennedy Airport, he persists in keeping to the right lane, letting car after car pass. Karla assumes he subconsciously, or maybe even consciously, wants her to miss her flight. She likes that he wants her to stay, and at the same time wishes she had taken a cab.

She was planning to check in early, but the way he is driving, she will be lucky just to get there on time. The traffic is horrendous. She forgot to buy Sominex so she can sleep on the plane. Sax says they'll sell it at the airport, but what if he is wrong?

"Watch out!" Did he see that Jeep coming? Should Karla have let him put her in the suicide seat? Will she die before she even gets to her plane? She rather likes the irony of that. Lufthansa made her tell them who should be notified in case of an emergency. She said Sax. But if he dies with her in the auto accident, whom will they notify?

Karla should have made out a will. But why? The lease for the Canal Street apartment is her only valuable possession, and if she dies, no one can inherit that. She would like to provide for Ron'l, because how will he live without her? Who would take care of him? She should have spoken to Ben.

"You will please, please, look after Ron'l if I die," she now begs Sax.

"You're not going to die. At least not anytime soon," he says blithely.

"Yes, but if I do."

"Yes, I will take care of Ron'l." Sax brakes hard; Karla jerks forward.

"If neither one of us makes it out of this car alive," she gripes, "Ron'l will be on his own."

"Just read the signs and tell me which terminal," Sax directs her.

Too many signs. Too many airlines. Allegheny. American. Avianca. They will never find Lufthansa. Then Karla will not have to go.

"Terminal C," says Sax, who, as usual, finds the way with no help from her. How can she go without him? She will be lost.

And what if he finds himself a replacement girlfriend while she is gone? Karla has seen more than one woman cozy up to him. "How do I know you'll still want me when I get back?" she asks.

"You have my word." Sax does not ask for her pledge in return. He accepts that this is something she has to do, a trip she has to take on her own. As if it's a perfectly ordinary event, he drives up to the departure area, slides out, opens the trunk, and hoists her bag to the curb. "You have your passport?" he asks.

"Yes."

"Ticket?"

"Yes."

"Credit cards?"

"Yes."

"Traveler's checks?"

"Yup."

"Then you're all set. And take this." He presses a $5 bill into her palm. "Give it to the man who takes your luggage."

A uniformed man already has her bag. "Ticket?" he asks.

Frantic, Karla gropes in her purse and finally produces it.

The man quickly flips through the pages, tears one out, goes over to a stand, and grabs a tag and a card. He slips the tag over her suitcase handle and hands her a pass, saying, "Gate twenty-seven A. Boarding will begin at six thirty."

It is barely five o'clock. She gives him the tip, hoping it is generous enough for him to make sure her suitcase ends up with her.

"Thank you, miss." He touches his hat brim and hurls her bag onto a conveyer belt. Will she ever see it again?

Sax is standing there, waiting.

They hug, Karla urgently pressing her body against his. This could be the last time they ever see each other.

He disengages and steps back. "You'll only be gone for two weeks," he reminds her. "Just two weeks," he repeats, as if reminding himself, too.

She nods, though she is about to cry. Because why, if it is only two weeks, does she feel so certain it is forever? And why, after Sax gets back in the car and drives away, does Karla feel as if a gigantic weight has been lifted from her?

CHAPTER 11

In the Frankfurt airport, the public address announcements are no
easier to understand in English than they are in German. The
luggage carts are free, but Karla's jams to a stop every time she
forgets to keep squeezing its handle.

Around her people wearing African head wraps, print body
wraps, and caftans swirl. Black-suited Hassids under the kinds of
hats children draw mingle with Muslim women, a few of the latter
swathed save for their eyes. Without noticing her, Indian men in
turbans and Indian women in saris rush toward Karla and away.

Other travelers of various ages and genders and nationalities
wear blue jeans with work shirts, blue jeans with denim vests, blue
jeans with leather jackets and square-toed shoes that identify them
as non-Americans. A dark-haired family with little kids speak a
language that clacks like castanets. And throughout the crowd, hurrying businessmen and women clutch their attaché cases.

Karla sleepwalks her way among this throng, feeling as if everything in her head is an echo, probably because of the Sominex she
pointlessly took on the plane. It did not dam up her excitement
enough to give her rest. Now, she follows unintelligible strangers
into and out of elevators and on and off moving walkways.

She reads the signs and, after asking over and over, *"Bitte, wissen Sie wo ist der Bahn für Karlsruhe?"* and then, *"Bitte, wissen Sie*

wo ist der Gleich für Karlsruhe?" because many people either reply in English or accompany their answers with unmistakable gestures, she miraculously boards a spiffy-looking train that slides off at 9:14 a.m., its exact departure time.

Before she discovered that the whole Dachau scenario was a fantasy, Karla often imagined Mutti on her way to the camp, crammed in a boxcar. No boxcar, today's actual train has seats very like those in the plane. The place assigned to Karla is at a table, nobody opposite. And since the folks all around her are speaking German and sound just like her mother chatting with their Canal Street landlord, a fellow German, instead of feeling as if she is in a foreign country, an exhausted Karla relaxes. For Mutti is here with her again.

And at this moment, like any child being taken somewhere, Karla is too tired to worry. Thus, once she has given the conductor her ticket and is positive she is on the right train, she becomes a bobblehead, jerking in and out of dozing. At each stop, she awakens, checks. Her purse strap is still twisted around her arm. She can read the station sign. Mutti's hometown, Heidelberg, is the next-to-last station before Karlsruhe, but Heidelberg will have to wait.

In Karlsruhe, Karla gets off the train and, after planning what she will do if no one is there to meet her—she has the address, she will find a cab, she will show the driver the paper with the address on it—she is overjoyed to see Lotte on the platform, peering and smiling as she spots Karla.

They each walk toward the other, Lotte with her arms out, Karla dragging her bag, until they are together and she lets go of the handle so they can hug. "I'm so glad to see you," she effuses, the intensity of her gladness a little embarrassing.

"It is wonderful that you are at last here," says Lotte, before she pulls back and they face each other.

"Yes." At least, Karla hopes it is wonderful.

Like someone whose mourning period is partially over, Lotte is wearing a light gray, not black, pantsuit that becomes her. "Let me help you with your bag," she says, and, as if she, too, finds their mutual inspection slightly awkward, she dives for the handle. "You must be so tired. These international flights . . ."

Too spent and too grateful to do much speaking, Karla follows her cousin and her suitcase out into a parking lot. She takes her place in the front seat of the kind of car Sax could identify. (Karla just knows it is not from Detroit and has a stick shift.) And once they click their seat belts and start off, she empty-mindedly gives herself over to whatever might happen next.

The German air, sky, ground, trees, and snow patches are all shades of gray similar to that of Lotte's costume. Nothing and no one expects any particular reaction from the newcomer riding by, observing. In any case, she is too sleep-deprived to comment when every so often Lotte points out, "That is the palace. . . . Over there, our famous Christuskirche . . . We are crossing now the river."

Karla appreciates the patter. Silences scare her, for who knows what might bubble up in them? Like now, when Lotte has stopped speaking and they are still here together. What is Karla supposed to say?

"Is that the Main?" She finally brings herself to ask.

"You mean the Main?" Lotte pronounces it "mine," which seems right, for this is definitely her turf, not Karla's.

"I guess so."

"No." Lotte laughs. "That is in Frankfurt. Ours is the Rhine."

"Ah." Karla should have known; she should have kept her mouth shut. So this time she simply allows the silence to linger, and that turns out to be just fine.

After quite a while, Lotte stops the car in front of a house set back behind a small, tidy garden where nothing at the moment is in bloom. As if all this part of the world is old, the bushes and ground and leaves continue the variations on gray, gray, gray. "Here we are, then," Lotte says gaily.

Too tired to match Lotte's enthusiasm, Karla trails her cousin to her front door. Inside, they go up a few stairs into a living room that, though hardly cramped, is hardly grand, either. Deep-set windows opposite the entrance let fish-belly-white winter light into a room without frills. The word "austere" comes to mind. Books in a wall of shelves provide the only color. The only artworks, four large Karl Blossfeldt black-and-white close-ups of ferns, are literal but somehow abstract, cerebral.

At least the armless, neutral-toned, upholstered, birch-framed sofa and two chairs have brick-red pillows tossed here and there on them. Punctuating the insistent calm, the pillows invite comfortable sitting. Not precisely arranged, the magazines on the coffee table are there to be enjoyed. But there is no clutter. Little sense of resident humanity.

"Cheese? Fruit? Bread? A glass of wine? Coffee?" Lotte offers.

"Nothing, thank you." Gassy and sleep-deprived, Karla shakes her head.

"Come, then. I show you." As if she has read Karla's mind, Lotte leads her into a bedroom dominated by a platform bed. "Because, you know, the best way to overcome jet lag in this direction is immediately to have a good sleep." She opens a door to an attached bathroom with foreign-looking plumbing. "This place, you will have all to yourself."

"*Vielen Danke. Danke schöen,*" Karla enthuses, before her cousin leaves her so she can at last pee, crap (as if releasing whatever remains in her of America), wash her hands, close the blinds, and crash.

CHAPTER 12

As Lotte predicted, by the next morning Karla has recovered from her jet lag. She enjoys *frühstück*, a meal whose meats, cheeses, breads, pickles, mustard, fruit salad, and yogurt seem more like a lunch than a breakfast. This is terrific, because she has always preferred lunch. Is that the German in her?

After Oskar goes off to work at court, Lotte and Karla clean up the dishes and head back to the station. Today they are to visit Heidelberg, where Mutti grew up, and, as if she is about to step onstage, Karla is keyed up.

Though the railcar they enter is not spiffy like the one on the train from Frankfurt, it is nevertheless clean and comfortable, and it, too, arrives and departs precisely on schedule. For this is, after all, the Fatherland, where trains run on time. Karla shivers.

"Are you cold?" Lotte asks.

"No." She is puzzled, because none of the passengers, eating morning hot dogs, reading newspapers, sipping coffee, seems unusual, and certainly not sadistic. Yet others just like them, indeed not really so different from Karla and Mutti themselves, rounded up people and slaughtered them.

A few get off at Mannheim. Others get on.

The trip from Karlsruhe to Heidelberg takes but forty-five minutes. Following Lotte's lead, Karla steps onto the platform. Here, she will find out what Mutti really was. Whether this will help Karla figure out who she herself is, is a question. This whole venture could be what Viv would call a *mishegoss*. But whatever it is, Karla is at this moment committed to it.

From the first moment, Mutti's town screams history. Old Heidelberg is antiquely Gothic, either because, unlike Karlsruhe, it was not bombed and rebuilt after the war or else because, in Disney fashion, it was replicated to *The Student Prince* specifications, just as Mutti replicated herself as someone else. In any case, Hilde Knecht grew up in this charming university town, her home an old one not far from the Holy Ghost Church.

With its beams and stucco, the attached house where the Mosts and Knechts once lived looks like pictures of Shakespeare's birthplace Karla has seen in travel posters. So this is the Saxon part of Anglo-Saxon, and being connected to such a place makes Karla feel a bit closer to Sax and his people.

"Many times, my sister and I visited here," Lotte says, as they stand across the street, assessing the building. "Come." She moves toward the place. "We are expected."

By whom? Ghosts?

Leave all hope, ye who enter here. As she steps over this threshold into the darkness of her mother's past, Karla recalls Sax's warning when he first came to her loft, and she realizes she never called him to tell him she arrived safely. But then, he would know that. And he has Lotte's number. If Sax were worried about Karla, he would have called her. Putting the thought of him behind her, once upstairs, she watches Lotte knock on a door, then listens to her own heart, and to footsteps.

A stubby German woman with hair like fog opens the door. "I was for you waiting," she says in English that is better than Karla's German.

Lotte introduces them. Karla awkwardly says, "*Guten Tag,*" and that is okay. Since Frau Müeller's face, breasts, belly, and hips resemble risen bread dough, she embodies motherliness, an impression enhanced by the homey odor—coffee, cabbage, cooked apples—she releases into the hallway. Lotte said the Müellers moved into the Knecht apartment in 1951, almost thirty years ago, but this Frau could just as well be Mutti's *mutti* welcoming Karla and Lotte into her home.

Such a woman would surely have greeted her beloved daughter's homecomings with a hug. She would offer fresh-baked apple strudel with *schlag* to her Hilde, just as Frau Müeller is offering it to Karla.

Not in the least hungry, Karla gets that if she does not accept, eat, and praise the offering, she will disappoint Frau Müeller. If only, with her roly-poly body and eager eyes, the German woman did not remind Karla so much of Mutti, waiting, always waiting in the loft for Karla to come home. If only Karla did not feel like a fly succumbing to a web's sticky embrace. But this is now, that was then. Mentally flicking off her discomfort, Karla agrees to sit down and eat.

"*Wie gut Sie sind,*" says Lotte, meaning, "How good you are," as the three of them take seats around the table in the small kitchen. Whether she is complimenting Frau Müeller or Karla is not clear; maybe both of them, Karla decides, smiling.

Fortunately, Frau Müeller speaks very little English, so Lotte has to do almost all the talking, leaving Karla to take in the fact that she is now sitting in a room where Mutti must often have sat when she was a little German girl in an apartment much smaller than the one on Canal Street but with the loft's same dim light and dark-painted tin ceilings, even the same rusty black-and-white (or at least whitish) diamond-patterned kitchen linoleum.

Though broken up into little rooms, instead of being one big space like the loft, in this apartment, too, a murky gloom permeates the air. So, somehow, Mutti managed to replicate in America, and to provide for Karla, the same dingy, unpretentious environment she knew as a child. As a result, this dwelling where she has never been feels very familiar to Karla.

Once they finish the coffee-klatch phase, Karla copies Lotte in nodding, smiling, agreeing, *"Es war gut, sehr, sehr gut,"* as she folds her napkin and stands up. *"Danke. Vielen danke."* Unable to tell whether she is anxious to see what else there is to see here or anxious to get away from the place, Karla just knows she is heavily anxious.

Frau Müeller is issuing a torrent of words, accompanied by easy-to-translate body language. She wants no help with table clearing and quickly herds them out of the kitchen, through a room where a swollen armchair reminds Karla of the one Mutti habitually occupied in the loft. They continue toward a windowless room, hardly more than an alcove with a curtain, instead of a door. There, Karla sees an iron bed just like the one she grew up with, a wrought-iron floor lamp, a fake-wood wardrobe.

Go on in, Frau Müeller's gesture says.

In this shrine there is space for only one person, two people at most. Nothing in here is new or seemingly even postwar. It is easy to visualize a little girl cooped up in this windowless closet, reading her beloved Karl May Westerns in bed.

Tears surged into Karla's eyes. Had she not tilted her head back, they would have slid over her cheeks.

"You perhaps want some time here alone?" the wonderfully empathetic Lotte asks.

Karla nods.

Left to herself, she sits on this bed and pretends to be the little girl who pretended to be someone else, only not yet. In this period of her life, with a mother probably much like Frau Müeller, Mutti was little Hilde, the merry child who made everyone around her happy.

No wonder she wanted to re-create exactly that setting in New York. And she managed that. Karla finally remembers having been happy, even carefree, in the loft. She recalls her pleasure when Mutti lulled her to sleep by crooning Brahms's Lullaby, the festive deliciousness of Mutti's *apfel* strudel, which was far superior to Frau Müeller's. Karla remembers the moment when, as a kid, she triumphantly showed Mutti how she had learned to switch from one- to two-footed skipping. To this day, whenever Karla is elated, she skips.

Now, sinking back into the mattress, she can almost hear the old stories, Struwwelpeter and Grimm. They are the same tales Mutti's mother would have read to her little Hilde—until one night, books could not disguise the sounds of sirens. Slammed car doors. Feet stamping up the stairs. Rifle butts pounding their neighbors' door. Karla's heart trembles. Was the Most family wailing? Begging? Numb? Did they acknowledge the Knechts' presence? Did Liesel cry out to Hilde, or Hilde to Liesel? Or did they ignore each other? Did Mutti watch the Mosts being forced into the caged back of a van?

Or did Hilde come home from school one day and simply find the door to her friend's house wide open? Did she rush inside to find familiar furniture, photos, and clothing strewn around or destroyed?

Who took the things the Mosts left behind? Did Mrs. Knecht collect a few treasures and bring them here for safekeeping? Could anybody just go into the emptied apartment and take anything they wanted? There must have been things there; Lotte said Hilde wore some of Liesel's clothes. How did she get them?

She might know when her cousin first realized her friend was never coming back. Lotte might even have had a friend or two of her own who disappeared. Would it be okay for Karla to ask her about that? If it was too personal, she could always back off.

Right now, Karla sees her mother huddling in the doorway to the street, just as Karla herself huddled across the street from the loft before seeing her grandfather that first time. Mutti would not know what was happening to her best friend before a new family quickly moved into the empty apartment. Talking to these people, asking questions, would be dangerous. They would be in league with the authorities. Unless the Knechts were careful, storm troopers would come for them, too; the other neighbors would know they were close to the Mosts.

Still, Frau Knecht or someone else kept Liesel's clothes. *Here*, Karla could just hear that person saying one day. *You always wanted one of these*, before she handed over to Hilde Liesel's favorite pink angora sweater: *You might as well have this one*. That could have been either okay or incriminating.

Wearing her friend's sweater, Hilde must have felt implicated in Liesel's disappearance. Yet the wool was so soft, so clingy; in it, she was being embraced. How could she not have loved this, part of her friend touching her?

Karla believes that the real woman who was the subject of *The Three Faces of Eve* automatically became each of the characters who inhabited her. But in the movie, when Joanne Woodward shifted from one character to the other, she knew that underneath she was still Joanne Woodward, an actress playing, not being, another person.

Did Hilde know that was what she, too, was doing? Or was she an Eve who, once she made the shift, simply stayed there?

No. Hilde kept the Knechts' photograph all those years. She concealed it and hid herself from the authorities. That had to mean she knew all along who she was. Taking on Liesel's identity had to have been a conscious decision.

If Karla had been the girl living here that night when the armed men came for her best friend, she would have burrowed under the covers and waited until it was all over. When there was absolute quiet, she would have emerged, thrilled to find herself safe. Could she ever have forgiven herself for that flair of joy?

Responding to an overwhelming urge, Karla roots around in her purse for a pen. Then she pushes up her left sleeve and starts to write the number 1 on the inside of her arm. She doesn't know what possesses her, but she is used to acting first and examining her actions only later. Was tattooing herself also Hilde's impulse of the moment?

The ballpoint against Karla's skin feels almost like a needle. To make the ink stick, she has to go back and forth repeatedly over the same spot. Soon her arm stings, and getting the spacing the same between the 1 and the 7, the 7 and the 8, the 8 and the 4, the 4 and the 3 is difficult.

Who was the person who etched the numbers on the Jews in Auschwitz? Was it a fellow prisoner? Or was it someone who went home to a family after work? Someone like Frau Müeller, maybe even Frau Müeller herself? If so, when she came home, what did she tell her family about what she had done all day?

Finished inscribing herself, Karla quickly pulls down her sleeve to conceal the numbers, just as Hilde must have concealed them. If Lotte were to catch sight of the ersatz tattoo, she would surely think Karla crazy, but, unlike Lotte's own mother, Lotte would never kick her cousin out of the house. She would more likely just look at Karla sadly and consult with Oskar behind her back.

At some point after her mother died, Hilde numbered herself. Unlike Karla, who inherited the loft, Hilde was kicked out of her home.

Someone packed her things—not her father, who was "away" either at work or in prison. Maybe Hilde herself did the packing, or the aunt, Lotte's mother, who had so many of her own worries. However it happened, Karla's mother turned into a burden, a person heavy even to herself.

How young Hilde was when her mother died! After that, Hilde's life as a child essentially ended. And so it makes sense that she would have worn black, in perpetual mourning for a self who still existed but no longer lived.

But why is Karla perpetuating this? With Mutti dead, she could begin her life again. Yet she has resisted a clean break and the new palette her clothing could have symbolized. Even now, Karla wishes Mutti were here not just in spirit but physically, so she could ask her why she did what she did, in hopes of understanding her own behavior.

Not that Mutti would approve of Karla's poking around in her past or be willing to talk about what really happened. "Just forget about it and do as I say," the person known as Liesel would have commanded.

Of course, neither of the Liesels, no matter what Karla imagines, is here in body. But, like garments draped on chairs and dropped on the carpet, facts lie all over this place.

Fact one: the actual Liesel Most never got to grow up. Fact two: she would have worn braids like Mutti always did—the hairdo of a child. Nipped in the bud and never to blossom, Mutti wore her hair in braids until her dying day; she created with them an eternal childhood. She got her daughter to take care of her, instead of vice versa.

So that could have been why, after she died, Karla immediately chopped off her own braids. She has never forgotten the sense that it was a mutilation, a crime she committed against herself, but now she wonders if she was pretending, as Mutti pretended, only instead of trying to remain forever a child, Karla immediately faked growing up.

Sighing, she gets off the bed and smooths the coverlet. She looks up at the small crucifix on the wall above the wardrobe. Here, in some sense, there is still a pre-Liesel Catholic Hilde to be conjured up, a person whom Karla can get to know. From this vantage point, she can actually see Mutti as a child.

Something about this room in Heidelberg calls for transformations. In here, Mutti became Liesel, and Karla feels herself changing, too. For when she was little, Mutti was a giant, righteous and powerful as any God. Then, even before she died, Karla's idol developed more than clay feet. She became hideously flawed, demented, demanding, worse than worthless. But in here, thousands of miles from home, Mutti is the Catholic kid who used to read and reread her Karl May stories.

It is she who told Karla that when she first arrived in America, she expected to find cowboys in New York City. What else did Mutti expect?

Pushing the curtain aside, Karla walks out of the windowless space that was her mother's "room." Numbers safely concealed under her sleeve, she makes her way back to the kitchen, rejects coffee but accepts a glass of water. No longer nervous, she sits down and listens to the two women, just as she listened for so long to Mutti and Viv. But instead of squabbling, these two, Lotte and Frau Müeller, are companionably speaking the German that makes Karla feel so thoroughly at home.

After a while, just as she did as a child, she speaks up, asking, "Is everything in that bedroom the same as it was when my mother lived here?"

Lotte consults with the frau. "*Ja*. In there it is," she confirms.

So Hilde chose to leave behind her Jesus on His cross. By that time, she was probably already wearing Liesel's sweater; had she already donned her friend's religion?

"Who lives now where the Mosts used to live?" Karla asks. There would be nothing of the Jewish family that remained, but still . . .

"Do you want me to see if we can go there, too, if not today, perhaps tomorrow?" the marvelously intuitive Lotte asks.

"Oh, yes, please." Karla wants to see everything.

❧

The rest of her first week in Germany passes quickly. Though Karla calls Sax and talks to him—it is night for her, afternoon for him— their talks cover only the surface of what she is doing, rather than what is really happening to her here. This, she can sense but not say.

Karla and Lotte return to Heidelberg, and Lotte arranges for them to gain entrance to the Mosts' apartment, its current tenant initially defensive.

"We were not here, not even in Heidelberg, when the rooms were taken," she says repeatedly in excellent English. "At that time, I was with my mother in Leipzig. Far from here. In East Germany. Very far."

Facing front onto the street, the Mosts' apartment is quite a lot nicer than the Knechts'—sunnier and therefore cleaner-looking. Liesel's room even had its own window. So was envy a factor in Mutti's decision to switch identities? Was it another way for her to claw her way up in the world? Many times she told Karla Jews were smarter than other people, that jealousy of their superiority motivated those who would destroy "us." Was she speaking out of personal emotion?

"Did you have Jewish friends of your own?" Karla asks Lotte when they get back to the house and she is setting the table while her cousin prepares the meal.

"No. Not really." As if engrossed, Lotte slices the meat that allows her to avoid eye contact.

"Me neither," says Karla, as shared guilt rises like mist around them.

❧

The numbers Karla inscribed on her own arm blur after her first shower and disappear after her second, but she feels no need to restore them. The sensation of the pen on her skin etched them into her so that now, though nothing shows even when she goes sleeveless, 17843 is still there.

The day Lotte takes her to the municipal hall, a gloomy, prison-like building that American occupation forces once used for their temporary headquarters, Karla can easily picture the homeless person who was her mother, the same age Karla was when Mutti died. On that fateful day, Mutti walked to this building, hauling her suitcase filled with the old books she later translated for Karla on Canal Street.

Did no American wonder why, if numbered, the not-so-little German girl was not skeletal? Or by that time was Hilde/Liesel so starved that she could pass for a camp survivor?

As she walks up the stone steps and through the shadowy halls, Karla lugs the imaginary weight of her mother's bag holding books and every one of her other precious belongings. She promises herself she will always have a bag packed with her own things. She practices saying her new name—Liesel Most, Liesel Most—praying that no one from her past will see her and blow her cover. Then she begins to move furtively, to be a person constantly in hiding.

"Are you all right?" Lotte asks, looking at Karla sharply.

"Oh, yes." Karla resumes her normal posture.

Back at the house in Karlsruhe, she and Lotte go to their own rooms, but today Karla closes her door, sits on the edge of the bed, mulls. Here in Germany, she can pretty much let go of Mutti's Jewishness, but what about her own? Yes, she has Nordic eyes, but her hair is rather curly and her nose rather substantial for an Aryan. Besides, according to the Nazis, anyone more than one-eighth Jewish—that is, with more than one Jewish great-grandparent—was a Jew. Karla has four Jewish great-grandparents, two Jewish grandparents, and one Jewish father. But Israel, and the Orthodox, say only the child of a Jewish mother can be a Jew. So is Karla Catholic?

Never baptized, she is not Catholic in the eyes of the Church. And though she admires the Virgin Mary as the most resourceful woman who ever lived and is blown away by Catholic pageantry, in churches and cathedrals Karla has never felt involved in anything the priests, their acolytes, or the parishioners (except maybe when they light wishful candles) do. Not like shul, where, when congregants kiss the fringes of their shawls and press them to the Torah, she feels that same reverence for learning embedded deep in her bones. So Karla still considers herself Jewish, no matter what the fuck anyone else thinks.

Does it matter that she does not believe in any God, Hebrew or otherwise? And that the Old Testament stories—Abraham's willingness to sacrifice his son is particularly repugnant—often strike her as cruel, vindictive, mythic, and inhuman? Or that, running down the list of Ten Commandments, she believes in only three? (One: anyone using the name of a god to justify acts is wrongly taking that god's name in vain; mere cursing does not count. Two: it is almost always wrong to kill people. Three: it is always wrong to bear false witness.)

But as far as "I am the Lord thy God" goes, says who? Some blowhard "I"? What could be more Jewish than skepticism and argument? Karla believes some parents should not be honored, some thefts and adulteries are okay, coveting is inevitable, and observing Shabbos, not to mention the laws of kashruth, should be optional.

Though enviously aware of the absence of Christmas and Easter in her life, Karla used to love watching Mutti light the Sabbath candles they blessed together. Karla still adores seders and Passover matzoh. She introduced Sax to gefilte fish and *gedempte fleisch*. The only brisket he had ever tasted was the corned beef his Irish mother boiled with cabbage; the only corned beef Karla had ever eaten came sliced on rye bread.

She has always identified herself as a female New York City

Jew. It's an attitude. For, maybe because she spent so much time as a child with Liesel and her family, Mutti did transmit Jewishness. After all, she took Karla to museums, not beauty parlors. She taught Karla to love books, to love music, to love art, to look down on sports. Mutti bragged about all the Jewish Nobel Prize winners; about Jewish dominance in medicine, law, science, entertainment. She said comedians needed to be mentally quick. No wonder so many of them were Jews.

So, what is the Jewish definition of listening? Waiting to talk. Interruption is not rude; it is inevitable. That war zone in which Karla grew up was a place where Mutti and Viv flaunted the same anger Sax's family bottled up. And as much as Karla is appreciating, even loving her cousins, and as much as she certainly agrees she is an offshoot of, and attached to, this German family, she cannot feel she is really part of them. Mutti left that crucifix behind.

With that suitcase under the bed, she trained Karla to feel temporary, nomadic, part of a flux, not a constant. What could be more Jewish than that? *Wherever I am, even in Manhattan or Jerusalem, I will always be the other*, Karla thinks.

The next day, Lotte suggests they stay in Karlsruhe so Karla can go with Oskar to visit the constitutional court. Karla suspects that her cousin, having noticed how she was carrying herself yesterday, is worried that she is getting too deeply into her mother's persona (like Hilde got too deeply into being Liesel?). Or maybe Lotte just wants some time to herself. Either reason is okay with Karla. After breakfast, she gladly accompanies Oskar to his work. Though the idea was Lotte's, seeing what he does interests Karla.

Once they are there, Oskar explains to her that the German constitutional court building and all the spaces in it are deliberately glass-walled so the public can see what is going on inside. "We have no secret proceedings here," he boasts.

Tempted to say that her mother engaged all her life in nothing but secret proceedings, Karla keeps still.

Oskar tells her that Germany is now at the forefront of the human rights movement. His country led the way for equal rights for homosexuals, for instance. Anyone who decides, after living in the country for eight years, to become a citizen gets all the benefits of German citizenship. She might want to look into this for herself. In fact, he tells her, because she was born before the law changed in 1975, she probably acquired dual citizenship at birth as the American-born daughter of an unmarried German mother.

Sitting outside at a café for a lunch that is his treat, Oskar clinks his beer glass with hers, and then, as they eat and drink, he speaks of the ironies of history. Though he is a judge and she is a nobody, he addresses Karla as if they are on par.

He points out that Hilde did more than assume a Jewish identity. From what Karla has told him, he understands that her mother chose a Jewish man to be her child's father. As a person trained in the Hitlerjugend, Oskar suggests this might have been Hilde's ultimate and very brave repudiation of Nazism. He speaks, in fact, as if Mutti were actually a heroine.

And, listening to him, Karla suddenly sees beyond the craziness, beyond the victimized little girl, to a woman with a certain bravery—even, Karla thinks, a certain integrity. Making a clean break, Mutti chose a new path for herself, and she stuck to it.

For the first time in forever, Karla is proud of her mother. She is proud of herself for coming here. She wonders what else, if anything, she will discover in her mother's land.

CHAPTER 13

On the ninth day of Karla's visit, the famous Johann arrives from Berlin at his parents' house. Everyone knows this because as soon as his car pulls up, he honks. Lotte immediately rushes to the door and opens it. Karla stands just behind her, watching his approach.

While his parents wear only blacks and grays, Johann flaunts a kelly-green cotton coverall over a canary-yellow turtleneck, with ketchup-red high-top sneakers. Pale, like his mother, almost to the point of translucence, he looks ghostly inside his bright costume but, his movements as fluid as a snake's, also manages to appear avant-garde, immediate, and even, in his own way, chic as he embraces Lotte.

Lotte pulls away and assumes her duty as host. "Here is your cousin, Johann." She properly introduces him first, as a mark of respect to Karla. "And this is Karla," she tells her son. But then, as if she were a magician conjuring up a giant rabbit from a hat, smiling triumphantly, Lotte snaps her fingers.

Karla laughs as she receives kisses from Johann on both cheeks. Only a few years her junior, her new cousin is clearly someone who, no matter how he is clothed—and no matter that, for some reason, he smells a little like cement dust—will always have style. Karla envies that.

"And this, Karla, is Magda," Lotte says.

With her lion-colored hair clamped haphazardly toward the top of her head, Johann's girlfriend wears denims and boots as if she sees no need to differentiate herself from all the other people who wear a similar costume. This, as well as the fact that she is carrying a video camera, broadcasts that she has more serious interests than mere fashion, Magda's look the kind that is never and always in vogue. "This is so exciting to meet you." Redolent of cigarettes (like Sax), she also bestows kisses on both of Karla's cheeks.

"Exciting for me, too," says Karla, who is also envious of Magda's timeless approach to fashion. What do she and Johann think of Karla's look, assuming she even has a look? She will have to see Magda's film before she has any idea how she comes across, but right now Karla does not know quite what to make of these two, who, only a few years younger than she, seem to come from a much hipper generation.

Following them into the living room of the house where he probably grew up, Karla cannot predict what impact, if any, they will, as a couple or individually, have on her. Ever since Oskar brought up the possibility, she has been toying with the idea of acknowledging her German citizenship, becoming fluent in the language, reversing Mutti's path, and moving back to Heidelberg. Karla can see herself making a life here, hanging out with these exotic but superfriendly relatives who are getting right down to the business that brought them here.

As Karla helps them and Lotte goes back and forth from the house to the car, bringing in Magda's equipment—lights, tripod, mysterious electronic boxes, cables—Karla considers whether she might want to emulate a class act like Lotte. She might pull that off. Karla has, after all, not just her German cousins as relatives; she also has everything she has learned in her courses and everything she has learned from Sax. Or, based on what she has learned from her grandfather and Ron'l, she might want to ignore all that class crap and become a hyper-high-fashion type like Johann, or supremely competent like Magda. Why not? As soon as Karla sees herself in Magda's documentary, she will have a better idea of what role she can play.

Having overseen the completion of the shlepping, Magda has already stationed herself a few feet away from Karla and is peering into and adjusting a video camera on its tripod. Magda is directing the angle, explaining to Johann the lighting and framing she wants. He sorts out wires and clips a microphone to Karla's leotard. Clearly, the girlfriend, not the peacock, is in full control.

So if Karla is going to imitate one or the other, Magda is the way to go. But what if Karla does not have to imitate anyone? Here in Germany, she might just break out a totally new version of herself.

She is having fun playing with the idea of leaving America, living apart from Sax, finding someone young, electric, as a mate. She might even become a new expat star. But, enjoyable as those fantasies are, Karla has seen no one in Germany remotely as attractive as Sax is. What's more, when they talk on the phone, all of her longs for all of him.

Karla is not the least interested in living a celibate life, and if she is going to be sexually involved with anyone, can she really find anyone more exciting to her than he is? It might be that the only good reason to leave Sax would be so she could have a baby, but if Karla agrees to marry him, she can probably get him to have his vasectomy reversed, his sperm still presumably present and retrievable, so she can't use the motherhood card to get out of the relationship.

The truth is, she does not want to dump the man, and she has no reason to do so. If Karla really wanted to move here, Sax would probably move with her. She whisks away the difficulties of shipping and installing his collection, the unlikelihood that he could keep his job. After all, this whole transfer thing is just a fantasy. But his commitment to her is a fact Karla treasures.

Her commitment to him is another story. Karla keeps fretting that she settled too quickly for the first man she ever slept with. If she had more sexual experience, she just might have found someone better than Sax. As it is, having shackled herself to him, she may, even now, be missing out. She is, however, murky when it comes to what exactly she might be missing out on, freedom all that comes to mind. But what does she need to be free to do?

Even hypothetically, she does not want to cut herself off from Viv, her grandparents, and Ron'l. A surmountable problem, Karla pretends. She will just join the jet set and travel back and forth. Then she won't have to worry about what else to do. Except that rushing around is not her idea of a great career, especially since her favorite activity is just "being." So, imagining now a life of constant transatlantic travel, she rejects it.

No. If she is going to do this, she will have to do it all. No more American family or friends, and no more Sax, either. Of course, no way is she going to run away from her life. She is no Mutti. Still, several very real questions do need answers, namely: How much of Karla is German? What, if anything, is she going to do about it? And somewhere, either in Europe or in the States, is there someone with whom Karla will be happier than she now is with Sax?

At this moment, Magda is explaining that she will be speaking from off camera, so, though her voice will be audible to Karla and the viewers, in the film only Karla will be seen. If she will settle herself comfortably in the chair, they can begin.

Obediently, Karla sits, placing her arms on the armrests. She waggles her tush and crosses her ankles. Because she has heard somewhere that this is the trick, she looks into the camera as if it is interviewing her. "Do I get final cut?" she asks the lens, whose shining, dark eye unnerves her. What is that thing seeing?

Instead of answering, Magda and Johann laugh.

So much for altering how she comes across; Karla will have to take her chances—a relief, really. Now she won't have to make any-one up.

"So," Magda says, assessing her. "Ready?"

Nowhere near ready, Karla nods, because, perpetually given to risk-taking, she is willing. She resists the temptation to close her eyes as if she were jumping off a height.

Magda opens with a challenge: "More than forty years after the war, what made you only now search for a German relative?"

Relieved, Karla easily parries with the truth. "Sometime after my mother died, I turned over her mattress and found this hidden photo." Fully prepared, she holds up the photo so the camera can zoom in. "It showed what clearly looked like a German mother and father with their daughter, and though the name written on the back of the picture was strange to me"—she turns the print side to the camera—"that daughter, Hilde Knecht, looked an awful lot like my mother." She flips it back.

"And this surprised you?" Magda redirects the camera from the snapshot to Karla.

"Yes, because, as you saw in her handwriting, it said, 'Maria Werner and Hilde Knecht, but I had all my life believed my mother was Liesel Most.'"

The day she discovered this new name, analyzing that writing was like trying to figure out the return address on a huge, not neces-sarily welcome, package. But now that she knows the story and has repeatedly told it, Karla believes Mutti enjoyed twisting bits of truth to make up her tales. She enjoyed making a fool of her own child. "These people should have been strangers to me, especially since the man is wearing a swastika armband."

How weird it feels to say the word "swastika" to a German in Ger-many! How ultimately victorious! Yet Karla is still pissed at suddenly becoming Karla Knecht. Couldn't Mutti have given her a name that didn't stutter? While her mouth moves around the familiar details of her search and its outcome, Karla looks past the camera's shiny eye toward Magda and Johann, hovering together in shadow.

Who are these people, really, and what do they think of her? Karla aches to win them over. Aware as she speaks of watching and being watched, she recalls how once, when Sax took her to the London Zoo, a woman came in wheeling a severely disabled, grown boy in a sort of giant stroller and a mother gorilla immediately stopped swinging from rope to rope and lumbered down to stare at the boy on the other side of the glass.

"Look," the boy's mother said. "She's looking right at you."

Now the camera is looking right at Karla and she wonders, before that gorilla noticed the boy, did the mother gorilla really not care what the spectators thought of her or did she just pretend not to care? After all, she was obviously aware of her audience, just as Karla is aware of Johann and Magda.

Aware of herself performing for the benefit of an audience she will never see, Karla yearns to be applauded. For just as Mutti could never admit that no one in her family was a hero, in Karla's mind, her life has somehow got to be seen, both by her and by everyone else, as special.

By now, she is getting off on talking to the camera, trying on possibilities as if they were dresses. Having always intended to star as the heroine of her own life, she feels born to do this very thing as she describes how she consulted Viv.

"And I asked her what she knew about the Knecht family and why Mutti had kept their picture, and she surprised me by asking, 'Why do you need to know?' as if it didn't matter to either one of us."

"But it did," Magda prompts.

"One seven eight four three," Karla replies. "That was my mother's number." She pats the place on her own arm, as if the numbers she penned that first day in Hilde Knecht's bedroom are still there.

"But that number did not belong to her?" Of course Magda sounds incredulous—anyone would.

"No. Dachau inmates had no numbers." The instant Karla says this, it occurs to her that she knows nothing of Magda's politics. Neither she nor Cousin Johann seems like a neo-Nazi, but who knows what they really think? In a worst-case scenario, they could use this video to bolster the argument of those who claimed there never were death camps, that the Holocaust was a myth.

"But," she emphasizes, "they *did* have numbers in Birkenau and my mother was *not* faking anybody's death, you understand. Liesel Most was undeniably murdered in Dachau," Karla stresses. "My mother was faking survival."

In uttering this truth for the first time, Karla believes it for the first time. Once Mutti became Liesel Most, at least a part, if not all, of the real Hilde Knecht was forever dead. No more merriment; no more making people laugh.

Which makes Karla a what? A not-Catholic or even Christian, not Jewish, not German, not exactly American, though American comes closest—and an orphan. The whole point of being American, though, is that you can be anybody. And Karla is no-how ready to be just anybody.

"And how does that feel to you?" Magda prompts again.

"My mother was a stranger to me, but she was no stranger to the girl whose identity she stole." Liesel Most, the girl who took the secrets with her into the grave—she, too, is part of Karla.

Soon after she got together with Sax, Karla explained to him that she had to work to earn money because she did not deserve the money her grandfather was giving her.

"That money is as much yours as your red hair is yours," Sax said, and, to this day, Karla remembers how, the minute she heard this, like mist rising from a pond, guilt rose off her and she felt deservedly wealthy. Of course, she is staying with Sax, but that has nothing to do with his money.

"And so you came here, not just to find your relatives but to be introduced to your own mother as well?" Magda asks.

"And myself, too." What belongs to this German-American half-breed, and where did it come from? This is what Karla has come here to find out. "Because it seems as if the more I find out about my mother, the more questions I have."

Whom or how to ask if the fact that Hilde cut herself off from her real relatives made her subsequent break with Viv an inevitable repetition? Did Karla inherit her mother's compulsion to isolate herself? Is that why she has been thinking of dumping Sax and decamping to Germany?

Questions clog her head. For it looks as though even after these weeks here, she will never know exactly when Mutti became Liesel, or whose idea it was for her to emigrate. Karla still doesn't know what part of her mother is buried in her, how large the stain is, or if it can ever be removed. She does not even know anymore if it is indeed a stain.

But especially now that Karla has sat on that bed and written on her own arm, she can see Mutti stabbing her needle into her skin exactly as she so often stabbed her needle into fabric. What Karla still cannot see is exactly what Mutti was saying with that code. "I still don't know who my mother really was."

"We could ask, could we not, does any daughter ever know who her mother really is?" Magda chuckles.

"Probably better than I ever did," says Karla, also chuckling, though God knows she is not amused.

The rest of the interview covers her general impressions of Germany and, specifically, her family here. Karla makes a point of saying how welcoming Lotte and Oskar have been, how at home they have made her feel. She says that speaking German, even badly, seems to come naturally to her. Asked what, other than the personal revelations, she liked here, she cites Oskar's tour of the German constitutional court and the fact that its workings are deliberately kept open to public view. "Sort of the opposite of my mother," Karla adds, "who hid not just her German life but her American life, too."

"Maybe we have all by now learned something about the evils of keeping secrets," Magda summarizes, wrapping up the video.

"Maybe," Karla agrees. And maybe not, she thinks off-camera. For between what she was thinking and what she was saying on the videotape gapes an abyss in whose depths feelings writhe. If Sax were here, she would talk to him about her sense that the words she uses act not as an outlet but as a cover to hide what she thinks and feels. He might say he can see under that cover. But who is to say it is not best to keep on keeping these vipers secret, most especially from herself?

The next day, Magda, Johann, Karla, and the camera go first to the Knecht apartment and then to the Mosts'. For much of this part of the shoot, Karla joins Magda for the voice-over, telling what they are seeing, how she interprets it, and what theories she has evolved about her mother's behavior.

When the nervous tenant in the Mosts' apartment reiterates her innocence about anything that happened before she took over that unit, delighted to have this chance to comment, aware that the apartment owner has impeccable English, Karla says, "Methinks the lady doth protest too much."

Magda gets a great shot of the woman's face, quivering with fury.

On their last day together, Karla leads Magda and Johann to city hall. "Here, in this big building, I could just feel what it was like for my mother, an orphan, estranged from her family, starving, with only books, bits of clothing, and dressmaking tools to her name. This poor kid had to persuade the American occupying authorities, who didn't even speak her language, that she was someone else so they would let her get to America to start over."

"Her story is unbelievable," Magda agrees.

"Yes, unbelievable," says Karla, bristling. "Yet, as it turns out, though it is untrue, it is at the same time true." She certainly did not make it up, if that is what Magda is suggesting by calling it an "unbelievable story."

"So, do you agree, then, with what your mother did?" Magda asks.

"Agree?" Karla pauses to consider. "Let's just say that after spending almost two weeks here, I accept what she did and, to some extent, who she was." But until Karla runs it all by Sax, she will not know what any of this means to her. She needs to evaluate her inheritance with him. For the last ten years, she has depended on his input.

"Perhaps that is the most we can expect," Magda agrees. "And whatever the outcome, I must thank you for giving me so much wonderful footage with which to work." Magda and Johann begin packing up, Karla's Warholian fifteen minutes evidently over.

But maybe it is only about to begin. Karla asks what she should have asked before she said yes to this project: "When you finish editing, where will this be shown?" Could it be aired on German television, or even in theaters? Might Sax be willing to travel with her to the Berlin Film Festival? She would so love for him to see this.

"It will be my dissertation," Magda says. "My professors will judge it."

"What will you call it?"

"*An Impostor's Daughter.*"

Karla has never thought of herself this way. Her mother was not just Nutty Mutti but an impostor, a member of a recognizable group, which makes her daughter feel a little less isolated. "Will you send me a copy?" Karla asks. She hopes that seeing what Magda has made of her will help her to go on developing this new sense of herself.

"Oh, yes, of course," Magda heartily agrees.

So the first "film festival" will take place in Sax's library, where Karla will see through his eyes, the camera's, and her own, how she has dealt with all this information. This video is going to show her at least a bit more of who she is. Karla already feels more certain of herself.

"Anyway, again, thank you so much," Magda says. "You were great."

"I enjoyed it," Karla admits, though how she will feel after she watches the film remains, like the footage itself, to be seen.

CHAPTER 14

With only two days to go before she leaves for home, and with her real business more or less accomplished, Karla can finally turn fully to the issue of Sax and their relationship. After all, she has not yet squandered her golden opportunity to see if sex with somebody else is as good as or better than it is with him. This was supposed to be her chance to have a fling with no consequences. Now, in the 1990s, only Holy Rollers go through their whole life having slept with only one person. What Sax will never find out cannot possibly hurt him, she repeatedly reminds herself.

Never mind that Karla has yet to come up with a likely candidate with whom to experiment, which is just as well. With Lotte or Oskar always at her side, Karla could not have done anything about it even if he had materialized. Besides, who goes to Germany to find a lover? France is, of course, another story.

The minute Lotte suggested they spend the next-to-last day of Karla's visit on a fun trip to Strasbourg, Karla enthusiastically agreed. In bed on the eve of the outing, she reviewed a montage in her head of old movie heroes—Jean-Paul Belmondo, Gerard Depardieu, Louis Jourdan—all so different, all so attractive. Something about French men, and even with Lotte there, Karla could dream.

But Lotte shows up at breakfast with one cheek grotesquely

swollen, as if she is suffering from a half case of mumps. "Of course, we must still take our little trip," she says, her voice distorted.

"Absolutely not," Karla contradicts, dropping her eyes to hide her revulsion at Lotte's facial distortion and her elation at being awarded an opportunity for who knows what possibility? "You need to see your dentist."

"Karla is right," Oskar agrees. "I will take her to work with me."

"But she has already been to the court!" Lotte points out, the two of them speaking as if Karla, the chore they must attend to, isn't sitting right there.

"Why can't I just go to Strasbourg by myself?" Karla's voice is louder than she intends because, embarrassed by her unseemly joy, she submerges it in a flood of anger, reliving all the times Mutti and Viv spoke to each other as if she were not there. What is she, then, just some invisible nobody?

"How would you manage?" Lotte asks, acknowledging her cousin's presence, a nice change from when Mutti and Viv ignored even Karla's loudest interruptions.

"I have a credit card and traveler's checks." Her smile is only in part about having money. "I'll buy a guidebook." The person who two weeks ago was terrified of being all alone in foreign territory is now itching for a single day of utter freedom among strangers.

"You must first take one of the boat tours," Oscar advises, as if the matter is already settled. "Then you will have an overview of the city and can further investigate what you want to see more of."

"But she doesn't speak French," Lotte protests.

"Won't many people in Strasbourg speak English?" Karla asks.

"Well, of course that is true. They will," Lotte admits.

"And what about Karla's German? They don't necessarily admit it, but they can all speak our language," Oskar adds. "You must take your dictionary and practice your German. You have already done so well in just your ten days here."

And so, on her last *Freitag auf Deutschland,* having left Karl-sruhe's grays behind her, Karla finds herself walking in French sunshine down the somewhat overly toasty center aisle of a glass-covered flatboat, searching a bit anxiously for a decent seat on one of the benches, now quickly filling with multinational tourists.

Ah, good! Spotting an empty row, she slides in, settles next to the rail, hears around her a chorus of words that have no more meaning than the seagulls' cries above the water roiling beside and beneath this boat. A nearby bridge looks as if it has its own troll, which makes Karla feel, even before her leading man shows up, that she is at this moment in a fairy-tale movie scene.

"May I?" asks her costar, not, after all, a continental smoothie, but a sun-blessed American around her age with backpack, chardonnay-hued hair, and tropical-sea eyes.

"Sure. Please join me." New Yorker that she is, Karla normally would consider someone who looks as all-out California as he does overly gilded (she and Sax might even laugh about that), but today the guy's insistent glow identifies him as a definite possibility. Still, she isn't sure whether nature built sunshine into this dude or whether his sunshine has been skillfully applied. Anyway, what does it matter? Taking him in, like taking in any work of art, delights her. "Where are you from?" she asks.

"Irvine, California."

No surprise there about the state, but the town is as unknown to Karla as Strasbourg is. The man's accent is not New England. Not Southern. But definitely educated.

"And you?" he asks, his smile revealing teeth as white as one of those salt licks in a New England pasture that Sax inevitably points out to her when they drive around Massachusetts. Sax has a thing about salt licks; this guy evidently has a thing about teeth whiteners.

"New York." For some reason, she doesn't feel like smiling back.

"What part?"

"The city. Manhattan." It always surprises her when anyone thinks there is any other part. Does Karla look like she is from Utica?

"Your first time here in Strasbourg?" His lips assuming a kiss shape, the Californian pronounces the town name like a native.

"Yes." Karla is impressed.

"Mine also." He surprises her.

But the fact that they are both here at this moment for the very first time in their lives means they are star-crossed. At least, she hopes they are.

He is Bil "with one *l*" Muir, no relation to John Muir, as in Muir Woods National Monument, where, Karla advises him, on a trip with her longtime man-friend, the scale of the sequoias and ferns gave her a whole new perspective on the earth and confirmed her infinitesimal place on it. "I mean, they really are awe-inspiring," she gushes, partly in relief at having confessed to being attached.

Tacitly agreeing that her coupledom is not a barrier to further palaver, Bil shares that he can't wait to get back to his part of the world, the coast around Santa Barbara being equally mind-blowing, not to mention Big Sur, farther north. He explains that he speaks French because his mother is French, and he is just finishing up a Fulbright year in Paris, with a quick tour of the rest of the country, before he heads home. So, after today, he is not going to be hanging around.

Perfect, Karla kvells as, from time to time, she glances at one of the church spires or other landmarks the guide is extolling in several languages, and at the geraniums in the flower boxes he does not mention, at least not in English. But this magnetic Bil Muir, with his delphinium-blue eyes, tops any other sight.

Originally from Eureka, California, he teaches in the School of Critical Studies at UC Irvine. He came to France to follow the trail of his heroes, Derrida and Lacan (Karla must remember to ask Sax who these people are), and to undergo a Freudian analysis here.

Bil Muir has his PhD in semiotics, whatever that is (again, Sax will tell her). His girlfriend of eight years dealt with their separation by making it permanent, which, though of course painful, gave him excellent material for his analysis. So, after eight months, Bil is grateful to her for affording him the opportunity to move on with his own explorations.

Karla quite likes the idea of being one of his explorations. She likes the built-in ephemerality of this situation. And the openness. She mentions that she has lived with Sax for almost ten years and that part of the reason she is here on her own is to figure out where they stand.

"Maybe I can help you with that," Bil offers, sliding down the arm he has draped over the back of the bench, to give her shoulders a prolonged squeeze.

Karla blushes from the breasts up. "Maybe you can." As alertly still as a bunny in a garden, she stays quiet and waits, thrilled to be atwitter.

"We'll just have to see." His arm remains firmly around her. Then his hand drapes down and his fingers move ever so slightly, like a fringe, in the vicinity of her nipple.

No doubt about it, the guy is good at this game. And maybe so is she. Smiling, Karla does not immediately lean forward to disengage herself, and when she does, both of them chuckle—each of them in on the joke.

After their hour on the cruise, they disembark down the gang-way and onto the dock, then the street. Neither says anything in the way of a goodbye. Rather, they stroll side by side along the river as if they were small boats, tied up and afloat, bumping gently into each other, then parting, only to bump again.

As they pass an attractive riverside hotel, Bil suggests they stop for lunch on its terrace. And why would Karla even consider saying no to that?

Seated at a table next to the flowing water, without so much as looking at the menu, they agree that in Strasbourg, one must, of course, eat pâté. Bil says that after meeting Karla, he is today feeling incredibly rich, so they must also order a Barsac to accompany the pâté.

Karla wishes that just for once, she could do her own ordering, but hey, she tells herself, at least this man knows what wine goes with what. And, once again, she feels herself to be in good—even, she might say, delicious—hands.

How easy it all is! Though Sax keeps coming to mind, Karla sees no need to tell this Bil anything more about his job, his art collection, his apartment. Saying this visit to Strasbourg is just a day-trip, she explains that she traveled to this part of the world to visit newly discovered German relatives.

In sharp contrast with her first meeting with Sax, years ago, Karla feels no urge to reveal her backstory to Bil. So she says nothing about her mother and her deceptions, or about her own earlier life as a maid. When Karla goes home, she will, of course, tell Sax about her discoveries on this trip, her doubts, and, to the extent to which she has any, her plans for what comes next. Where, if, or how this Bil will fit into her narrative remains to be seen. All he needs to hear is that she takes courses, relating mainly to art history, at NYU and Columbia. What Sax needs to know, she will decide later.

Right now, lolling at this table next to the water—who knew Strasbourg was an island?—Karla concentrates on spreading the marvelously creamy pâté on crusty but not at all dry chunks of baguette. She savors the richness in her mouth, absorbs bliss, favors her body over her mind.

No need even to speak as Bil reveals that his father was a small-town lawyer in Eureka, right near the Oregon border. His mother is a violinist who plays at weddings, bar mitzvahs, anniversary parties, funerals. She taught Bil to revere Beethoven.

"My mother was a Beethoven fan, too." Karla chews, savors, swallows the intense flavors and textures, hears in her head the Beethoven violin concerto's joy-filled rondo.

"I still haven't found Ludwig's superior, if there is one," Bil says.

"Me neither," she agrees, as she sips the perfect, though rather sweet, wine, which gleams like the spring sunlight inside her and outside as well. She drinks in the nonstop sunlight Mr. Quintessential California is exuding.

But then Karla pulls back a bit—there could still be complications. "Any kids?" she asks.

"No." Bil explains that although he has had a number of long-term relationships, in one of which his girlfriend had a two-year-old who, for five years, was like a daughter to him, he has never, as far as he knows, fathered a child.

"Do you still see the girl who was like a daughter?" Wondering if there are others he doesn't know about, Karla immediately identifies with that little girl who thought of him for five years as her dad.

"No. It seemed best to make a surgical break," he explains, apparently not too worked up about having dumped the seven-year-old along with her mother. Karla finds repellent the ease with which he dismisses the "daughter's" presence in his life. What a contrast with Sax and Fleur!

Right now, Bil explains, he is just devoted to reconstituting himself. For the three years preceding his Fulbright, he had to work on getting tenure, an up–Mount Everest climb, especially for a WASP male; finally, after publishing a major article in the *Journal of Cognitive Semiotics* last year, he was the one white guy in any UC Irvine department to be granted a professorship.

"Congratulations," Karla cheers, with a touch of envy. She has no clue about the meaning of the words "Cognitive Semiotics," or much interest in the subject of his "major article," but she does understand that this man has won himself a significant lifetime job.

"You have the most amazing eyes," he says, suddenly, turning to gaze steadily into them.

"It takes one to know one," she counters, seriously laid back now, what with the wine, the sunshine, the travel-poster ambience. Lifting her glass, she toasts him and his startling blue eyes.

"Maybe, but your eyes are unique."

"That's what Sax always says," she replies.

"He's a wise man."

"Yes." But what would he think of her now, flirt-teasing with this California luftmensch? Sax always claims that, above all, he wants Karla to be happy. So how can he possibly complain when her entire past splits off like a melted glacier and slips down into a dark sea? How can anyone begrudge Karla when, marooned in this richly delicious anticipatory now, she has never, ever been happier?

Anything Sax never knows and never finds out can never hurt him. Karla is on an island, cut off from everyone. When she crosses back over to her family, she can leave whatever she wants to behind. Right now, the golden wine Bil is pouring into her glass promises further joys. Still, laying her hand over the glass, she motions for him to stop. "I think this is enough."

"Why? The day is young."

"Right. No sense in getting too sloshed to make the most of the rest of it," she points out. She has no interest in losing control. If she goes ahead with this thing, Karla has to mean it.

"What would you like to do next, then?" He accompanies the invitation in his eyes with a slow circling of his fingers on hers.

These touches radiate through her whole body. "What do you have in mind?" she asks, as if she does not well know.

"I was thinking a postprandial siesta might be in order."

"Where?"

"We could book a room right here."

"But we can't leave Strasbourg without seeing the cathedral, can we?" she teases, not believing for a minute they'll make it to the church.

"I'm quite sure the cathedral's not going anywhere." He chuckles. "Besides, what time do you have to get back?"

"I didn't tell them a specific time," she admits.

"When's the last train?"

"Not until eleven." She blushes.

"Wonderful. It's only three o'clock now. That gives us all afternoon. Then we can take in the cathedral and have a last supper." He makes the whole thing seem fated to be.

And it does feel preordained. Bil is the man Karla has been looking for, her chance to get it on with someone she never has to see again. She remembers reading that Heidi Fleiss, the Hollywood madam, said her clients didn't pay to have sex; sex these days was easy to get for free. Instead, Fleiss said, "they pay us to go away after it's over." But what if he or she doesn't want to go away?

Karla dismisses the thought. Once whatever happens today between them is over, this Bil is the type who will most assuredly go away. For free.

"Wait a minute, though." She taps the brakes. "What about we stop at a drugstore first?" For she is not so carried away that she is about to do anything unprotected.

"No sweat." He waves away her fears. "I've got that covered, so to speak." Chuckling, he flashes a shiny little packet from his pocket.

"Great," Karla says, crossing her fingers, because having sex with a guy who walks around perpetually prepared is as much a minus as a plus.

Exactly what is she getting herself into? Karla is not sure this Californian is not carrying equality for women too far when he has already figured her half of the bill plus tip, set down his half for lunch, and risen to his feet while waiting for her half. *But listen*, she tells herself as she counts out the money, *you can't call yourself a feminist if you don't hold up your end.*

A few minutes later, standing inside the hotel at the reservation desk, instead of giving in to the romance of the moment, Karla confronts her own reservations. If she puts this charge on her credit card, Sax might see it. "Exactly how much will it be?" And when will she set Sax aside so she can concentrate on the guy at hand?

Her half comes to 30 euros, more than she has with her; ever in her head, Sax warns her not to cash a traveler's check in any hotel because they rip you off. Karla cannot at this point ask Bil to take her to a bank. This whole experiment is threatening to drown in a tsunami of practicalities. Defying Sax and cashing the damn check, she lets herself be fleeced.

If she is to go through with this Bil thing, Karla has no choice. She cannot leave a paper trail. An adventure is bound to cost something. *Please God, it should be only money,* Karla silently begs, as she enters a teeny-tiny elevator seemingly made for pretryst kissing.

There she discovers that, though Bil looks like salt and sun, up close his scent and the flavor in his mouth suggest a hint of swamp. Bad gums, Karla diagnoses but, after a slight recoil, decides not to notice.

Normally she would explore a new hotel room, check out the soaps, shampoo, shower cap, look for a robe, and lean out the window to take in the view. Today, she stands just inside the door, watching as Bil pulls the shutters together, closes the two of them in shadow, approaches a bed that takes up most of the room.

How different this is from her first time with Sax! No Oscar Peterson or Modigliani to set the mood, just this guy kicking off his sandals, sliding out of his shorts (no underpants), whipping off his T-shirt, and flipping back the duvet as, condom in hand, he flips himself faceup on the mattress.

Is this speedy efficiency the Californian's idea of foreplay? The body he reveals is indeed an athlete's, tanned except where he evidently wears a Speedo, and lean, muscled, strangely hairless but for a brown nest out of which a pecker thinner and longer than Sax's is already lifting itself.

How will that thing feel in her? Karla wonders, as she seats herself on the edge of the mattress, her back to him, and carefully removes her shoes. "You'll have to excuse me." She gets up, goes into the bathroom, shuts the door. Will he hear if she locks the door? He will probably not come in, but eventually she will have to come out. Leaving the door unlocked, she hurries to take off her clothes; that way, even if he does appear, she will not have to strip in front of a stranger.

Bil is still on the bed. And once she lies down next to him, Karla immediately immerses herself in the old magic of skin on skin, but, rather than joining her, Bil seems to be going through some sort of checklist.

He begins with a fairly deep kiss, followed by a writhe. Next comes nipple tweaking until he gets each one to shrivel; then, giving each a quick lick, he abandons her nipples to attend to the tender unrolling of the condom from its packet.

When he places Karla's hand on his freshly wrapped prick, she enjoys its heat, skimpiness of girth, and surprising length, but the feel of rubber is a turnoff, caressing pecker skin one of her all-time-favorite pleasures. No matter. He has moved on to renewed tongue flicking, this time between her breasts, then down the line, pausing at her navel, before heading right through her bush, between her labia, to her clit. And there is no denying, gum disease or no, Bil's tonguing feels pretty good down there, so Karla automatically gets juicy on her own.

But by the time she figures out that she just needs to close her eyes, fondle his head, go with the flow, maybe moan a little, he has sprung back up, face-to-face, and is slipping his schlong into her, springing it in and out a few times, before rolling over to set her on top. "Ride 'em, cowgirl," he commands.

Which she does, until something inside her flashes. Then she relaxes on him and he rolls her back over and, grabbing her ass, pumps himself to the finish. She waits a few minutes before she works herself out from under him and heads for the bathroom.

"You okay?" he mumbles sleepily.

"I'm fine," she lies.

Once in the bathroom, Karla throws on her clothes, just as she did that first morning with Sax, but this time there will in fact be no follow-up. No visit to the cathedral or amorous supper. Not that she is angry at Bil. Karla certainly played her part and then some in the seduction. But now that she really gets the difference between making love and having sex—after her first time, she mistakenly believed that was what she and Sax had done—she is overwhelmed by revulsion, an urge to vomit without the ability to do so.

Much as she would like to unload this disgust onto Bil, she knows that would not be fair. It belongs only to her. She has betrayed Sax, who trusts and loves her. An hour or so of elation has cost Karla her self-respect.

Without writing a note for the Californian, who lies there easily asleep, but leaving a euro for the chambermaid, which, as a former maid, Karla always makes a point of doing, she glides past the opportunity (will he add another euro? Probably not) and out the door, which, with a sort of sigh, clicks behind her. As if it can shut out what just happened.

She did to Sax what his wife did, though not with his brother. Still, how devastating a second betrayal would be to him! But how else could Karla find out for sure how she feels about him? And how now will she face him? Sax was the one person in the world to whom she could reveal the subterranean truths of her being, but now she will always have to be on guard, to hide from him her treachery. For a couple of hours of pleasure, she has sacrificed her own need to be open.

She wanted a day she could keep like a photo, a private experience she could show off for kicks to herself. Instead, she is taking home an event she will have to keep from a man who can read her unspoken thoughts. If Karla is not to do irreparable harm, she will have to lie to Sax. She will have to convince him she is telling the truth. She will have to get away with this.

CHAPTER 15

S ax does try to enjoy his time without Karla. After seeing her off at the airport, still in Queens, he picks up a rack of barbecued ribs with sides. When Pam dumped him, like a penitent monk, he went on Metrecal; this time, back in the apartment, indulging himself, he pigs out on mac and cheese while watching football.

You couldn't wait, he hears Karla, his Ms. Watch Your Cholesterol, accuse him. *The minute I turn my back, you go redneck.*

Even when she's not here, she makes him laugh. Yet without her, the apartment depresses him. Sax cannot bear to look at his beloved Modigliani.

The next day, he drives up to Greenwich to visit Fleur and her family. Glad to see his daughter thriving and pleased to spend a little time with his grandkids, Quattro and Priscilla, Sax nevertheless comes home appalled.

How could a child of his be content living in the snooty country-club environment Sax finds so stultifying? Initially, he saw this transformation from pothead masochist to suburban yuppie as an improvement. Now it seems like one of those Faustian arrangements: no more suicidal acts means no more individuality, either. Clinging to the rules of status quo, Fleur could be any WASP matron.

Did Sax teach her nothing at all about how to live an exciting life? Where are the artists in her circle, the thinkers? And where oh where is Karla when Sax needs her? What is she doing? And, most critically, with whom is she doing it?

Is this trip of hers really about delving into her mother's past, or is it Karla's chance to reshape her own future? How could Sax, achingly aware of the thirty years between them, blame her if she left him for a contemporary? It is not as if he can picture himself with a ninety-year-old. No wonder Karla has left him. Even less committed to him than Pam was, at least officially, Karla could already have found his replacement.

He returns from Greenwich to the apartment's unmade bed, the satin quilt on his side pushed aside diagonally like a conch shell, the pillow and spread on her side neat, anonymous, vacant. On his first evening alone, repeating history, he again resorted to Oscar Peterson, but, instead of providing company, the music came across as a dirge. So now Sax suffers in silence.

He waits until three thirty, nine thirty Karla's time, to call. When she answers, her voice, here in this room momentarily, comforts him. Then, because she is actually thousands of miles away, Sax yearns even more intensely for her.

She tells him her flight was uneventful. Cousin Lotte and Oskar are being wonderful. She has already learned quite a bit of German. He tells her he spent the day in Greenwich.

"How was it?" she asks, interested as no one else is in his encounters.

"Fleur seems to like it," he says, unable to convey over the phone his combination of delight in his daughter's happiness and his horror at the conformity required for that sort of happiness. He wants to describe his own alienation from the scene, but, clearly excited, Karla is saying, "Tomorrow Lotte is taking me to the house where Mutti grew up."

"That should be interesting," he replies, especially in comparison with his upcoming workweek — nothing new planned there.

"I'm pretty psyched about it," she says.

"You'll let me know how it went?" His own question strikes Sax as containing more than a hint of desperation.

And, apparently responding to that, Karla assures him, "Of course I will."

"Good."

"Until then," she murmurs, by way of a goodbye. "Love you."

"Me, too," he ungrammatically confesses.

"Under the circumstances, your being in a funk is understandable," Sax's shrink maddeningly tells him. "You feel as if you've been abandoned."

"I *have* been abandoned."

"Do you really think she's not coming back?"

"Odds are she will," Sax admits.

"So your feelings do not reflect the reality."

"So you're saying my feelings don't make sense?"

"Who says feelings are rational?"

Who indeed? "So what am I supposed to do about them?" Sax is already bored with getting up in the morning, eating breakfast, going to work, exchanging pleasantries, eating lunch, showing up here, making money, eating dinner.

"Boredom is a cover-up," his therapist has said in the past. Now he counsels, "After you acknowledge the feelings, you let them go."

"And then?"

"You figure out what you want to do next."

Sax wants to see Karla home. And, he reminds himself, in nine more days he will. He will. But how will he welcome her?

As soon as it occurs to him that he can surprise her with something wonderful, he immerses himself in catalogs. He can buy something new that will enchant her. A Pollock? A Warhol? What is out there that they can both love?

That evening, he sits at his library desk, nursing a scotch and flipping pages until, glancing up, he finds the answer to the question of what they will both love in a silver-framed Christmas picture of his grandson. Sax has heard of nieces and nephews older than their uncles and aunts. He has heard of men who had vasectomies successfully reversed. Surely the chance to conceive a baby would be, for Karla, better and cheaper than a Warhol. And whether or not they ever marry, their baby will bind them together forever.

Sax knows so much more now. Raising another kid will give him his chance to do the job right. Sax pictures teaching his son or daughter—makes no difference to him—to play tennis, to sail, to love fine art, and, most important, to believe in the values his mother and father believe in, kindness above all. Sax won't have to counter Pam's conventionality or her repulsive snobbery. This new child's parents will actually love not just their offspring but each other.

In the next phone call, all atwitter, Karla tells Sax she met her cousin Johann and his girlfriend, Magda, who has started making her documentary about Karla's search for her German roots.

"Terrific." Sax smothers his excitement over his own secret: tomorrow morning he is to see the urologist.

After the examination, they sit, the doctor on the far side of his wide desk, Sax with his back to the door. "So?"

No doubt intended as a sunny smile, the doctor's momentary on-off teeth baring gives him the look of a cornered dog. "We can certainly try to do a reversal," he says. "But there is no guarantee of subsequent fertility."

"That doesn't sound encouraging." But Sax does not let himself sag.

"The success rate for this surgery depends on how much time

has passed since the vasectomy." The doctor consults his notes. "Yours was almost thirty-five years ago."

"Yes." Which, until this minute, Sax thought was a good thing.

"At most, you could expect only about a 30 percent chance that, at this point, you could ever father another child."

"Not very good odds."

"They might not be as bad as they sound." The doctor again flashes his teeth. "The fact that you have already produced one child is in your favor. Even if blockages have developed, we might be able to harvest enough viable sperm for an in vitro fertilization. In the last ten years, we have made considerable progress using that procedure."

"That hardly sounds romantic."

"Or inexpensive." This smile is more of a wince. "But it can be effective. And meanwhile, should you elect to go ahead with the vasectomy-reversal surgery, we could schedule you for what is usually an outpatient procedure that takes from two to three hours, with an hour or so afterward to recover from the anesthetic."

"And how long before I could resume sexual activity?" Sax automatically frames his question in medico-speak.

"Assuming all went well, two to three weeks. If you think you'd like to go ahead with this, we can schedule it for sometime next week." Tilting his head toward his chest and raising his eyebrows, the doctor looks simultaneously disbelieving and hopeful.

"I'll have to think it over." Sax is not going to greet Karla the minute she gets back with a three-week moratorium on sex—that's for sure. But he can offer her a 30 percent possibility of getting pregnant. He can pay for a test-tube fertilization. And if all that fails, he can still buy her a Warhol.

∾

The night before Sax's last Saturday on his own, his partner's wife, Arlene, calls to invite him for dinner and bridge with Sandi, her widowed sister. "You do play bridge?" Arlene checks.

"Haven't for years," says Sax, and doing so now would probably mean yet another dose of the paralyzing boredom that has afflicted him since Karla left.

Boredom is a cover-up, he can hear his shrink again reminding him.

"That's okay. As long as you know the basics," Arlene says.

"To be honest, the basics are that Karla is coming back Monday," Sax explains. "I'm not really an eligible match for your sister." But he cannot think of anything better to do Saturday night, another Greenwich visit a depressing prospect.

"I know, I know. And so does Sandi," Arlene says. "But she can really use a little diversion at this point, even if it's just for a home-cooked meal and an hour or two at the bridge table. I suspect you can, too. Besides, Rick will be thrilled to have his buddy with him."

Not that Rick and Sax get to say much to each other at the event.

"So, what turns you on, Sax?" Concealing the no-nonsense, sharp intelligence she cannot help revealing once they get to the bridge table, Sandi is older and more substantial than Karla and, though skillfully done up, less interesting-looking, but she is not entirely unattractive as she gets off the first salvo in her barrage of questions.

"I guess I'd have to say art," Sax admits.

"Do you have a particular kind of art you like best?" Laughing at her own question, she seemingly works hard to come across as an absolute airhead and, judging by her décolletage and natural endowments, a potential sexpot.

"More or less contemporary, primarily," he says.

"My idea of great art is Norman Rockwell and Grandma Moses."

Sandi guffaws. "My late husband used to get after me about what he called my 'plebian taste.'" Widowed at thirty-eight by a drunk driver, she is now, after fifteen years as a single mother of two, a veritable fountain of giggles.

"Nothing the matter with Rockwell and Moses," claims Sax, who suspects that Andrew Wyeth would also be this woman's cup of tea.

But no matter. Sandi greets this remark, too, as if it is howlingly funny, though nothing anyone is saying is anywhere near as amusing as her laughter might suggest.

Her ha-ha reactions call attention to the stupidity of Sax's choices; surely, going to a movie, any movie, would have been less oppressive than being here. This woman, with her forced jollity, is trying so hard to charm him, but her nervousness is contagious. It infects him, and having to pretend otherwise is exhausting.

Nevertheless, when at the conclusion of the all-but-endless bridge game (could it really be only ten thirty?) Sax declines to share a cab ("It's only a few blocks; I'll just walk, thanks"), and Sandi then suggests they meet tomorrow morning to play tennis, Sax, with that automatic politeness he despises, promises to show up at ten at her club. He rationalizes that it will be good to get some exercise, and a tennis game will use up at least a chunk of his last solo Sunday.

You sure tennis is all this date is about? Karla asks in his head.

"Absolutely positive," Sax says out loud. And he laughs.

On Eighth Avenue and Twenty-Fifth Street, in a particularly undistinguished box of a building, Sandi's tennis club requires a climb up a steep, wide, poorly lit stairway. But once he reaches the courts, Sax is pleased to see, through glass walls, that they are Har-Tru, his favorite playing surface.

Sandi, in a tennis outfit that shows off her busty figure and long legs to advantage, is waiting by the desk. "Good morning, good morning," she bubbles, as if her words needed repeating.

"Morning," Sax grudgingly rejoins, before offering to chip in for his half of the court. She really is quite attractive and undoubtedly, once you get to know her and she relaxes, not all that overenthusiastic.

"No, no. I've got this one. Your money's no good here," Sandi says.

"Thank you." Sax quite likes the idea of free tennis.

He likes the actual tennis as well, because, just as she did at the bridge table, Sandi holds her own on the court. Sax has to use a good bit of his arsenal to defeat her six-three, six-four. By the time they finish playing the two sets, he has worked up a good sweat.

They agree to meet, after they shower and change, at the Starbucks just across the street. Sax figures he owes Sandi at least a cup of coffee. In fact, at an earlier time in his life, he would have suggested a matinée.

After all, why not? Judging from the signals the widow, so abruptly deprived of her conjugal rights, is sending out, she might enjoy a no-strings-attached hour or two with him. And Sax might then feel himself less in thrall to Karla. But what is the point? Every single thing he has thought or done in the ten days since she has been away was diminished by not having done it with, or told it to, Karla. Sleeping with Sandi is not going to change that.

All Sax wants from this woman is a chance to talk about Karla and to say how much he misses her. To get that, he is more than willing to hear about Sandi's longing for her dead husband. Loss, after all, is what he and she really have in common.

In the locker room, after Sax showers, he towels off and gets himself mostly dressed. Then, as he sits on a bench, pulling on his socks, easing his feet into his loafers, he realizes he is being approached by a dark-haired, tattooed bodybuilder type wearing shorts and the kind of tank top more often seen in wrestling than a tennis match.

"You bangin' Sandi?" this guy asks.

"What?" Sax assumes he must have misheard.

"You bangin' Sandi?" He repeats his question, a bit more loudly this time, as if Sax's hearing is the problem at hand.

"I thought that's what you said." Quickly shoving his sneakers into his tennis bag, Sax shoots to his feet so he is at least on the same level as this jerk, which, though it makes him feel considerably less vulnerable, does not prevent Sax from grabbing the bag and preparing, if necessary, to try to smash this bozo's face with the shoe bag before the he-man pulverizes him. "But you'll have to excuse me." Sax nods toward the locker-room door. "I'm leaving now."

Wordlessly, the muscleman steps aside.

In the coffee shop, instead of describing Karla and his longing for her, Sax describes his questioner. "Heavyset, dark, surface-of-the-moon facial skin, heavily tattooed, in his forties, bodybuilder. Does that sound like someone you know?"

"It sounds like someone I used to know." Sandi emits more of her volcanic har-hars.

"Yes. Well, you might want to keep your eye out for him," Sax advises. "Even look into a restraining order." This warning is all he is going to do to protect her. For, even before the creep became a factor, Sax planned never to see Arlene's sister again. He is already looking forward to telling Karla about his locker-room confrontation, laughing with her about it, making sure that whatever happens in the future, she is smart enough to avoid weirdos like the muscleman. "The guy struck me as potentially dangerous."

"Point taken," Sandi agrees, now serious.

"Good." At least Sax did that much to help her.

The next day, during the drive to the airport, Sax keeps checking his watch. More than two hours before her plane is due. Still, a
car, hood up, belches steam and gathers rubberneckers, and a lane
closing in 1,500 feet slows traffic for 1,500 eons, each delay feed-
ing his impatience. Finally, after negotiating a maze of byways, he
enters a vast lot and zigzags from row to row before at last sliding
into an empty slot. Sax gets out of the car, makes a mental note of
its location, and follows the signs to the terminal. By the time he
emerges, he has less than an hour to go.

Sax is waiting at the gate when Karla at last appears. The reconnecting of two powerful magnets, their hug reminds him of places
he has been, places he wants to go back to, places he is just finding.
"Welcome home," he says, as fervently as a born-again greeting a
new convert.

"It's good to be back," agrees Karla.

But, after searching his face, her eyes shift so Sax cannot help but
see how different she is after only two weeks away. More self-assured
than the old Karla, this person with nervous eyes has something
to hide. What that might be is all too obvious. The only question
is, with whom and how significant? "So, how was the experience
overall?" With her bag in hand, Sax forces himself to look right at
her. Damn it, he has to find out where he stands, even if his heart
is not in it.

"It was really terrific." Karla meets and holds his gaze.

Turning away, Sax does not actually fall to his knees in thanks;
he only feels like doing so because, with luck, whatever she did with
whoever it was is now an incident in the past.

In the weeks ahead, Sax will just have to do what he did not do
with Pam: observe Karla closely. He will have to watch for phone
calls at odd hours, calls she rushes off to take in private, races to
get to the mail first, gaps in the stories of her days. Sax sighs. How
nice it used to be during all those years when he did not have to be

constantly on guard! But then, he should know by now that nothing lasts forever.

"What was the best part of the trip?" he asks.

"The visits to Mutti's apartment. I felt as if I was getting to know her for the first time," Karla answers, with unhesitating enthusiasm.

Which probably means that what she said is true. Her delving into history trumped her delving into . . . what? It could not be adultery, since they are not married, but it sure could have been infidelity. "Meet anyone of interest outside the family?" The masochist in Sax needs to know.

"Not really." But her blush tells its own tale.

"Well, there was certainly an interesting development here while you were gone." Sax slides behind the wheel, taking charge even as he regrets his own cowardice. Fucking Sandi might have been fun; at one time, he would have enjoyed that sort of peccadillo. "But it can wait until we get home."

"Oh, come on." Now Karla is having no trouble looking right at him. "Tell me what happened."

"Later." One thing he is sure of: when he talks to her about his potential surgery, Sax is going to give her reaction every ounce of his attention.

CHAPTER 16

So here they are, the two of them, just as they were that very first time almost ten years ago, seated opposite each other at Sax's kitchen table. But tonight neither of them has to cook. Instead, their egg drop soup is delivered with sweet-and-sour pork, shrimp, broccoli, water chestnuts, brown rice, even fortune cookies. Karla and Sax have only to raise food to their lips and talk.

But what to say? They are no longer strangers. Yet, in some funny way, tonight each is a brand-new person.

Karla notes a slackening around Sax's jaw, and that not just his hair, but his face, is also gray. He looks older than she remembers from just two weeks ago. Or else she is just now realizing how much he has aged over their years together. But instead of being a turnoff, as she has always assumed his aging would be, Sax's paleness, the wrinkles around his eyes, the expansion of his forehead where there used to be hair, fills her with a tenderness that is all but unbearable. She stands between this man and death.

She wonders what he is noticing about her. Sax is studying her as if she were a document in which every single word is of vital importance to him. Much as Karla loves this attention, she fears it, too, for she knows she has to be careful what she says and exactly how she says it. She has to be on guard without looking as if she is on guard.

"I wanted to surprise you with something marvelous when you got home," he is now telling her.

"That's so nice." She reaches across the table, grasps his hand, then releases it. "But oh, God, I didn't think of bringing you a present." The idea never occurred to her. It isn't as if Sax needs anything, but he might have expected at least a token gift. Karla should have thought of that.

"You brought me something terrific." He is still looking at her speculatively over the rim of his glass of scotch. "In fact, you are the best present anyone has ever given me."

As if they weigh a ton, those words land smack in the middle of Karla's gut. Clearly, he means them, and just as clearly, she does not deserve the compliment. She has betrayed him. But she must not look guilty.

What a relief it would be to confess, clear the air, start fresh! Karla knows she would feel so much better. Unfortunately, she is also pretty sure Sax is feeling much better not knowing for sure what he is clearly suspecting. Her need to protect him from pain trumps her need to confess. "You're not too shabby yourself." Loving him to the hilt, she laughs off that dangerous, tell-all impulse.

On the plane home, sipping wine, she'd considered possible approaches to the Bil Muir episode and decided that if she didn't mention him at all, it would feel strange. Karla loves telling Sax about everyone she encounters. And she looks forward to his take on semiotics, tenure, Fulbright fellowships. She wants Sax, as opposed to Bil, to be part of as many of her life experiences as possible.

So she plans to mention the man she met in Strasbourg. She thought about turning him into a friend of Johann's and opted against that. When Sax meets her German cousins, as Karla assumes he inevitably will, he might just mention the "friend," who could come back to haunt her. And, probably as part of Mutti's legacy, Karla inherited her understanding that to lie successfully, one has to tell as much truth as possible. That way, later, there will be fewer lies to trip her up.

So Sax's Bil Muir will, whenever she resurrects him, be the actual Fulbright fellow Karla met on the Strasbourg boat tour. She will be interested in the fact that even though he, too, is an American, he is in many ways foreign to her and entertaining. So he and she will have their pâté-and-Barsac lunch together. The whole event will be exactly as it really was—minus only one hour. Surely she can manage that.

She frowns now in anticipation, then forces herself to smile.

"What's so amusing?" Sax pounces on her.

"Nothing. I'm just happy to be back." Consciously guarding her secret, Karla feels the balance between them shift. For the first time ever, she, too, has a self; she is a person in her own right.

"Tell me about what happened while you were away," Sax says again, with that peering, assessing look.

Steeling herself, Karla gives a day-by-day account, emphasizing the family, the visits to Heidelberg, the filmmaking. She naturally ends with her last day, the day on her own in Strasbourg. She tells him about Lotte's toothache and Bil Muir, and she finds out that semiotics is the study of "meaning making" and the consequent consideration of words as symbols. Karla adds how very "California" the guy was.

"And what did you two do after lunch?" Sax zeroes in.

Saturated with a welcome calm, Karla says, "He and I went our separate ways." She aims her eyes at Sax's, hits the mark, and does not flinch. "Bil to Paris, me back to Karlsruhe, then home." New to the awful business of deception, she saves a sip of wine for afterward. Right now, she has to be totally clear-headed.

"You're quite sure there was nothing more to it than that?" Sax looks at her piercingly.

"Should there have been?" Karla brazens it out.

"Never mind 'should.' How about 'could'?"

"Sure. But there wasn't. And how about you? What did you do while I was away?"

"I counted the days until you came back."

"I'm really glad to hear that." Now she can finally go for that blessed swig of wine.

"So, are you ready for your surprise?" he asks, temporarily appeased.

"Totally." With the worst behind her, she is ready for anything.

"Last week I went to the urologist to see about reversing my vasectomy." Talk about a pregnant pause! Sax takes this moment to scoop up some soup.

"And?" Astonishment rushes through Karla; he wants to do this for her. And she . . . What does she really want? "What did the doctor say?"

"The fact that I've demonstrated prior fertility is a plus." Sax holds his palm up as if to dam her expectations. "But the fact that the original procedure was done so long ago is a minus. All sorts of scar tissue has probably developed."

His pessimism is infectious. And maybe for the best. It was one thing to long for a possible child, and quite another to imagine having an actual kid to raise. "So nothing is certain." Karla will, like the shrimp she now tries to grasp with her chopsticks, continue wavering. Still, it means so much to her that Sax is willing to try for a baby. And the shrimp does, after all, make it into her mouth.

"As they say, nothing is certain except death and taxes."

Karla will later remember his saying this, but right now she merely chews, before joking, "You mean there's only a conceivable chance I'll conceive?"

"I suppose, one way or the other, naturally or with medical intervention." As if he is determined to detect the secret she is hiding from him, he studies Karla.

She holds back despair, for surely, at some point, he will trust her again. "What do you mean by medical intervention?" It sounds like torture, and who can blame him, but no way is he ever going to see anything on her face that will reveal that hour in France. The price for doing what Karla did is that, having been untrue to Sax, she no longer has the luxury of being truthful. This subterfuge is something she will have to maintain for the rest of her life.

"Even if the reconnecting, which is called, get this, a vasovasostomy, doesn't work," Sax is explaining, "they might still be able to harvest—don't you just love the language? —enough sperm to use for a fertilization. Makes it sound like I've got acreage where the handy farmer will reap and sow."

"I don't care how they say it. It sounds very encouraging." The spark in Karla flares up unchecked. In her life, so much profound has happened to her, either in bed or over a meal, and this conversation is no exception. She might get her cake, be pregnant, and have Sax, too. She might get away with her lapse. Warily, she eyes their two fortune cookies and picks up the one that double-points more or less at her.

"But, Karla, let's be realistic about this," he warns.

"Of course." Though it is never a good sign when Sax addresses her by name, she shrugs. What exactly does he mean? Does he realize she took a chance on getting pregnant with someone else's kid? Is Sax having doubts about being a father again or about Karla's being his kid's mother? To recapture her happiness, she takes another healthy swig of wine as Sax continues to warn her against any optimism. "Our child will have a father in his midsixties, with a life expectancy of maybe ten years."

Karla will later remember that prediction, too. At the time, she thinks it grossly gloomy. "All I know is, our kid will have a terrific dad."

"If you do have our baby, you could well end up"—Sax sticks with his relentless doom and gloom—"having to raise him or her on your own."

"You mean like my mother raised me?" All her life, Karla has sworn she would never be a single parent. But never in her life has she felt as she does now.

Not only did she manage on her own in foreign countries, she is also getting away with the Bil Muir episode, whatever its downside. And Sax still loves her. Karla snatches up her fortune cookie, tears the cellophane with her teeth, cracks the wafer, unfurls the message, and reads, "'Big events are on your horizon.'" "See, I told you," she crows.

"I notice there is no mention of just what those big events might be," says he, dowsing her flare-up of happiness. "The events could be big disappointments. And don't forget, there's another downside to this whole thing." Sax keeps hammering in the negatives. "If we go ahead with it, we will have to have a three-week moratorium on sex."

"Right after we've just been through a two-week moratorium." Karla grabs this gift opportunity to stress that point. "I don't know if I can handle it." She pushes up from the table, goes around, presses herself behind him, strokes his chest, soaks up his scent, openly craves him. "When would this new moratorium go into effect?"

"Not until after I see the surgeon." His head follows the movement of her hands.

"So, what does your fortune say?" Karla asks, as if it is going to determine what happens next.

Sax breaks into his cookie and, chuckling, reads, "'Never question love.'"

"Fabulous advice." She taps his shoulder, as if with a magic wand.

"Maybe so." Finally capitulating to her glee, he grins up at her.

"Then why don't we get busy?" She steps back, yanks her skirt off over her head, and, twirling it like a banner, marches out of the kitchen and down the hall.

No need to look. Karla senses Sax, as he must have sensed her following behind him that first time. But tonight she is the one leading the way into the room where their own personal masterpiece is still radiating sex.

Tonight's lovemaking is no repetition of past couplings. Along with the physical hunger that, as usual, overtakes her, this time Karla allows the full torrent of her emotions to run through her hands to Sax's ears, his jaw, his shoulders, his spine, his ass. Her mouth pours love into his lips, his nipples, his cock; the soles of her feet caress his calves.

Eyes all the while closed, she loses track of where in the bed they are, heads up, down, sideways. She just feels their sway of sea, thunder of drums, gusty winds, the fountain of fiddles and tickly harp fish, the insistent crescendo of desire, and, most arresting, the small flute-wail that emerges repeatedly from her own throat.

Never before has she heard this music. Never has Karla felt this abundance of feelings, which she wholly owns and tonight wholly gives over, unlocked, unguarded, unrationed. How different sex was with Bil and even with Sax before this! Whatever happens next, no one can ever take this exchange of love in word and deed away from them. Karla knows that for sure.

Tonight Sax has at last agreed really to share his life with her. Tonight he forgives her for the sin he clearly recognizes she committed. Tonight he is opening to her the chance to make a family. Tonight, for the first time in her life, she knows she is right where she belongs.

Tonight she, Karla, takes this man, Sax, to have and to hold, for better or for worse, for richer or for poorer, to love and to cherish from this day forward, until death do them part.

CHAPTER 17

Within days, Sax and Karla are immersed in pre-op, op, post-op, stitches, no sex, ice packs, no sex, pain pills, constipation, no sex, sperm retrievals, sperm counts, no sex, sperm analyses. Busy with one medical appointment after another, Karla tells her friends and relatives nothing about what they are up to, because there would, after all, be no point in Sax's having surgery if she is infertile. There is no point in getting anyone else's hopes up until they know more. As it is, it's hard enough for them to keep their own excitement under control.

The gynecologist, a white guy with an Afro begins by asking Karla about her sexual history. She confesses to not having much experience (if she is never confessing to Sax, Karla is certainly not going to tell this stranger about that one time with Bil). The doctor seems not to care one way or the other, as, apparently, only one answer interests him: when Karla says that, despite her regular twenty-eight-day menstrual cycle, she has never used any form of birth control and never become pregnant. This, he says, could be a bad sign, but since Sax is certifiably sterile, it is probably unrelated to her ability to conceive.

He sends her to a lab. There, they take her blood to test it for female hormones, thyroid hormones, prolactin (a pituitary hormone that will tell her if she can ever breastfeed), and God knows what else. Fortunately, all Karla's hormone levels are within the normal range. She has cleared the first hurdle. Her next involves coming back to the lab twice more, a few days before and a few weeks after she has a period, so they can test for follicle stimulating hormones, luteinizing hormones, estradiol, and progesterone levels.

No problem with any of those, either, but Karla is beginning to think that, never mind the Virgin Mary, given the huge range of variables, any conception is a miracle. She is tempted to drop into every church she passes to light a candle.

At her next gynecological appointment, the doc slides a maxi-prick wand up into her vagina with disconcerting ease. When did Karla get so welcoming up there, and is that solar system on the video monitor really hers? Who knew she had a universe inside her?

"You're a perfect specimen," the doc pronounces, slipping his magic wand back out.

Having never thought of herself as a specimen of any kind, Karla is still elated to know that she is perfect, by which, she assumes, the doc means she can get pregnant. That night, the discussion with Sax of possible names goes well. He is fine with Michael, after Karla's father, and they both like the name Lucinda for a girl.

Either way, from now on Sax is at bat and Karla is his chief rooter. Can her guy hit a homer in the bottom of the ninth? She often finds herself looking up at the sky and begging help from anyone up there.

The fluid the urologist aspirates following his first incision contains zero sperm, so he explains to Sax that he is ineligible for a vasovasostomy, in which the vas deferens is simply reattached.

"Va-va-voom," Karla jokes that night to lift his spirits. "No vasovasostomy."

The doctor said this was not an unexpected result. Instead, he will simply perform an epididymovasostomy, which means he will cut the vas deferens to get rid of any obstructions and connect the end directly to the epididymis, or coiled tube behind each testicle. "Under these circumstances, epididymovasostomies are common," he says.

"Do you suppose all urologists stutter?" Karla asks on the way home.

At this point, Sax is still able to laugh.

But three weeks after the more complicated surgery, there are no sperm in the fluid sample. "It can take as much as a year to come back," the doctor explains.

More or less listening to him, Karla hides her disappointment inside a noncommittal expression while, nasal and reedy as an oboe, a voice spins out of the doctor's mouth, a cocoon from which once in a while a word like "spermatozoa" emerges. But mostly it is just sounds.

"And if nothing changes?" Sax looks as if a friend has just died.

"We'll cross that bridge when we come to it," the doctor replies.

Hardly reassuring, yet the urologist insists his tests are far from infallible; occasionally, semen with what seem to have a zero sperm count produces a pregnancy. So, during the next months, they try to maximize fertility. Karla takes her temperature four times a day. Within an hour after it goes up, whenever possible, they have "ovulatory receptive" sex. Sax actually likes rushing home from the office at odd hours "just to cooperate."

Other couples find the process stressful, but Sax and Karla pretend their sporadic matinées are episodes in a hot, super-clandestine affair.

Still, every month after every one of her relentless periods arrives and every one of Sax's tests comes back sperm-negative, Karla is glad she did not get her grandparents' and Viv's hopes up. And though she keeps on taking her temperature, she has lately found that when it is elevated, she has to push herself to call Sax, because she is loath to set him up for yet another disappointment.

At the end of the year, the doctor informs them that, though Sax is most likely incapable of fathering another child, they can always try for an in vitro fertilization using donor sperm.

At which point Karla can no longer dredge up a joke.

"In all honesty," Sax says that night over the inevitable scotch, "I'm more disappointed for you than I am for myself. I'm just sorry I've let you down."

Of course, Karla immediately reassures him he has not let her down; it really doesn't matter. They are still whoever they are, and hasn't that always been enough?

Still, even as he goes on to say that if she really wants this, he will consent to try in vitro with donor sperm (which might or might not work), she realizes her choice is obvious. She can saddle Sax with a kid that is not his, dump him, or resign herself to never having a child. And if she does not make her decision soon, Mother Nature will decide for her. By now, Karla has come to understand that good old Mother Nature never stops working.

So in bed, while Sax sleeps, Karla lies beside him, fretting. In January, she turns thirty-six. Only a little younger than her mother was when she died. Karla always thought that by this time she would have at least one child, but all she has is Sax. Admittedly, that is quite a lot, but everything is too late. The tick of her biological clock is thunderous, but she cannot see herself leafing through a photo album, picking a sperm donor, bearing a two-dimensional stranger's kid. Adopting would be better. But what would be the point?

She tells herself over and over, hoping at some point to believe it, that her life is not just about motherhood. She does not need the complication. She has little time, and she is not going to waste any of it mourning a kid who never even existed. Karla has far too much on her plate. She has to make Ron'l understand how careful he has to be, Arthur Ashe dead of AIDS and not even gay.

So much right now is out of Karla's control. Some guy drove a car bomb into the World Trade Center. People are being mailed explosives, losing their hands. And what is she doing about it? Karla has all she can do to show up for class. Have her shoes resoled. Memorize the two-part invention before her next piano lesson. Buy Viv and Joel an anniversary present.

Viv was right: if she was going to leave Sax, Karla should have done it years ago. Now she loves him too much and, worse, she owes him too much. With or without a kid, she is stuck with him. But if Karla is going to be that unthinkable thing, a childless woman, the pressure on her to take up some occupation to give her life meaning is intense. Attending classes and doing errands will not cut it. Ironically, Karla, who wanted to defy Mutti by being just like Viv, is ending up to be just like Viv after all, and it turns out Mutti was right—there has to be more to life, and Karla will just have to find out what that is.

Every day she hauls herself out of bed and goes about her tasks. Abstract Impressionism at NYU. New shoes not that much more expensive than new soles. How about a mirror for Viv and Joel? Karla will roast a chicken for Sax's Valentine's Day dinner. Ron'l is having a big birthday next month, so she'll make him a party, too.

She is now thirty-six and a half and that much closer to death, with no lasting accomplishments. Karla is desperate, not so much to have a child as to have the purpose that being a mother would automatically give her.

They are still trying, still seeing doctors. Over Sax's objection, having insisted on going to the appointment with him so she can hear for herself what the doctor says, Karla asks the urologist about the weird lump that looks like a shoulder pad perched on top of Sax's left shoulder.

Narrowing his eyes, the urologist examines it. He pokes at it. "A lipoma or a benign fatty cyst, probably nothing to worry about," he assures them.

"Good. Then we can go home." Sax is already rebuttoning his shirt.

"He only said it's probably, but not definitely, nothing to worry about," Karla points out.

"No good doctor ever says 'definitely,'" the doctor says, laughing.

"Well, how about this, then?" Repelled by the look of the bulge on Sax's shoulder, Karla presses the expert. "If that thing was on you, would you have it removed?"

"Yeah. I guess I would." He has the grace to look sheepish.

Yet Sax insists that he doesn't believe in cosmetic surgery. He prefers just to live with his flaws. However, Karla is not sitting still for this. For she failed to protest when Mutti ignored her swollen legs. She failed to act when a doctor might have saved Mutti's life. This time, not willing to accept Sax's obstinacy, she nags him until he finally agrees to see a surgeon.

Utterly hairless, the new doctor looks like a walking thumb. He speaks as if nothing is more routine than the removal of a lipoma, but first he schedules Sax for an X-ray and a follow-up visit.

"Just as we thought," the thumb says the next time they see him. "The lipoma is benign, unimportant, but there is something that shouldn't be there." He fastens an X-ray to a light screen and points to a tiny, well-defined oval in the clouds framed by ghostly ribs. "I'd say it's no more than three point five centimeters."

Teensy, whatever it is, Karla thinks, as he expresses "guarded optimism" and recommends first an MRI and then a biopsy.

Later, recalling that visit, she finds the word "optimism" ironic and the word "guarded" prophetic. But on that first day, blissfully unaware, Karla just knows that whatever this thing that should not be there is, it is going to be removed forever. And that will be that.

The "something" turns out to be a malignant tumor that orig-inated in the lung. An adenoma. Sax has stage 4 lung cancer. Because it has migrated outside the lung, it is inoperable.

So Karla's decision to stay with him is irrelevant; Sax is leaving her. It is too late for him to stop smoking. It is pointless to berate him for his addiction. They both know he is going to die of this disease.

The first oncologist says that if none of the treatments work—and there is always a chance they will—Sax should live for at least three and very likely as long as six months or more. How much time he has left is impossible to predict with any accuracy. Life's indirection both gobsmacks Karla and clarifies her position: here she thought she and Sax would be bringing a new person into existence, when instead she will be seeing him out of it. No more worrying about what to do next. No more wishing for a baby. She must squeeze as much joy as possible into every second she and Sax have left. Except for him, cancer, and treatments, the world drops away.

They make an appointment with Dr. Chachoua, the hotshot Egyptian oncologist who specializes in lung cancer at NYU. "He's tip-top," Joel confirms, and gives Karla a copy of *Invictus* that says, "I thank whatever gods may be for my unconquerable soul."

But Karla wants more than Sax's soul; she wants all of him.

Looking around the specialist's waiting room on the day of their appointment, she expects heavy-duty lung cancer defeat. Instead, she sees cozy chairs, current magazines, a machine dis-pensing coffee, tea, herbals, hot chocolate. Karla cannot tell, unless a sunken face, wig, turban, or oxygen-tube mustache makes it obvious, which people here with them are the patients and which are the sidekicks.

And where in this collection of cancers is the tragedy? The technician who comes to get a plump, Hershey-brown woman for a blood test asks her, "Why isn't one of your boyfriends here with you today, Grace?"

"I gave us all a day off, them and me." Grace laughs.

As does everyone, especially a gaunt woman with velveteen hair.

Meanwhile, Sax, an ankle perched on his knee, is leafing through *Newsweek* as if the real news is there and not in what the expert doctor will say—not that they immediately see him. As if who is going to pay for the treatment is more important than whether or not it exists or will work, they first meet with someone to discuss what kind of insurance they have.

Welcome to reality, kid, Karla thinks as, back in the waiting area, Sax picks up another magazine and, oddly resigned, she brews herself a Styrofoam cup of tea, uses her teeth to free a graham cracker from its cellophane prison, sits down, nibbles, sips, waits.

Neither she nor Sax is surprised in the doctor's office when the graying, fifty-five-ish expert confirms Sax's diagnosis while making it clear that what sort of person any of them is is irrelevant to this meeting. All they will ever have to talk about with each other is cancer.

"What will dying be like?" Sax asks.

"It's different for everyone," replies the oracle.

And, sitting there, Karla mutely despairs. This hotshot with a heritage famous for its tombs is not even hinting that Sax is not about to die. He is not promising to keep him alive. Karla knows Sax is on his way out, but at the same time she does not want to stop semi-believing he has years of life ahead of him. For the doctor is recommending treatments, one of which could miraculously work.

And in fact, the treatments do work by providing a routine for them, a life raft that keeps them afloat. In the weeks that follow their NYU consultation, the cancer center becomes their home away from home; faces become familiar as everyone, patients and staff, dips into the ever-filled candy bowls as if they are all celebrating Halloween, all teetering on the brink of becoming something else.

There does turn out to be reason for optimism. Radiation stops the tumor from eating into Sax's spinal column. Chemotherapies reduce his bone lesions. From the beginning, Mutti raised Karla to be her caregiver, and now she resumes that role as if caregiving is what she was always meant to do.

Karla sits beside Sax whenever poisons are hooked up to flow into him. She sees to it that he has cold drinks, a sandwich, chips, applesauce, and candy corn. Together in the cancer center, they picnic and treasure even the dullest aspect of the normal, for normal is the opposite of dying.

However, from the very first day, Karla knows and Sax knows, and they each know the other knows, that this disease is going to kill him. But not in three months, and not in six months. When, then?

They discover that, like people walking a tightrope, those facing a diagnosed death are entirely absorbed in what they are doing. And in Sax's case, moving toward the end of that tightrope stretches time, as, in the weeks and months that follow his diagnosis, his cancer turns out to be about waiting.

They wait for biopsy results, blood test results, MRIs, PET scans, CAT scans, bone scans, doctor's reports, doctor's appointments, doctor's calls, chemotherapies. They wait for anything besides death to wait for. Meanwhile, in just four months, Sax morphs from sexy dynamo into frail old man. They do not notice this happening. They just, now and then, recognize the total effect.

Sax and Karla do not realize, the final time they make love, a date neither of them can afterward remember, that it will be their very last time. She continues to hope that once the right treatment takes effect, the disease will go into remission, Sax will rejuvenate, and they will go back to all-encompassing sex. But even without physically doing so, they are constantly making love.

"I don't care what the prediction is—these protocols [one of the new words she has learned to use] sometimes work," she tells him again and again. "Someone is in that 2 or 3 percent; it might just as well be you."

But instead of speaking, as they always used to, about art, politics, office and family gossip, fears, finances, ambitions, possibly having a child, now they discuss symptoms and schedules.

Taxotere, the second chemo, seems at first to be working, as does its successor, Iressa, a drug that for 10 percent of the people who take it is a virtual cure. "And 10 percent isn't nobody," says Karla, reminding Sax that one patient who was a doddering eighty-pounder made a complete return to normal life.

They consult a Chinese doctor who, having trained at NYU, combines ancient Asian remedies with modern approaches. He tells them to continue as they are but with a new diet: no root vegetables, refined flours, sugar, or dairy products, only organic poultry and meat, lots of soy and fish, and protein shakes.

Karla delights in preparing these concoctions. At last, she has exactly the right job, and she is doing it. Sax is astonished by how things taste; he describes his meals as "eating in Technicolor."

Without discussing possible miracle cures, they do not fly to Mexico for laetrile. They do not go along with the Mount Sinai specialist who wanted to do surgery. "That operation could help Mount Sinai," Sax says, "but not me."

Desperate for an alternative to the inevitable, they remain insistently rational.

Months later, in a therapist's office, when she realizes that every single person is born worthy, Karla will be astonished by how much effort she has spent on trying to prove she deserves to exist. And when, finally, in that same office, she accepts that she may never have a child, and will in any case never have the childhood she still craves, she weeps. Mutti will always be her mother; there will be no do-over.

But did Mutti in fact fail? Seeing herself through Sax's eyes,

Karla finds her caregiver training comes in very handy. In fact, feeling so good about what she is doing, she isn't sure she would want to be different.

In August, she and Sax can still go to Shakespeare in the Park, but afterward they speak about how Sax is feeling, not about the play.

"We need to talk," he tells her in early September.

"Sounds ominous." She stops applying moisturizer and turns to face him.

"About getting married." These days, easily chilled, he is wearing pajamas to bed.

"Kind of a last rite?" How she misses his naked skin on hers!

"You could say that."

"So, is this a religious thing?"

"No. Economic. Married to me, you will inherit the bulk of my estate without having to share it with Uncle Sam," he explains.

"Oh, God." She closes her eyes. "I can't stand this."

"You don't have to, you know," Sax says. "In fact, this might be the right time for you to leave."

Karla eyes snap open. "And that's what you'd do? Run away if I was dying?"

"If I were thirty-six and you were almost sixty-five?"

"Yup."

"No." Sax shrugs. "No, I probably wouldn't."

"Then what makes you think I will? What makes you think I don't want to take care of you?" After all Sax has done for her, Karla finally has her chance to give a little back.

Again he shrugs.

"Oh, Sax. Don't you already feel married to me?" Tears thicken her voice.

"But if we were legally married, you'd inherit the whole bundle."

"I want you, not your money."

"Right, but that's not an option."

"So who would our marrying be for? You or me?"

"Both of us."

"But why now?" Never before has Sax seriously proposed to her. Karla hates the idea of a wedding tied to a death.

"Because I want to leave you serious money."

"I already have enough money." And Karla cannot explain her profound certainty that marrying him now would be unlucky and unwise, just as it would be unwise to try to tell him this. For Sax would just pooh-pooh her superstition. "But if you really want to get married, of course I'll do it." At this point, she will do anything he wants.

"It would be for you, not me," he says.

"I want to benefit from your life, not your death."

"So, it sounds like you want a no-nup agreement."

"If that's okay with you."

"More than okay." Smiling, Sax relaxes and slides into his side of the bed.

"Good." Karla scooches next to him, her head on his chest. "Thanks to you, I've had it very easy."

"I'd like you to go on having it very easy."

"That's very generous of you, but I'm already married."

"Sleep on it. Then decide whether to make it legal."

"Sure." Karla has seen people suck up to Sax; she knows what they think of her. Once, when she was carrying on a pleasantly flirtatious conversation with a painter, a busybody took it upon himself to tell the artist, "You should know that Karla is Saxton Perry's significant other" (but a nobody in her own right, the shithead implied).

As Sax's widow, a word totally alien to her, Karla would always have to wonder whether people liked her or the big bucks he left her. There would never be a way for her to know for sure. Sax has always said having a fortune is oppressive. And he's been the one to worry about paying taxes, insurance, maintenance fees. Karla has never even had to figure out who and how much to tip at Christmas. The thought of making investment decisions terrifies her. With reality stretching like razor wire across her path, she acknowledges how privileged she has been.

Not sure she is ready to give up the trappings of her present life, once Sax is safely asleep, she gets out of their bed and prowls. No need to turn on lights. She knows this apartment. Yet, opening one of the bronze doors into the dining room, she still feels like a guest, rather than an inhabitant; she could be a customer entering a bank vault.

Before, when she imagined her wedding, she used to wonder, *Should I go to Vera Wang or Kleinfeld or ask Ben to design my dress?* But at this point, forget about the dress—the real question Karla has to ask herself is, would marrying a dying man make him better or worse or have no effect? Probably no effect, at least on the cancer. So, what *would* a marriage do for him or her?

On the plus side, Karla could show off to everyone that Sax loves her enough to make it official. The minus is that most people would assume she is a gold digger. Of course, Viv and her grandparents would be thrilled if she married Sax and then he died. Imagining them gloating, Karla cringes.

The next morning, she tells Sax, "I've slept on it."

"And?"

"I still don't think it's a good idea for us to get married right now." If, please God, Sax recovers, then their marriage would be a perfect celebration. "Let's get you better, and then we'll talk about it," she promises. "And if you still want to . . ."

"You don't want to consult a lawyer now? Someone who could protect your interests in my estate?"

"No. I'm not worried about what you'll leave me." Even if he leaves her nothing, she can afford to be quixotic. She has Ben. That reassures Karla but worries her, too. In turning down Sax's proposal, is she reenacting Mutti's rejection of Ben and his millions? Was Mutti actually right? As it is, Karla is dependent on her grandfather. ("Rich or poor, it's better to have money," as Viv likes to say.)

"You should know, then, I am leaving you a life interest in the apartment and its contents," Sax says, "subject to a condition subsequent."

"What does that mean?" When other people are talking this sort of gibberish to her, she will have no one to ask what it means. Even if she isn't officially a widow, Karla is going to have to learn the language of money. But at least Sax is still here to teach her some of what she will need to know.

"You can live here as long as you want," he explains, "but you won't own the place and can't sell it."

"What's the condition subsequent?"

"If you move out for more than a year, the apartment will automatically belong to Fleur."

"What if I want her to have it before then?" It already feels to Karla like a mausoleum in which she is buried alive. Truth be told, the whole building has always struck her as stodgy and degritted to the point where it is generic. *I am the embodiment of wealth*, says its blank granite exterior. But Karla, the child of polyglot Canal Street, longs for funk, expressiveness, vitality.

Remembering how the stink of fish repelled her on her first time here, she now finds herself longing for the kind of rot out of which things grow. The whole point of Sax's building and others like it is to wall out anything that will change the way things are. Karla craves flux.

"You can always give up your interest at any time," Sax says.

"Good," says Karla, hoping he does not suspect that what she really wants to know is what he is going to do about the paintings, in particular the Modigliani.

Sax does not say, and Karla does not ask.

One night over drinks, he says, "I have to tell you something."

She leans forward, expecting to hear something profound.

"The Procrit can lead to diarrhea," he tells her.

❧

By fall, instead of conversing, during dinners they are watching *The MacNeil/Lehrer Report*. In late October, Fleur and Cotty come for a meal of oysters tetrazzini made with soy powder, instead of milk; at this point, Karla is serving only easy-to-swallow foods. They talk about Fleur's next baby, due in May; they already know it is a boy who will be named Saxton Perry II.

"Poor kid," Sax says, with an unmistakably satisfied smile.

Karla gulps a lump of tears. She was the one who was supposed to be having the baby. When she first heard the news, she silently screamed, *Why Fleur and not me?* But now, having long ago made her peace with Sax's daughter, Karla can be a little glad and a little hopeful, because if Fleur can have a kid at forty-five, pregnancy might still be a possibility for Karla, too. Sax is the one who is dying. "As my mother used to remind me," and he has so often quoted her, "life is for the living."

Not long after that evening, Karla helps Sax get out of a cab and then gives him her arm so he can cross the sidewalk, make it into the Frank Campbell Funeral Home, and reach the elevator. Upstairs, proceeding slowly down the hall, they meet a smoothly eager, surprisingly young man who, upright, narrow, and bending toward them, reminds Karla of a human-size praying mantis.

He leads them to his office, where, after they are seated, Sax explains that he wants to be cremated. Rubbing his hands with irrepressible glee, the mantis discusses options. Sax chooses the least expensive, and the mantis seems unperturbed.

On the way home, Sax complains, "What a racket! They make you buy a coffin in which to be incinerated."

Karla nods numbly, as if she were in an audience, seconding something said onstage.

As the weeks go by, challenging her own versatility, she concentrates on cooking foods he can manage—tofu, ground chicken, salmon soufflé—but it seems as if Sax is beyond noticing, until one night, his voice soft and sandpapery, he says, "Thank you. You are very good."

Clearly, he is talking about more than the food.

"You bring out the best in me," she replies, blushing. For, she realizes, this has always been true. He helps her to be a good person.

Or at least a semigood person. Karla does not tell Sax she has started thinking about when and where she will move once he is gone. She still pays rent on the loft, but she is not sure she could stand living there again.

She does not ask what provision Sax has made for his collection, or who will get the Modigliani.

She definitely does not discuss with him the personal ad she is thinking of putting in the *New York Review of Books*, despite her real grief, or maybe as an antidote to it: "Dilettante seeks diligence. Forget photo; send references."

Karla does not say, either in the make-believe ad or to Sax, that she despairs of finding a partner while she is still capable of having a child. She does not speak of the possibility of repeating history and, with donor sperm, giving birth on her own, possibly in the loft. She does not admit that she cannot keep herself from at least planning for, though she is not looking forward to, her life without him. But it may be he knows without her saying—at least, so it seems when, out of nowhere one day, he says, "Be careful. Remember Sandi's stalker I told you about. You don't want to get involved with anyone like that."

"Right," she agrees, vehemently swearing off sex without love. Never again.

By Christmas, Sax is taking a nap every afternoon, managing only purées and protein milkshakes yet still seeming pretty much like himself. Karla cannot keep her hands off him. "I'm stockpiling," she tells him.

In January, she dreams she is lolling on a lawn with Fleur's husband and Sax, imitating *Le Déjeuner sur l'Herbe*, Karla naked, Sax and Cotty wearing velvet suits. Only Sax is gagging. But that part isn't a dream. Roused, Karla switches on the light and sees him swaying on the edge of their bed, retching.

"You want some water?" she asks urgently.

"No," he whispers, dropping back down beside her.

The next morning, she wakes up nauseated and achy, as if she drank too much at the dream picnic.

From that night on, she drinks the scotch Sax at one time loved but is now forbidden. And, because she will be no good to him if she is exhausted, Karla begins taking sleeping pills, alternating three different varieties to avoid addiction. Often she thinks about how flight attendants warn passengers that when the mask comes down, you must put yours on before you put one on your child. If she is going to help Sax, Karla has first to take care of herself.

By February, five months after the doctor predicted six, Sax needs her to brace him before he can get out of the bed. Her heels planted, her hands tight around his wrists and his clasping hers, she leans back to balance his rise to his feet before, holding on to her forearm, he shuffles to the toilet. In this way, though they can no longer make love, physical intimacy continues and actual intimacy deepens.

"Do you know why I love you?" Karla asks.

"You love me because I let you." He astounds her by not needing to be told.

How much easier to give love than to receive it! But Karla is learning.

On Sax's sixty-fifth birthday, able to make it down the hall to the dining room for what turns out to be the last time, he drinks a glass of the champagne Fleur and Cotty brought over—without complaining, as he has been complaining for months about other wines, of its bitterness.

Karla has to hand it to Fleur; she saw behind Cotty's plaid trousers and canned enthusiasm—the man actually says things are "neat"—to his profound goodness. They toast the namesake they all believe Sax will never see and then toast the two grandchildren he adores.

After they leave, Karla asks accusingly, "How can you leave me?"

"I will never leave you, Karla," Sax swears.

Moved beyond tears, she knows this is true. Whatever happens to her now, he will be with her.

When, unable to stand or even sit up, Sax whimpers if anyone touches him, the hospital sends over a hospice nurse, who catheterizes him. Now he never needs to leave a bed whose special air mattress, designed to prevent bedsores, writhes and hisses.

On March 21, Sax does something he has not done for days: he speaks without being addressed. "You are beautiful," he tells Karla, enunciating each word separately.

"You mean your eyes are going bad," she replies, and instantly wishes she had not reflexively joked. For he must have thought for some time about what he wanted his last words to be, and of course he was not referring to her looks. But Karla cannot accept that she is beautiful or even okay. For she cannot save Sax.

The next day, his breathing rattles. "Cheyne-Stokes respiration," the doctor diagnoses. "Won't be long now. A day or two at most."

"No. Not Cheyne-Stokes. Agonal breathing," the hospice nurse contradicts, as if this makes a difference. In any case, she makes sure Karla still has the number where she can be reached twenty-four-seven.

Sax keeps breathing.

When Karla goes to the bathroom, she hears, with a wall between them, that Sax's breathing sounds as cozy and familiar as the large percolator they used to use for parties, back when they had parties. But sitting right next to him, watching his head jerk back as he struggles to haul in oxygen, she feels the agony in every "agonal" inhalation.

The doctor claims Sax is not in pain.

He keeps on breathing.

The doctor's day or two becomes three, then four.

As if he is either ashamed of his inability to offer further help or angry at his patient for revealing that fact by dying, the oncologist stops communicating.

And what, after all, remains to be said? In a chaise next to Sax's hospital bed, Karla lies, listening to the on-and-off special mattress hiss and the awful gasps for air.

From time to time, Ron'l, Viv, Ben, Adele, or one of Sax's business associates stops by. Karla is particularly grateful if anyone brings her a meal she does not have to plan or prepare.

Fleur frequently provides a dinner. "I hope you know how much we appreciate what you're doing for Dad," she says one afternoon in the kitchen after she's visited Sax.

"It's the least . . ." Karla shrugs off the gratitude. "But listen." She makes sure their eyes meet. "Are you okay?" After all, this woman once tried to take her life.

"Yeah," Fleur says, her voice furry with tears. "I'm just glad he and I got to make our peace before all this."

"But you'll miss him," Karla insists that she face that reality head-on.

"We both will," Fleur acknowledges.

The hospice nurse comes each morning and each evening to empty the catheter bag and take Sax's vital signs. Karla keeps watch, dozes, writes Sax's obituary, and lists the people she will call when he dies. She waits, goes to the toilet, comes back, waits, dozes. Everyone waits.

Finally, on the fifth morning, when they are alone, it occurs to Karla to lift Sax's hand in hers and reassure him, "You've taken good care of me. It's okay for you to go. I will be all right."

Sax sucks in one loud breath.

Karla waits for another.

There is none.

Recalling her unwillingness even to look at Mutti's dead body, Karla thought she could never kiss a corpse, but, kissing Sax's cool forehead—even when his mouth remains twisted around his teeth in a terrible last effort to haul in air—she feels no more disgust than she feels placing a period at the end of a sentence. This is their goodbye.

Then Karla takes her list to the phone, dials Fleur, and says, "He's gone."

"I just knew it," Fleur says. "Ohh." She sighs. "We'll be right there."

"Good," says Karla, in a voice that seems to come out of her but to belong to someone else. For, like Sax, Karla has left the body whose eyes read the list, whose fingers poke the numbers, whose mouth speaks to the hospice nurse, Viv, Ben, Ron'l. Without Sax, the woman who is doing these things is empty.

CHAPTER 18

Hours after Mutti died, Karla turned to Viv, who took charge of the burial arrangements and introduced Karla to Joel, her new husband, and the grandparents Karla had never met. Immediately, Ben, Adele, Viv, and Joel helped Karla get through the weirdness of being on her own. So she has never really experienced a death alone. But this time, whether she is with Viv and her grandparents or anyone else, Karla realizes John Donne was wrong. Every human *is* an island.

Today's memorial service at the funeral home, and then its aftermath at the Colony Club, flow around her. As Sax's ex-wife, sister-in-law, and the club member who has arranged for them to be here, Pamela, exuding graciousness, has taken charge. Normally, this would have irritated Karla. But today, aware of what is going on, she is here in the way a mannequin would be here. If someone were to knock her over, she would notice but not care.

Karla notices that, as sorry as he is about Sax's death, Ron'l cannot help bubbling, for last week, Ben finally promised to hire someone to model it for him if Ron'l makes a human-size design. "This be my big chance," Ron'l keeps saying. "My big chance."

Far from offending her, his excitement in the face of her sorrow seems just right to Karla. *At least someone here is happy*, she thinks, shaking her head whenever a waitress offers her something she would under other circumstances love to drink or to nibble. But at this point, Karla prefers not to chew. She has trouble swallowing. When she tries to, she does not taste. But she can still observe.

Fleur and Cotty stand with Pam and Oliver, who, ever punctilious, offered Karla practiced civility before creating this distance that she welcomes. They are the blood mourners; she is the outsider. Except for Karla's usual stalwarts (and really, how profoundly has she ever known any of them?) and a couple of people from school, most everyone here is connected to Sax. But that's okay, Karla thinks. More is required of a participant.

Many of those in Sax's business crowd still consider her "the maid." In fact, her favorite of Sax's partners, Rick Goldman, comes up, gazes at her with his droopy comedian's face, and says, "Oh, Cinderella, how we will all miss your prince!" as he gives her a heartfelt hug.

Cinderella nods, but noncommittally.

With everyone, Karla maintains her composure and her distance. She is here and not here. People pause in front of her to offer her their sympathy. As if speaking from far away, she thanks them. Art dealers tell her they are "sorry for her loss," in reply to which, instead of saying, "You mean *your* loss, don't you?" she again and again murmurs the expected: "Thank you. Thank you for coming."

Karla is surprised when Bessie Shelton, whom she hasn't seen since they took classes together, approaches her.

"I know how it is." Bessie looks into Karla when she says this, for she was a widow and she does know what will help. "I'll give you a call in a few weeks," Bessie promises. "We can go to dinner."

"I'd like that." At least as much as Karla, in her deadened state, can like anything.

That night, back in the blessedly empty apartment-tomb, she tells Sax, *I never realized how useful going through the motions can be.*

Most people think going through the motions is the same as living, he replies, before he goes back to being dead and she continues to be not precisely alive.

The next day, a lawyer brings over a copy of Sax's last will and testament. Fleur inherits everything—just over $200 million—minus $5 million Sax left in trust for Karla. Aware that had she agreed to marry him, her $5 million would have been a hundred, Karla is still glad she resisted going that route, for Fleur needs to know she came first, and Karla needs Sax, not his money. Not that she isn't getting a bundle of it. The lawyer says her share should easily generate an annual income of $150,000. And Sax has also willed her the Modigliani, plus money to insure it, which, even if Karla sells the painting, she will get to keep.

So Sax has seen to it that she will never need a job or be forced to decide what to do. But, forced or not, she will have to figure out a new role for herself; rich, longtime girlfriend of a dead man is not going to cut it. Right now, she has no idea what will. Yet she must decide, and soon, though at this point she is unable to decide anything at all.

Once again alone after the lawyer has left, she wafts from room to room, locating her lover in the bronze doors she swings open, in the dining room's massive silence, and in the den's cigarette air. Karla knows now she would never have left Sax, but she has already gone beyond her dilettante phase. She has played the three c's: cleaning lady, concubine, caretaker. Those roles, at least in her case, have now, as they say in the corporate world, been phased out. So what's next?

Looking for work is the worst job in the world, Sax says.

No, it isn't, she contradicts him. The worst job is deciding what job to look for. Having to figure that out without him here to help her infuriates Karla. She would have come to this point soon enough. Sax's death has simply accelerated that necessity. It is almost as if he took himself out of the picture to make her get on with her life as an adult.

What she will be when she grows up may still be a question, but that she is now about as grown-up as she will ever be is probably a fact. However, whatever he intended, it is not yet a fact that Sax is gone.

Here in his library, celebrating the impending birth of his namesake, cadaverous yet joking, he is lifting his glass of bubbly and toasting to the future. Healthy, he is waiting for Karla in the bedroom, lusting, his eyes giving away his intentions.

For months, her time has been all about him. How many years, months, weeks, days, hours did Sax have left? Would he suffer? Could she take care of him?

Today, when she has answers to those questions, Karla faces new ones: What should she do in the short and long terms? Where should she live? If she decides to move, when should she do it? Who the hell is this great caretaker without a Sax to care for?

Karla can just hear "The Story of Old Women," a poem by Tadeusz Rozewicz that Joel once read to her, saying, "I like old women ugly women mean women they are the salt of the earth . . . not disgusted by human waste . . . old women, ugly women, mean women . . . only fools laugh at old women."

Three weeks after Sax dies, Karla receives a package from Germany. Not that long ago, she would have been pleased by this, curious about it, eager to consult Sax. Now, whatever is in this box comes to her as yet another chore. Wearily—every single act demands so much effort—without even looking at the return address, Karla slits the tape, opens the flaps, and finds, nestled in Styrofoam caterpillars, a video. Ah, yes, of course. From Magda.

A relic from another world, another life, Karla's two weeks with her German family a century ago, and yet she can feel herself sitting in Lotte's chair, facing the camera, holding the photo, answering Magda's questions.

And now? Sax was the one who knew how to work the VCR. Karla will have to figure it out. She resents this but is grateful; at least he was organized. So there, in his desk files, a folder marked "VCR" contains a manual.

"Turn on your TV and tune in to the video input," the instructions advise.

Huh? None of the trillion buttons on the VCR remote that Karla studies says anything about video input. So what now? She sort of remembers Sax fiddling with the TV and cable remotes. Retrieving both, she hears him warning her, *Don't just randomly push buttons,* as she randomly pushes, until, at last, a tiny video message appears in a corner of the television screen. So there, Sax!

Next she is supposed to "open the drop-down panel." This is not, however, as simple as it sounds, but Karla assumes, as she claws at the thing, that it will not require a screwdriver. And indeed, once she depresses the right button on the VCR itself, the door to the slot majestically descends.

"Insert the tape." Which way does it go?

Looking into the machine and checking to see where spools would fit, this, too, Karla manages to figure out correctly. A triumph of sorts, she supposes, as she shuts the flap. For on the television screen, in the same grays and not quite whites she remembers from her cousin's Karlsruhe living room, sits a woman who has to be the Karla she was then, sitting in a chair. This person is answering questions, showing a photo.

The new, now Karla sits back and steels herself to examine her ancestor. In the film, she is surprisingly attractive. Only because she knows very well who it has to be, Karla detects in her a little bit of herself, but something rather German about her and the way she lifts her upper lip when she speaks also resembles Mutti.

Not that long ago, had she perceived any similarity between her and her mother, Karla would have freaked out. But now she feels like she has spent years and years trying to keep out a supposed burglar who, all that time, was actually living unconcernedly in her house. Karla might as well accept Mutti's presence in her as inevitable, no?

I'd say so, Sax says.

So, now that you've seen Magda's documentary, what else do you think? she asks. *Am I okay?*

How many times do I have to tell you? Sax asks, with his customary irritation. *You're beautiful.*

He makes this sound like an insult, Karla thinks, as she sits in Sax's library, watching the part of the tape when she is in Heidelberg. She imagines Sax and Mutti sitting at a kitchen table, that venue where so much significant in Karla's life has been discussed and determined, swapping stories about her.

Did Mutti ever visualize herself in that room where she grew up, or is it only Karla who pictures her there? The camera lingers on the crucifix over the bed. Karla still cannot understand what growing up with that dagger-like object pointed down at you every time you went to sleep would have been like. Nor can she see Mutti crossing herself.

When the short movie is over, showing off her new skill to her ghost audience, Karla ejects the videotape. Then, exhausted from learning and doing and grieving and watching and simply being, she rises to her feet.

When she was participating in Magda's project, Karla thought this video would eventually show her, and Sax, too, who she is and what she could be. Instead, it gave her a glimpse of who she was — nice-looking and seemingly self-possessed. And though she aches for Sax to be here assessing with her, even though he is not physically present, after watching her video, Karla at last perceives that not being great is not the same as not being okay.

It could be that nothing will ever tell her who she is. It could be there is nothing to tell. What, after all, is the point of her? What is the point of asking? No one expects an ant or an antelope to have a point. Maybe it is arrogant to think a purpose is necessary for humans. Animals, vegetables, minerals just are, exactly as, right now, Karla just is.

In Germany, being filmed, she fantasized that this video could make her a star. Now she wonders who will see it and how they will react. Is Magda pleased or disappointed with how her film turned out? Does she think Karla's story reveals anything useful to anyone else?

There isn't anything, Karla is surprised to realize, that she wishes she had said but left out; there isn't anything she rues having said. In front of the camera, she simply told her story.

When she called to console Karla over Sax's death, Lotte naturally did not mention the documentary. But if Lotte watched it—and it is hard to believe she did not—what did she think of her cousin on the screen? What did any of the Germans expect from their American kin? And did Karla deliver?

Neither she nor Lotte may ever feel comfortable discussing it with each other. But someday soon, Karla will bring it up, even though right now it seems to her that, like her home-movie father sitting on his pony at his sixth-birthday party, she is merely an image, recorded at a moment in past time.

And sure, this particular minute, when she is leaving Sax's library to go down the hall to the kitchen, may feel unreal and endless. Karla by now gets, she gets in her gut, that no moment, not this one or any other, with or without her in it, is endless. So what then?

CHAPTER 19

During the following months, Karla knows what must be done, and, still on automatic pilot, she does whatever it is. She meets with Sax's accountant to discuss the procedure for filing tax returns. She gathers the materials the accountant tells her she will need; she practices the piano; she shows up for her lessons.

She goes to the lawyer's office and discusses the making of her own will; she will leave half her money in trust for Ron'l and the rest to Viv. When the lawyer calls to say he has prepared the document, Karla returns to the office and, witnessed by the lawyer and his paralegal, signs the new will.

In the apartment, she writes a personal response to each condolence note. She picks her courses for next semester.

The day Karla walks by a store window and sees a bright yellow suede vest she would have bought for Sax, a wave of grief drenches her. But only hours afterward, she cannot keep herself from thinking that though Sax's diagnoses annulled any chance of his again being a father, his death reopens the question: Does she still want to be a mother? Karla has always sworn she would never have a kid like Mutti did, but if she uses donated sperm to get pregnant, her baby will also have no father. What choice has she? Right now, though her clock relentlessly tick-tocks, the thought of having sex with anyone other than Sax disgusts her. Yet in bed every night and every morning, she yearns to make love.

And something in her keeps pressing, so, as she walks down city sidewalks, she finds herself staring at infants scrunched against their mother's chests. God, how she wants a baby nestled against her!

Karla visits Fleur and the new Sax, first in the hospital, then at home. Trying to be helpful, she takes the two older children to McDonald's for lunch. Quattro has to show her how to fasten his sister, Priscilla, into the car seat. He has to explain that he does not weigh enough to sit in the front next to Karla. An inexperienced driver, she has to back Fleur's car and its precious cargo out of the driveway. She has to negotiate the route to the Golden Arches.

Walking through the parking lot holding the children's hands tightly, she has to make sure neither darts away and gets run over. She has to make sure her bag doesn't slide off her shoulder and hit Priscilla in the head. Karla has to elbow the restaurant door open without letting go of a hand.

Inside, she has to decide what to eat. The kids already know they want Happy Meals.

Clambering onto a booster seat in a booth after Karla has collected their food, Priscilla tells Karla she must go get more packets of ketchup and more napkins. Karla has no idea where these things are. When she returns to the table, she has no idea what to say to this little couple, or how to react when they sit there, staring at her expectantly.

"Everything okay?" she asks.

Quattro shrugs.

The children take between fifteen minutes and forever to eat. Karla has never seen anyone select french fries as precisely as this little girl, who picks out each, one by one, and dips it just so into the puddle of ketchup she squeezes from yet another packet in the pile Karla has repeatedly to go back to replenish. The kid has yet to touch her burger. Should Karla urge her at least to taste it? At this rate, they'll be here into dinnertime.

"She stole my napkin." Quattro shoves Priscilla

"I didn't," she wails. "It wasn't anybody's."

"We have plenty more napkins." Karla holds up the six-inch stack.

"But that one was mine," he claims.

"How were your McNuggets?" Karla asks, as if she gives a rat's ass.

At long last, she gets to dip napkins in a cup of water and, to the children's noisy dismay, wipe the sticky mess off their hands and faces. Karla gets to clear the table. She gets to shepherd the two of them through the parking lot perils and to fasten them back into Fleur's car.

That night, she tells Sax she might be better off not having a kid. They're exhausting.

But yours will be different, he promises.

At least, so Karla hopes. But is Sax telling her to go ahead and try to have a baby, or is she just talking to herself in his voice?

When she visits her grandparents for weekly dinners, she says nothing about a possible baby or about her conversations with Sax. They ask how she is doing, and she replies, "Fine."

Two months after the memorial, Karla lunches at the Harvard Club with a woman from the Harvard Development Office. (*Notice how fast they latch on to you?* Sax asks.)

A few days later, she has dinner with Bessie Shelton. Afterward, slightly sloshed after drinking their manhattans, they go to a movie that Karla might once have enjoyed, but now, sitting next to someone whose hand she cannot clasp saddens her.

Still, grateful for Bessie's attention and for the prefabricated structure of her life that allows Karla to pretend she is the same person she used to be, she negotiates her hours.

Then one afternoon she sees a slender, dark-haired man crossing

Madison Avenue ahead of her and hurries to catch up, thinking for an instant that this stranger is Sax, until she stops dead to stifle her tears.

A few weeks later, a sixty-ish man and a midthirties woman enter the restaurant where Karla is waiting for Viv. The couple are holding hands. This time, Karla's weeping is too powerful to stifle, for she assumed she and Sax would be like that, too. She has trouble calming herself before Viv arrives.

Viv, that level-headed stalwart ("a cluck," Mutti insists), phones every day to say that by no means should Karla consider living in the loft on Canal Street—too depressing. She should find a place near Viv and Joel on the Upper West Side. She should get an apartment in Brooklyn Heights, or in the Village if she is looking for arty types. Gramercy Park is a great area. There are some lovely condos in Fort Lee. New Jersey is actually nicer than Karla thinks.

Every day a new idea. And every day Karla assures Viv she is thinking it over. Indeed, on Sundays, sitting in the den, sipping Sax's scotch, she reads the *New York Times* Real Estate section. Open House. Prewar. Sun-Filled. Sophisticated. Not one of these adjectives applies or appeals to her. But staying here, especially if she has someone else's kid, would be too weird—yet Karla cannot leave, for this is where Sax lives.

Finished with the papers, she wanders from room to room. Though it has been years since she moved in, this apartment was always his and it still is. Now that he is gone, Karla cleans, dusts, vacuums, and scours because she likes going over the place inch by inch; she likes again being his maid. And as she polishes, she tells Sax how great his choices were and are. She tells him what the latest appraiser said. She tells him his namesake has learned to smile. She tells herself she has to get busy if she ever wants to see a baby of her own.

Karla moves into Sax's side of the bed to occupy its gaping

emptiness. Her half quickly becomes a nest of magazines and books. In the den, instead of facing his absence, Karla sits in Sax's chair.

Each day, as if she were one of the appraisers sent to the apartment by the lawyer or the insurance company, Karla chooses a painting, an etching, a print for serious and detailed study. How she still loves the doors and Sax's story of their acquisition! Remembering it, she is again at Quo Vadis, having dinner with him. But three months after his death, she is here.

When she is finally ready to confront the Modigliani, from which she has been studiously averting her eyes, the nude's flesh glows exactly as it has always glowed. Affronted, Karla glares at her. How inappropriate for that bitch to look unchanged! Yet had it not been for her, Sax would never have noticed Karla. Now it is time for both that painting and Karla to start their new lives.

Seized by a sudden spate of determination, Karla races into the bathroom, retrieves Sax's terry-cloth robe, and flings it open on top of the bed quilt. Then she climbs up, unhooks the portrait from its S hook, and, taking care not to drop the ungainly painting or to fall on it, she carefully lays the nude facedown on top of the robe, flips the satin comforter around the frame, and thumps off the bed to the floor.

Then she calls Ron'l and asks if he will please bring her some clothesline. It is time to get moving. Not that Karla is ready to leave Sax. But she must right now have someplace to repair to that is all hers.

She stares at the anemic rectangle on the wall that her painting has up to now hidden. Then she heads to the library, pours a scotch, sips, and waits in silence until the house phone rings and the doorman announces Ron'l.

"Send him up," Karla says, heading for the front door.

Ron'l steps out of the elevator wearing a cowboy shirt and boots, the clothesline she asked for looped like a lariat over his shoulder.

This man is there for her. Tears shoot into Karla's eyes. Sax said he loved her because she loves Ron'l.

"What you fixing to do now?" he asks.

"Come." Embarrassed by her unseemly gratitude, she grasps his arm. "I'll show you." She leads him to the bedroom. "Help me tie this thing up." She snakes clothesline under the quilt and Sax's robe, and, Ron'l on one side of the bed and she on the other, they pass the line over, under, and around the Modigliani, working their way up until Karla ties double square knots and cuts the line. Focusing on the job at hand while she still has the resolve, she turns the trussed painting, and they pass more line up, over, and around it the long way.

"Where we putting this?" Ron'l asks when they finish.

"Canal Street," where Karla, after all, began.

She had been living with Sax for almost a year before he spotted the suitcase under their bed. "What on earth is this thing?" He kicked it out and snapped it open.

"Nothing. It's mine." She rushed over and snatched it away.

"You going somewhere?" he speculated, looking suspicious.

"Only if I have to." Embarrassed by being caught with this vestige of Mutti's paranoia, she could not meet his eyes.

"But you're ready to escape from me without notice."

"No. This isn't about you."

"My brother's already spoken for, though there'd be a kind of exquisite justice if you did break up those two." Sax was joking, but his pain was obvious.

"I'm not going anywhere. I swear it. The packed suitcase— Mutti called it a valise—is just an old habit."

"Oh?" He looked skeptical.

"In case someone comes for me."

"And who would that be?"

"I don't know. The SS. I've got shoes, clothes, so I could go into hiding." Said out in the open, the escape plan sounded as completely off the wall as it was.

"The SS," Sax repeated. "Storm troopers?"

"American-style." Karla actually snickered. "Remember, my mother faked her identity. She really was afraid she'd be found out."

"And the cops were supposed to hang around while you carried off your suitcase and made your escape."

"Something like that," she admitted, seeing for the first time the idea's wacky impracticality.

"Here," Sax handed her an American Express card made out in her name. "I've been waiting for the right moment to give this to you, and this is obviously it."

"Why?"

"In case you need an airline ticket or a hotel when you're hiding out."

Whatever happened to that valise? she wonders now. It's probably in the basement storage bin. She will have to go down there and check. She will have to take it to Goodwill.

"You had you supper yet?" Ron'l asks.

"Later." Though, now that he's mentioned food, she realizes she is seriously hungry. "Just help me grab this thing, will you?" She does not mean to sound angry, but unless they get this done while she has momentum, she will go back to drinking scotch in the library. They will eat two of the dinners from the freezer. And that will be that for today.

Downtown, sliding herself out before she eases the painting from the cab, Karla catches herself automatically checking upstairs for Mutti's signal light to tell her it is safe to go home. God, Karla hopes

Sax didn't see that, even as she still longs for someone who will constantly look out for her.

In the old days, Mutti never missed a thing. Sax watched Karla, too. Now, with no one paying attention, she realizes her life could be an endless opportunity to make mistakes. But it could also be Karla's chance to do something great. *Every solution has its costs*, Sax says.

Climbing the dark stairs, she wishes he were the person going up backward with his corner of the painting, but that is Ron'l. When they reach the landing, Karla unlocks the door and they carry the painting inside.

Once it is propped against the mirror, Ron'l darts over to scoop the orange satin *schmatta* he's been working on off the sewing table.

"That's okay," Karla assures him. "You can leave it where it is. And you can still work here, even if I do move back." She shivers at the thought of living here and of sharing her space. "But right now, I think you should go home."

"You want I cut you picture open first?" He is ready to attack the Modigliani.

"Thank you, but no." She will do her own unwrapping.

"You don't need no supper?"

"Not yet."

"Ain't nothing but diet Kool-Aid in the icebox."

"That's okay." The mildew plus Mutti-pee stink has already killed Karla's appetite. Viv was right about even the air here being filthy. Karla pushes Ron'l toward the door. She really will have to find somewhere else to live. "I'll go out later for groceries." And cleaning supplies. She prods him out, shuts the door, turns around to face the room.

The chair in which Mutti sat for the last two years of her life is empty. If Karla sits in it, either she will squash the terror lurking on that black cushion or it will engulf her. Karla flops into the seat and remembers that even before Mutti got sick, Karla asked her once, "What will I do if something happens to you?"

"You'll manage," Mutti promised.

"How?"

"Have I taught you nussing, then?"

Looking around, Karla sees that her education—reading, figuring, cooking, cleaning—was never about the day "they" came for them but, rather, about now. Before this, like any parasite, she attached herself to Viv, her grandparents, Sax. But today, she has this place and this chair and the portrait, still tied in the quilt.

Well, she might as well get the unveiling over with. She gets up, picks at the clothesline, and curses her double squares. When the knots finally give way, the quilt and the robe drop and, like Botticelli's Venus, Modigliani's nude rises out of satin and terry foam.

After propping the frame back against the mirror, Karla sinks back into Mutti's chair. *You okay with where she is?* she asks Sax.

Jesus Christ, he erupts. *You don't need my permission.* His voice is a slap that brings her to her senses.

The only permission Karla needs now is her own. So what is she going to let herself do?

Her Modigliani glows as brightly as ever, but at this point Karla is responsible for her well-being. And there was that robbery at the Isabella Stewart Gardner Museum. So she will have to get an alarm system installed. Until that is done, she will have to stay here to guard her painting. *And then*, she realizes, *I will be another Mutti. Stuck.*

Goaded by this nightmare possibility, Karla pushes herself to her feet. She hauls the armchair to the door and bumps it over the threshold. She hurls the cushion to the bottom landing and, with the rest of the thing tipped against her back, thuds down.

Outside, no one looks as she drags her burden to the curb and slaps the cushion on it. Twilight casts over it a thin overlay as rust-colored as her own hair. Frightened by the encroaching dark—who knows who is hiding in it? —Karla runs back, takes the stairs two at a time, bursts into the loft.

Of course, nothing has changed, no one is there, and the nude is just as she was. And, despite the chair removal, so is the loft's stink, which by now has seeped into Karla, too. She rears back, kicks off her shoes, tears off her skirt, unpeels her leotard, and hurls it onto the floor.

No dawdling in the shower, no caressing of her parts. Just good warm water and a cracked soap bar that, touched by wetness, springs to life.

Stepping out into the unheated air, Karla feels some of her sadness spiral with the water down the drain. How much zest she still has! Even her hunger impels her, as a brisk rubbing with a stiff, scratchy, inadequate old towel wakes all of her up. Clean as she now is, she resists putting those smelly clothes back on.

She needs something to wear this minute that does not reek. Does it really have to be black? Karla picks up Ron'l's orange satin. She lifts his Big Chance to her nose and sucks in a deep breath. Miraculously, the cloth has not absorbed the loft stench. So what loomed for all these years as a momentous decision—when to start wearing color—becomes obvious.

Karla thrusts out her hands and examines two big, slippery squares sewn together on three sides with a slit at the top and an opening at the bottom, into which she sticks her head so it is between the back and the front, or maybe between the front and the back. Either way, she wriggles out up at the top, punches at the side seams, locates holes for her arms.

Naked inside this icy cloth djellaba, she shivers. Will Ron'l mind her wearing his creation? And what about the gods? So many times, Viv has told the story of the night Karla was born—how Mutti immediately clothed her all in black, even to the diapers. So many times, so many people urged Karla to try wearing colors.

Now the floor remains firm under her feet. No thunderbolt comes down from above. Instead, as if she were one of those vacuum-packed coffee cubes, once opened Karla immediately grows larger, looser, messier. And with the satin's golden glow on her, the person reflected in Mutti's full-length, three-way mirror is, like the unlocked coffee, potentially delicious. Thanks to Ron'l, Karla finally shows off in her reality what her Modigliani nude has only in paint. Oomph.

How ironic! With neither a bang nor a whimper, Karla's apparent lifetime mourning ends just when her actual mourning is at its most acute. *Yet another unexpected twist*, she thinks, turning away from the mirror. Raised to be forever a girl, she has become a woman who understands that "happily ever after" is a copout. Cinderella's prince, no matter how reliable, could not last forever. So what then?

She could have ended up as a conduit for her mate's heirs. She could have spread around her good fortune, used it all to feather her nest, gone to business school for an MBA, learned how to manage her vast riches, or died ignorant. Her kid could have invigorated a moribund royal line, or Cinderella Junior could just be more of the same old, same old.

Only one thing is clear. This present Cinderella, aka Karla Most, has to figure out the "what next" of her life, and the answer is here, staring her in the face. If Karla sells her Modigliani, she can buy herself a lot more than a fabulous apartment. As if coalescing, the endless possibilities—all those art classes, hanging out with dealers, watching Sax negotiate—have been flowing into a chute, and she finally perceives that just about everything she has done for years is tumbling in one direction.

Karla can go into the art business, acquire her own collection, open a gallery. Remembering her joy in working with paint, paste, potatoes, she can give that pleasure to other people. She can look for a bilevel space for talented upstarts to show their work on the lower level and periodically present a hands on—how to combination of art lectures, demonstrations, and workshops upstairs in the brand-new Prototype Gallery.

"What do you think about that?" Karla asks the nude, who smirks conspiratorially because she probably understood all along that once Karla runs her own gallery, she can determine her own hours and can unearth and champion new talent. There is a precedent for that: Peggy Guggenheim, Paula Cooper. And now Karla Most can take what they did to the next level: turn spectators, and not just the privileged ones, into creators. She can promote not just the selling, but also the making, of art.

She can also find a partner and have his child or, like her mother, be brave enough to raise a kid on her own. Now that she is on the verge of thirty-seven, Karla's immediate impulse is, with or without a partner, to get herself knocked up. And once she has taken care of that, to find and talk to the right people about how to establish her Prototype Gallery. Karla owes it to Sax, as well as to herself, to make the most of everything she has.

She has other talents she will mine. Like a cork, no matter how often or how deeply sunk she is, she shoots back up to life's surface, her irrepressibility a big plus. She can love and be loved. How much more should she expect of herself?

The very little she's done for other people over the years— helping Ron'l stay in his apartment, supporting Sax through his dying—made her feel worthy. So she will have to help more people, but not in the abstract. Actual people.

Outside, tires scream. Cars crash.

Karla rushes to the window. A taxicab and a van. Smashed glass, crumpled steel. The drivers now out of their vehicles, filling the air with "fuck" and "fucking asshole." No one looks up. But as Karla watches from above, a sand-colored hound strolls over to Mutti's chair, lifts his leg, and pisses. After this contemptuous spattering, the mutt scratches the pavement and saunters away.

How could he? How could she? Karla flies downstairs. Picturing a garbage truck grinding up Mutti's chair is like seeing it grind up Mutti herself. Karla bursts outside, aware of how nutty she must look in the garish satin, with her sopping hair, the sidewalk cold and sandy under her bare feet, as she drags the chair across the sidewalk and prepares somehow to lug it back upstairs. If Hilde's Heidelberg bedroom is intact, shouldn't "Liesel's" New York apartment be intact, too?

Why? Karla has the sense to pause and ask herself. *You think you're maybe God? You can bring her back? There is no bringing back,* Karla thinks, as, careful to keep it from contaminating Ron'l's creation, she prods the stinky chair back to the curb and leaves it.

Upstairs, the door sighs behind her. Karla trembles under the slippery cloth; she trembles from the chill and because she is scared. It is finally time to give birth to herself, and where better to do that than here, where she was born the first time? Only now, Karla can finally get out for good.

She can become a mother, open her gallery, find another great lover, model for Ron'l, do it all. *Right on,* Sax agrees, though whether he means this ironically or not, and whether the words are his or her own, she has no idea.

Did he will her the Modigliani as a sign? Did he mean for her to keep it? Or what? Karla looks up at her nude, who glows inside this cage of darkness. Staring past her into the three-way-mirror, she sees that she herself is more like the famous Klimt woman.

Backed by that mosaic of money, this person is not looking for another man to rescue her. Even if she does link up with someone wonderful, she will go on being her own caretaker. And the thing Karla needs to do for herself right this minute is to get her inheritance and herself the hell out of here. For there is no way to clean out of this place its dark history.

Glad she never ended the loft's phone service, Karla calls Ron'l and belatedly asks if it is okay for her to borrow his satin dress.

"You the one in my mind when I make it," he says. "How it look on you?"

"Come see for yourself and help me take my painting back uptown."

"You sure?"

"I realize now it's where she belongs. At least for right now."

"We going to eat first?" Ron'l asks.

"After we get her back." Karla hangs up the receiver, rewraps the portrait in just the quilt, and reties the knotted clothesline, saying, "Sorry about that," as if the nude can hear her. Then, putting Sax's bathrobe on over Ron'l's orange satin, she again views her mirrored self in this crazy getup.

Moving closer to the image, Karla stares into the pale eyes Sax found so remarkable. And she sees someone she has always known but never before met: a person who finds it easy to look into other people's eyes; a smart New York woman with a pretty interesting backstory; a redhead who, with a little face paint, will look absolutely smashing in cranberry or amber.

Turning away from the mirror, she brushes the grit off her soles and stuffs her feet into her shoes. She glances at the tangle of black clothes she is leaving behind. Then she hoists the portrait, grabs her purse, pauses at the door, takes a last look.

The loft is a murky box holding very little. Karla is more than okay with moving away from here. Though she may come back now and then to visit, she will never again inhabit this place, and neither will Mutti.

Karla goes out to the top of the stairs, twists her key in the dead bolt lock, grips her painting. *Okay*, she thinks, *so I am a meshugge-ner's kid. Well, what's a crazy woman's daughter like? Truth be told, a little crazy, but then, isn't everybody?*

That is not all she is. Karla carefully places one foot, then the painting, then the other foot, down each step, one at a time. Right now, she is headed for another life. A good one? With a child? Only one way to find out, she reminds herself, as, finally, she gets to the bottom, opens the street door, presses it with her hip.

Then Karla steps out onto the sidewalk and into this world that assaults her with vital rot: the compost of cabbages, bus exhaust, fish; the thereness of pavement; the city clatter, honk, and grind. Hungrily, she waits for Ron'l, ignores the chair a few yards away, enjoys the promise of orange juice for her parched mouth.

And, Karla asks herself, how can she possibly feel this anticipatory if Sax is dead?

Why not? he asks.

Why not indeed? For, thanks to her mother, she is alive.

And, catching a cute passerby's eye, Karla does something she has not done in weeks. She laughs.

ACKNOWLEDGMENTS

Official editor: Annie Tucker

Unofficial editors: Claire Gerus, Deb Grossfield, Jeffrey Miller, Jon O. Newman, Susan Rand Brown, Diane Hockstader, Pamela Awad

Comembers of the Storrs Writing Group: Denise Abercrombie, Jon Andersen, Lisa Butler, Carol Chaput, Jim Coleman, Joan Joffe Hall, Anne Flammang, Alison Meyers, David Morse, and John Surowiecki

ABOUT THE AUTHOR

Ann Z. Leventhal is the author of *Life-lines*, a novel about a wife who runs away with her husband's mistress. Her short stories, articles, poems, and reviews have appeared in *Vignettes*, *The Georgia Review*, *Prairie Schooner*, *Christopher Street*, *The New York Times Book Review*, and *Publishers Weekly*.

SELECTED TITLES FROM SHE WRITES PRESS

She Writes Press is an independent publishing company founded to serve women writers everywhere. Visit us at www.shewritespress.com.

A Cup of Redemption by Carole Bumpus. $16.95, 978-1-938314-90-2. Three women, each with their own secrets and shames, seek to make peace with their pasts and carve out new identities for themselves.

The Belief in Angels by J. Dylan Yates. $16.95, 978-1-938314-64-3. From the Majdonek death camp to a volatile hippie household on the East Coast, this narrative of tragedy, survival, and hope spans more than fifty years, from the 1920s to the 1970s.

Magic Flute by Patricia Minger. $16.95, 978-1-63152-093-8. When a car accident puts an end to ambitious flutist Liz Morgan's dreams, she returns to her childhood hometown in Wales in an effort to reinvent her path.

A Drop In The Ocean: A Novel by Jenni Ogden. $16.95, 978-1-63152-026-6. When middle-aged Anna Fergusson's research lab is abruptly closed, she flees Boston to an island on Australia's Great Barrier Reef—where, amongst the seabirds, nesting turtles, and eccentric islanders, she finds a family and learns some bittersweet lessons about love.

True Stories at the Smoky View by Jill McCroskey Coupe. $16.95, 978-1-63152-051-8. The lives of a librarian and a ten-year-old boy are changed forever when they become stranded by a blizzard in a Tennessee motel and join forces in a very personal search for justice.

The Geometry of Love by Jessica Levine. $16.95, 978-1-938314-62-9. Torn between her need for stability and her desire for independence, an aspiring poet grapples with questions of artistic inspiration, erotic love, and infidelity.